DARK SIGHT

THE DARKWORLD ORIGINS

Pyros (Logan)
Ailuros (Kailin)

~

THE DARK SIGHT SERIES

Dark Sight
Cursed Sight
Vissarion
Shadow Sight
Dark Prophecy
Cursed Prophecy
Shadow Prophecy

~

THE APSARA CHRONICLES

Immortal Bound
Gods Ascendent
Dominion Falling
Vengeance Born
Last Legion

~

A SEASON OF ASH AND BONE

Heartfyre

~

DARK SIGHT

THE DARK SIGHT SERIES 1

ISBN-13: 978-0-473-42927-0

DARK SIGHT

USA TODAY BESTSELLING AUTHOR

T.G. AYER

CHAPTER 1

When Allegra received the call from Nike Rehab sending her to her latest patient, she went with dour reluctance and not even an iota of impending doom.

Had the Fates been kind to her, they'd have allowed her a tiny premonition. Maybe even a palpitation or two. Or at the very least, a tiny butterfly's flutter.

But Allegra got nothing.

She'd driven past the ancient, and mostly abandoned, temples of Apollo and Athena, and neither had seen fit to provide her with even a little foresight.

Allegra slammed her sandaled foot on the brakes as she neared the wrought-iron gates guarding her client's mansion, the car making the turn onto the cobbled, elm-lined driveway with a sputter and a hiss.

Struggling with the clutch on her battered old Branson A Class, she came to a shuddering stop only a few inches from the sentry, who stood stiff-spined and expressionless before the gate.

Going to have to have a talk with Senator Branson one of these days. Of all the things to leave car production for, the man had chosen airlines. And she'd once thought him one of the smartest minds in the world.

Allegra pulled the brake, prayed it would hold, and opened the car door. Grabbing her small black leather purse, she looped the strap over her shoulder and alighted.

After slamming the car door shut and sending a prayer to Apollo that it would remain so, Allegra faced the mansion and smoothed down the front of her pale pink pantsuit. She kept her work attire low-key, but wealthier clients tended to require a classier look, even on the hired help.

Tossing the long matching organza shawl over her shoulder, she checked that her bland blonde hair was still neatly within the high ponytail on the top of her head. She faced the guard who stood in the already-strong mid-morning sun, even though the row of trees lining the short driveway provided sufficient shade.

The Breslins were of the level of wealthy where style bordered on the ridiculous. The latest craze, among those blessed with money, was house-staff dressed and treated as slaves had been in ancient times. When Allegra had read the article on the elektroweb, she'd sworn the world was going mad.

Slavery had been abolished centuries ago, and today the wealthy were bringing it back, even if they were just pretending. Allegra tilted her head to look up at the polished ebony abs of the sentry.

He wore leather sandals, a pleated red skirt, a pair of bronze armguards that glinted in the bright sunlight, and a bronze helmet topped with a bouquet of blood-red feathers.

And pointed a very sharp spear at Allegra's left eye.

The guard glared at her, his expression hard enough to shatter diamonds. "In the name of Darius Breslin, state your business."

Apollo save me.

Allegra pasted a smile on her lips. "I have an appointment with Citizen Breslin. I'm Allegra Damascus."

No response.

Allegra gave it another try. "His *physio*. For his torn tendon?"

She pointed at her left arm, annoyed now with the show-and-tell. They were expecting her, but she still had to jump through hoops to get inside.

The man's expression didn't change as he shifted the sharp edge of the spear to a slightly less-deadly position.

At her left boob.

"Proof of identity."

Man of few words, huh?

Allegra dug inside the little bag at her waist and withdrew her Nike Rehab ID badge. She handed it over, and waited, watching his muscles bulge and shift as he examined the plastic card.

A soft breeze rustled through the trees, ruffling the red plumes on his helmet. It also lifted the hem of his short pleated skirt, revealing an expanse of toned, muscled thigh.

Allegra averted her eyes.

At last he gave the card a nod, then handed it back to Allegra before reaching for a button on the fence wall.

Automatic gates. No surprise.

Breslin, the handsome darling of international tennis, had won gold at the last Olympic Games. Seriously, the man was deemed so attractive that the Vestal Virgins were clamoring for the Olympic Games Events to return to the ancient rules of compulsory nudity for all participants. His win had garnered him huge support in the New Germanic States, including an advertising deal as the face of Daimler-Benz, the reigning leaders in international automobile manufacturing.

Cursing Branson, Allegra jumped back into her vehicle and gassed the engine, crossing her fingers and hoping it wouldn't die on her. Allegra thanked the Fates when the heap of metal grumbled its way along the long drive up to the villa.

The avenue, lined with a row of tall firs on each side, took

Allegra up the hill to a classic Greek-style mansion. It resembled a massive temple with gigantic white pillars guarding the front face of the residence.

Hades would be proud of such excess.

At least the entrance wasn't bracketed by a second pair of sentries.

Must be a limit to slave ownership in these parts.

The old Branson coughed out a cloud of black dust as Allegra brought it to a halt. Allegra frowned as she exited the car as gracefully as she could, and wondered if the car was finally in its death throes.

It would be an annoyance because automobile-shopping was her pet hate. Reason she'd held onto her first car all this time.

Hitching her bag higher on her shoulder, Allegra grabbed her leather case which contained her oils and cloths, shut the door with a solid thunk and climbed the majestic flight of marble stairs to the double-doored entrance.

The Breslins had made a determined effort at majesty with the gaggle of expertly-cracked statues of armless, nubile gods, satyrs and nymphs, the males all well-endowed.

But the result was nothing less than tacky, and nothing more than fake.

No judging, Allegra. Keep your mind on the job.

The door opened and a tall brunette met Allegra's gaze. Honey eyes studied Allegra from head to toe. "*You're* the physiotherapist?" An arched eyebrow dared Allegra to confirm. Her bearing, and her clothing, said lady-of-the-house.

Portia Breslin.

Allegra eyed her short skirt. It ended just above the knee, with generous folds of silky fabric draped loosely from her waist, across her breasts and over her right shoulder.

"Yes. Allegra Damascus from Nike. If there's a problem, I'm sure the agency will send some oth—"

Portia raised an imperious hand, silencing Allegra. After a moment in which the skin on her forehead puckered and her lips pursed, she gave a cool nod and spun on her heel.

The fabric trailing the floor behind her was the only thing gracing her bare back.

Fashion these days.

Allegra's hostess led her deeper into the building, exiting into a square courtyard fringed by apple trees and dotted with stone benches.

At the center was a pool of clear water that reflected the sunlight like shards of glass. On a cot beside the pool lay the magnificent construction of muscles, limbs and pheromones that was Darius Breslin.

His skin gleamed a dull gold from baking in the strong Fornia sunshine, and he didn't seem to notice, or care, that he was slowly getting burned.

Guess you have to suffer for true beauty.

"Darius, darling. The therapist girl is here."

Allegra eyed the woman as she crouched beside her husband and gently helped him up. Citizen Portia Breslin, the pretty and very jealous Breslin wife. Some of the gossip mags - not that Allegra read such trash - claimed Darius had a taste for more than just one woman at a time.

Where there's smoke?

As Portia leaned over, the fabric slipped off her shoulder and dropped to her waist, exposing her from neck to navel. Neither blushing nor blinking, she tossed the fabric back over her shoulder and lifted her chin to give Allegra a nod.

Maybe being flashed will be the highlight of my day. Please let it be so.

Allegra stepped around the cot and came face-to-face with Breslin, and was surprised to be unaffected by his stunning manliness.

Just as well, since he was a client. Despite his undeniable beauty, Allegra barely blinked an eye.

Instead, she introduced herself.

Breslin gave her a noncommittal nod. "Before you touch me, I'll need some sort of reference."

There was that arrogance she'd been expecting. Stardom gone to his head just like Hercules. "The Nike Agency is very diligent in vetting their therapists—"

Breslin lifted a hand into the air, mimicking his wife's earlier movement. "Who have you worked with?" At Allegra's puzzled look, he sighed and spoke very slowly. "Anyone . . . that I may know . . . that I can ring up and confirm with?"

Allegra swallowed the profanity that threatened to spill from her lips, prayed for the strength of a Minotaur, and said, "Of course. There's Ronnie DeLuca, the—"

"The baseball player? The one who coaches the Nova Roma Tigers?"

Allegra nodded.

Allegra's clientele was mostly the rich and the elite. An unusual achievement for someone so young.

Fortunately, her very first client, after she'd completed her training, had been Olympic sprinter Adnan Suleiman, son of a friend of her late father's. Suleiman had taken gold in the five-hundred-meters at the Olympics that year and his win had launched Allegra's career.

Demand for her services had skyrocketed, with the who's-who in the sports and movie industries asking specifically for her.

Ronnie DeLuca had been one of them.

Allegra disliked name-dropping but she had to get this job done and get out of here.

Who knew what else these people were into.

Breslin seemed satisfied, his eyes grazing over her chest and hips in appreciation, despite his wife's proximity. "You may begin."

Squelching a sigh of relief, Allegra said, "Where would be the best place to perform the therapy?" She glanced around the courtyard looking for somewhere in the shade. "We should be out of the sun. I don't want you to get dehydrated."

"He's been drinking water." Portia commented coldly. "And you will start when we've verified with Ronnie."

"Portia."

All he uttered was that one word and Portia turned on her heel and hurried off. Seconds later, four attendants – *pretend-slaves* - entered the courtyard holding the four poles of a makeshift tent, shade offered by an elaborate handwoven tapestry carpet.

Was this a thing? Or was Portia smarter than she looked?

The four slaves, two men and two women, all wearing nothing more than a pleated silk skirt which hung low on their hips, secured the tent. Then the men left while the two women took up positions at each side of the cot, awaiting their master's needs.

Allegra avoided looking at the two topless women and said, "Citizen Breslin, I'm going to need you to lie on your back."

As he resettled himself, Allegra dropped her purse beside the cot and turned to her case to snap open the lid. She withdrew a bottle from the rows of herbal rubs; cold-pressed olive oil infused with cloves. She didn't think his sun-baked skin would handle anything stronger.

"First, I'll manipulate the muscle a little, to gauge the tension and inflammation. It shouldn't hurt, but let me know if it does."

With the cot so low, Allegra was forced to kneel, placing herself gingerly on the roughly-hewn terra-cotta tiles.

Movement at her side confirmed the return of the jealous wife, and the woman's cold silence confirmed she'd made her telephone calls. If she only knew that her precious husband did nothing for Allegra's libido.

As the wife and slaves watched, Allegra reached out to place her hands onto Breslin's shoulder joint, studying the swollen muscle and reddened skin.

The agency had advised his condition when she'd received the job; a partial tear. Rehab should get him back to normal as long as he behaved sensibly, and followed his doctor's instructions to the letter.

Based on the available evidence, Allegra expected nothing of the sort.

She placed her hands on his shoulder, palpating the muscle and concentrating on the feel of tissue beneath his skin.

She'd planned on running him through a series of low-key exercises to ease him slowly into the rehabilitation process.

But the moment she touched Breslin, her vision shifted. The light changed, searing sunlight replaced by a dull moon shaded by inky clouds. The pool sat half-filled and was covered in green slime, and the courtyard lay deathly still.

Before her lay Breslin, but this time there was no cot. His lips were parched and bruised, blood caking small cuts where he'd broken the fragile skin.

"Citizen Breslin?" she gasped, unsure of what had just happened. "What's wrong? Are you ok?"

A voice echoed in her ear, like something from a dream. "What's the matter with you?"

The voice was indignant and irritated, but in her vision, Breslin had barely opened his mouth. She drew closer. "How can I help you?" she asked again, but he didn't seem to hear her.

And yet he answered. "Water."

The word crackled from his throat, the sound hoarse and pained. His skin was flushed, droplets of perspiration covering his forehead and bare chest.

She frowned. "You have a fever. What happened?"

"Help," he called again, but even Allegra could hear his energy fading, his resolve dissipating.

He turned his head to look at her, his eyes glazing over slowly until she knew he was dead. And he'd died staring at something beyond her shoulder. Allegra shifted around and let out a cry of horror.

Someone tugged her shoulder, hard enough that the vision disappeared and the sun shone in her eyes.

She was lying on the ground, both the Breslins glaring at her in annoyance, the two slaves curious enough to break the rules by openly gaping and tittering.

Allegra pushed herself into a sitting position and put a hand to the back of her head. "What happened?"

"You hit your head on the stone," said Portia unsympathetically.

"When you had your vision." Breslin.

"It was more like a fit."

Breslin glared at his wife and she closed her mouth.

Allegra stared up at Breslin who looked so different from the dying man she'd seen mere moments ago.

"What happened? What did you see?" He seemed to be the only one interested. Of course, Allegra had mentioned his name during the vision.

She blinked, still disoriented, then looked at the spot on the floor where he'd lain dying.

"You were sick. Dying." She hesitated before saying the last word in a whisper. "Died."

"What?"

"You . . . you were feverish . . . dying of thirst. You kept calling for help, but there was nobody to help you."

"What is this crap, Darius? Tell her to leave." His wife's cold expression indicated she'd had enough.

"Let her speak, Portia."

Again the mention of her name shut her up.

Allegra looked at Darius, shaking her head as he said, "Did you see the future?"

Excitement edged his voice. Like most people, seers fascinated him with the possibility of knowing his future. But Allegra didn't think he'd want to know this particular fate.

"It wasn't really the future. I don't know what it was. You didn't look any different. Like it could be today or tomorrow, or in the next few months."

"And what did you see?" he asked again, as if the second time around he'd get a different answer.

"You died here. Alone."

Breslin paled and the courtyard fell into a cold silence despite the heat of the sun.

Portia scoffed, folding her arms and giving Allegra a sneering smile. "Is this some sort of prank? You a SeerGram or something?"

Allegra looked at Portia but she didn't have the heart to reveal what else she'd seen.

"I'm sorry. I don't feel well." Allegra got to her feet, grabbed her bags and straightened, staring at the couple stiffly. "I have to go."

She fled the house without a backward glance.

For some unearthly reason, her car started on the first turn and she drove off, terrified of what she'd seen, terrified in case Breslin gave chase for more information.

The sentry at the entrance opened the front gate for her, oblivious to the drama that was probably playing out inside the mansion right this minute.

As Allegra turned onto the main road, she gave the house one last glance. She'd made it out in time. If she'd been there any longer, Portia's bitchiness would have pushed Allegra to tell the vicious woman the truth.

That Allegra had seen *her* death, too.

When she'd turned to look at what Breslin had been staring at the moment he'd died, Allegra had let out a horrified cry. Portia must have sat down on the stone bench at some point. She'd been lying on her back, hands hanging to the ground on either side of the narrow seat.

With two black crows sitting on her chest, pecking out her eyeballs.

CHAPTER 2

*I*f Apollo were to walk up to Allegra and ask her what she wished for most in the world, it would be a do-over of this entire disastrous day.

Not that she was stupid enough to believe in great mythical beings, but it was a nice little daydream.

Allegra sighed as she stared out at the deep blue of the heaving ocean and sipped at her cup of bitter, dark coffee. The *Neptune* overlooked the harbor, a restaurant that boasted long waiting-lists for their sought-after tables.

These days, seafood was one of the most prized delicacies, especially lobster, crawfish and squid. The chef at the Neptune knew people who knew people, ensuring his menus always contained near-unattainable ocean fare.

Except for the one time with the pufferfish liver.

Good thing Senator Nordstrom survived and had considered the experience invigorating.

At least the Dark Ghana was helping to still Allegra's shaking fingers. Xenia had better arrive soon because Allegra didn't think she could stand one more moment alone with the tumult that was her current thoughts.

A tinkling of laughter from across the room announced Xenia's arrival and Allegra smiled as she watched her dearest friend in all the world cut a line between the densely-packed tables, like a great airship on her maiden voyage.

The lady's entourage consisted of Pepper, her adorable golden retriever, whose tail began to sway with intense vigor the moment he set eyes on Allegra.

She smiled as the pair made their way toward her.

Xenia owned the room, dressed in a floor-length turquoise silk skirt with one of those weird wraparound flowy tops in which Allegra could never figure out where arms or head went. The bright colors only enhanced her deep brown skin, which made Allegra green with envy.

To other people, Xenia was a little flamboyant, but to Allegra she was the best friend a girl could have.

Pepper danced around the table, catching his lead amongst the legs and forcing Xenia to let go of the strap. He stood on his hind legs and placed his chin on Allegra's thigh, begging for attention.

Usually Allegra would scratch his head and mutter unintelligables to him. But today she just said, "There's a good boy," and ignored him. Pepper seemed to take the hint and returned to his mistress's side.

Xenia sank into the plush seat opposite Allegra and pushed her dark red sunglasses high onto her head. They served to hold back the expanse of black curls that was offset beautifully by a pair of glittering jade earrings.

Allegra leaned close and studied the stones. "Tell me those things are not real."

"Pfft," said Xenia. "You know we don't do fake." She fingered the stones, which served only to intensify the rich brown of her skin.

Allegra rolled her eyes because they both knew Allegra herself did fake, since a physiotherapist's income did not often run to genuine jewelry. Xenia, of course, could splurge with her parents' money because there was too damned much of it.

After ordering a sweet Lanka tea and a bowl of water for Pepper, Xenia studied Allegra's face. "You have to tell me what's wrong. You're looking all pale."

Allegra snorted. Her own pale skin could put milk, lilies and clouds to shame. But Xenia was only seeing what she herself felt. Stressed, tense, worried.

And afraid.

Allegra inhaled softly then waited as the waitress arrived with tea and water. The girl set the drinks down, one on the table with a polite smile, and the other on the floor with a barely disguised grimace.

Allegra straightened her spine as the waitress hurried away. She met Xenia's eyes without a smile. "I have to tell you something. But you have to swear you will not freak out."

Xenia nodded solemnly. "I swear."

Allegra studied her friend carefully. She could read right through her lies. Allegra's lips thinned. "Swear on Hera."

"What?" whispered Xenia, her dark skin flushing. "*That* bad?"

Pepper's head popped up, nosed propped on the edge of the table, watching her with doleful eyes.

Allegra nodded, unsmiling.

Xenia blinked, and swore on Hera.

Allegra told her everything that had happened at Darius Breslin's mansion.

While Xenia processed the tale, Allegra sipped more of her coffee and stared at the white-topped waves, wishing she could just ride out into the sunset and live forever where the sun met the sea.

Dreams are for kids.

"And," Xenia leaned close, "how are you coping?"

Allegra hid her shaking hands beneath the table and smiled. "I would have been okay - I think - if I hadn't had a second . . . episode . . . with Connor Kiriakis just now."

Something cool and wet nudged Allegra's shivering fingers, but she drew her hand away from Pepper's nose. As well-meaning as he was, she wasn't in the mood for the dog.

He gave a small whine and returned to place his chin on the table at Xenia's elbow.

"Hades almighty." Xenia swallowed. "What happened?"

Allegra sighed and leaned forward. To an onlooker, the two women would have appeared to be friends meeting for lunch and a gossip. And usually, that was exactly what they were.

Today was different.

And something was telling Allegra that *nothing* would ever be the same again.

"Kiriakis has a hamstring injury."

"He still deadlifting?" Xenia sipped her tea, then petted Pepper's head to get his nose off the table.

"At sixty-four he shouldn't be, but who can tell him anything?"

"So what did you see?"

Allegra swallowed hard. "He was dying too. In the same way. Fever. Dehydration. Sores around his mouth. He was on his yacht and it looked abandoned." Allegra ran her fingers through her hair and groaned softly. "What in Hades is going on? I'm going crazy, aren't I?"

"Did you tell him?"

"Kiriakis? Why would I do such a thing?" Allegra's laugh was mirthless. "I managed to maintain my composure, thank Apollo. The last thing I need is to upset the sweet old man."

"Allie, you did the right thing, and maybe it's best to keep this under wraps for a while."

"Who would I tell? You think I want a long line of people at my door bringing me chickens and lambs to read their entrails?" She sighed and sat back, pressing her fingers into her forehead.

"What am I going to do? How can I possibly do my job like this? I can't work if every time I touch a patient, I see his horrific death."

"Come on, Allie. You are being a little dramatic. Maybe you're tired, or just stressed. And besides you've always had forebodings like this. You managed so far without going loco. Maybe it's nothing more than an overactive imagination."

Had anybody else said those words, Allegra would have been furious, but Xenia knew her enough to know her past too. Allegra's parents had died when she was sixteen, leaving her in the care of her parent's closest friends—Xenia's parents, thank goodness.

Allegra had had a terrible dream in which she'd seen her parents' deaths, but when she'd told her dad not to go out that night, he hadn't listened. Instead, they'd driven off and died in a collision with a fuel tanker on the highway.

Since then, several times similar premonitions had aided her and Xenia in avoiding trouble, so neither of the girls would be ready to fob them off in totality.

Again, she sighed. "Maybe you're right."

Wishful thinking.

Xenia tapped one azure fingernail on the table in front of Allegra's hand. "I have an idea."

"Which is?" Allegra asked, returning her focus to the undulating surface of the ocean.

"Touch me," said Xenia. Allegra snapped her gaze to her friend's face, alarmed. Xenia merely raised her eyebrows encouragingly. "Tell me if you see anything."

Allegra studied the serious edge to her expression. "Er . . . I don't think so."

"Why in Hera's name not?" Pepper danced in a circle and whined. Xenia shushed him.

"Because the last thing I want to do is see your death."

CHAPTER 3

$\mathcal{A}$llegra flinched, having spoken the words a little too loudly.

She scanned the tables around her, relieved to find her outburst had gone unnoticed.

Inhaling softly, she said, "Maybe it's nothing, but if these . . . visions . . . are real, then I do not want to see how you die."

Xenia grinned, unaffected by Allegra's morbid reaction to her suggestion. She waved a hand at Allegra, dismissing her concern. "Don't be so melodramatic. What's the worst that can happen? You see my death? We all have to die someday. Besides, maybe you could save me from whatever awful demise you see." She lifted her shoulder, her shrug simultaneously nonchalant and elegant.

Allegra leaned forward, a little suspicious that her friend was hiding her own concern all too well.

There. Xenia was a good actress, but Allegra knew her long enough and well enough to read between the lines. The odd expression in her eyes, the almost imperceptible tightening at the side of her mouth.

Two things that confirmed Xenia was having a silent freak out.

"That's BS and you know it," Allegra snapped. "I've been right too many times in the past for this to be my imagination."

"Come on, Allegra."

Allegra tilted her head and stared at Xenia. Lifting a hand, she raised one finger. "The time I told you not to go to Oliver Randall's party because I had a bad feeling and the cops ended up raiding the place for underage drinkers."

Xenia rolled her eyes.

Allegra lifted a second finger. "The time I didn't go on the field trip to the Amazon Rainforest because I had a strange dream about people dying, and the class contracted Hepovirus and Claude Braga and Ernestine Filian both died from it."

No eye-roll this time.

Allegra lifted a third finger. "The time I tried to stop my parents from going to a business dinner because I had this strange vision about bloody broken glass-"

Xenia raised a palm. "Okay, fine. I get it." She sighed loudly. "But it doesn't change anything. You need to verify that whatever it is you're seeing is the real thing."

Allegra had already lost the will to fight. Maybe Xenia was right. After all, it made sense to find out, on the off-chance that she'd suddenly developed a seer's power. If these visions were based on some form of reality, it would mean that those people really were about to die.

And maybe, just maybe, she could warn someone.

Xenia reached across the table and took Allegra's hand. Though she instinctively jerked away, Xenia didn't allow her to let go. It wouldn't have mattered anyway, because just the touch of Xenia's skin sent Allegra straight into another vision.

Allegra blinked hard, staring around her; Xenia's garden, the large expanse of stunning roses and rare flowers, surrounded her. A pale hand reached across the stony path before Allegra and she moved toward it.

Xenia lay on the grass, shaded by a large plant, her face swollen, her breath coming in short bursts. Her parched lips were cracked and oozing fresh blood, and her beautiful hair was soaked with fever sweat. She was staring up at the single flower that drooped from the plant beside her.

A gigantic purple bloom was larger than Allegra's head, and so dark it was almost black. And as she watched the flower dropped from the stem and floated to settle on Xenia's chest.

But Xenia was dead before the flower landed.

Allegra sighed and opened her eyes. She stared at Xenia, her vision misted by a film of hot tears.

Xenia didn't comment on Allegra's emotional reaction. Instead, she schooled her features and asked, "What did you see?" keeping her voice calm and neutral.

Allegra wasn't buying the act. She blinked away the tears and swallowed hard. She wasn't sure she wanted to say the words out loud, but Xenia squeezed her arm again.

Allegra flinched, expecting to be hit with a vision again, but this time nothing happened. Except for the wave of nausea filling her belly.

"Sorry," whispered Xenia.

Allegra smiled and shook her head. "It's fine." She reached out and held Xenia's hand, ignoring the roiling in her stomach. Allegra stared at the dusky skin starkly contrasted to her own paleness.

The two girls were so different and yet they'd lived most of their lives as close as sisters. And Allegra owed it to her friend to be completely honest with her.

Taking a deep breath, she said, "I saw you in your garden. You were lying on the ground beside one of your weird flowers."

"Was I dead?" Again with the bland expression. Good actress.

Allegra nodded.

"Any idea when this will happen?"

Allegra shook her head, unable to voice the words because of the huge lump in her throat. She was still trying to get over the fact that she'd just seen her best friend die.

Xenia freed her hand from Allegra's now vice-like grip, and rapped her nails rhythmically on the table - a habit of hers from way back when they were in school - her eyes staring up at the ceiling as she considered something. Then she looked at Allegra and said, "Which flower was that? Describe it."

Allegra frowned, trying to remember anything specific about the bloom. "It was huge for one thing."

"How big?" Xenia stopped rapping.

"About as big as my head I think."

Her friend nodded, her skin a little gray now. "Color?"

"Purple. So dark it was almost black."

Xenia's eyes widened a fraction, and she let out a breath that Allegra hadn't even realized her friend had been holding. "I just bought that. It's called Agrippina Noctus. It blooms once every decade, and only at night."

Allegra leaned forward, her ears buzzing. "So when will it bloom again?"

Xenia's features tightened, and she looked a little ill herself. "In three months, give or take a week. The bud has only just appeared."

Allegra's shoulders slumped as she felt the fight drain from her body. "That's not good."

"Understatement."

"You see? This is the very reason I didn't want to test it on you. I don't think I can handle the burden of knowing that so many people are going to die from the sickness. Especially the people I love."

"So the symptoms . . . were they similar?" asked Xenia. Allegra noticed that she didn't include herself in the question. She could understand why; it would make it more real.

Reluctantly, Allegra nodded. "Dehydration, fever. Dying of thirst." None of the deaths were a pretty sight and Allegra was determined not to elaborate.

She watched in silence as Xenia called a waiter and ordered a couple of brandies. Allegra didn't bother to remind her that it was the middle of the day. To be honest, it was probably the best idea. Her nerves too needed calming.

Both girls sat in banter-free silence as they waited for the drinks to arrive. Even though Allegra noticed her friend's hands shaking, she refrained from pointing it out. When the waiter arrived, they lifted their glasses and downed each of their single shots in one swallow.

Allegra laughed as they thunked the glasses back onto the table. "We should have told him to make it a double."

Xenia snorted. "That's all we need right now. To get smashed while the sun is still shining."

Pepper got to his feet again and nuzzled the girl's elbows, first trying to gain Xenia's attention, and then Allegra's when his mistress nudged him away.

Without thinking, Allegra reached out and patted him on the head. The vision was unexpected, especially since she'd automatically assumed that this new ability applied only to humans.

The handsome golden retriever limped down a deserted road flanked by storefronts with shattered windows and a scattering of tire-less rusted cars. Pepper's usually-rich golden coat was flea-bitten, his ribs poking painfully through his skin.

Allegra recognized the area, a side road that led into the marina with the Las Suertes harbor in the distance. The waters were dark and silent, garbage and random debris floating on the oily surface. The ships docked at the piers listed to one side, all rusted and abandoned, except for a flock of silent gulls.

Dear merciful Apollo.

Allegra snatched her hand away, unable to hold back a mournful sob. This time a nearby couple turned to stare at her undesirable public display of emotion. She ignored them and looked at Xenia.

"Pepper?" asked Xenia, looking away to inspect the ocean before Allegra could answer.

"He was alive," Allegra spoke softly, "but barely. Starved, alone. The whole waterfront looked abandoned."

Xenia stared at her, forlorn, her expression dark and scared. "He would not be all alone if you still survived. I know that much. You haven't seen yourself . . .?"

Allegra rubbed her middle finger over her left wrist, where the blue veins shone through her pale skin.

Nothing.

"It doesn't seem to work like that. But being able to see it coming does not make me immune." She swallowed. "Pepper looked so forlorn. But whatever happened, it didn't kill him."

Xenia's hand moved over the dog's head in a protective gesture. "Small comfort when he's left hungry and alone."

Allegra reached for her friend's other hand, this time uncaring if she received another vision. "It won't come to that. It'll be okay."

Xenia nodded and sniffed, giving Pepper a quick glance as he whined and looked up at her. He knew his mom's moods, and crying wasn't something Xenia did often.

Cause for concern.

"I know it will. You've always been able to take the correct precautions, and those who did listen to your warnings . . . they were safe. You just have to see what you can do to stop *this* from happening." Xenia watched her face, waiting for Allegra to respond. "Right?" she urged.

Allegra nodded, her neck muscles tight. "Exactly. And usually my feelings are about stuff that happens soon. Like today and tomorrow." Xenia was nodding, making Allegra feel a little more confident. "That gives me more time to find a solution. And these visions? They didn't seem like an immediate threat. And the future . . . it isn't written in stone . . . so there is hope we can do something to avoid it."

Both girls fell silent, pondering the potential for failure.

Allegra's stomach twinged. She didn't like the idea that people's lives rested on the decisions she was about to make. If only the gods had not abandoned humanity. Had they still cared Allegra would have been able to pray for help with some chance of success.

Of course, a growing minority of people argued the gods had never existed in the first place. Whatever the case, humanity was on its own. There was nobody for Allegra to turn to.

Yet, surely the fate of the world couldn't rest on her shoulders alone?

CHAPTER 4

The house felt claustrophobic.

Allegra was so on edge after the visions that she'd canceled all her standing appointments and sent a message to the service to refrain from sending her any new clients.

Call it cowardice, but Allegra couldn't stomach seeing anyone else die a miserable, bloody death. Not until she figured out what she was going to do about it.

Now, she sipped nervously at a cup of coffee as she sat on her deck. Dark angry waves battled it out on the distant horizon, the shadowy black smudges marring the pure beauty of the cobalt sky. The ocean heaved and plunged, navy blue clouds skidding overhead.

The view only amplified her grim mood.

At last, she threw the dregs of her coffee over the railing and watched the liquid splash onto the rocks below, creamy brown hitting black jagged edges and splintering into hundreds of tiny droplets. The sight made her shiver.

She felt like those droplets, torn asunder by visions that she couldn't understand, visions that made so little sense to her.

Allegra spun on her heel and headed inside, depositing the cup in the sink without bothering to rinse it out.

She went down the hall to her study, and took a seat at her desk. Sometimes she worked there, in the airy room that used to belong to her father Aleks. She filled in forms and submitted paperwork on Nike Rehab's fancy new system.

Flipping the switch on the heavy base of her personal computer, Allegra waited as the machine whirred and clunked. Finally, a few minutes and a whole lot of beeps later, the square monitor revealed a dark screen and blinking white words requesting her password.

Punching it in on the rectangular keyboard, she used the mouse to click the browser sign on the main screen and waited for the program to load.

Allegra tapped her fingers and stared out of the window. Beyond the glass panes, the apple and orange trees in the orchard called to her. She loved walking through the trees in the mornings, sipping her coffee and checking for ripe fruit.

Not today.

Today, when she looked at the trees, all she could see were rotten dying branches. Her imagination of course. Her visions had seemed to point to human deaths only, as Pepper and all flora and fauna seemed to survive whatever scourge was eradicating the humans.

The computer bleeped and she typed in words related to her visions; thirst, blood, starvation, death. The search engine brought up a range of results and Allegra spent the next few hours skimming through them and taking notes, devoting all her free time to research.

Fortunately, her modest trust fund and what little savings she'd accumulated, allowed her to take some weeks off until she got to the bottom of her deadly visions.

Not permanently, of course.

But then, what did *permanent* mean at this point? What was money anyway if everyone was about to die?

Allegra shook her head, wondering where that morbid thought had come from. She'd seen the deaths of a few people. That did not mean everyone was going to die.

She had to know more about what was going on.

But the more she researched, the less she understood. The symptoms pointed to a flu- or a pox-like disease. The festering sores and boils had suggested a pox or leprosy, but none of those diseases had existed for centuries. Not since the Black Plague which had decimated the population all across the world about five hundred years earlier.

People had learned their lesson then, and steps had been taken to keep cities and homes cleaner, to install water-filtration systems and implement sewerage control. Hygiene had long since become a top priority for most governments.

Allegra studied the websites on public health and began to draw a clearer picture of what she'd seen. She compared the symptoms of the dead and dying to the symptoms she'd seen in her visions and came to only one conclusion.

A strong contagion, similar to the pox but much more virulent, causing complete incapacitation of affected patients.

She frowned, scanning the sites again, an idea brewing in her head as to her next step. Contacting the government's Disease Control Department.

A sharp, almost angry knock sounded at her front door, and Allegra instinctively jerked her hands from the keyboard. Irrationally, she felt almost guilty about her browser's gloomy content.

She sat at her desk for a few moments, reluctant to open the door. Maybe whoever they were would just go away if she refused to answer?

A second knock echoed around the house, this one more peremptory, a little sharper.

Allegra sighed, got to her feet and switched off her computer, before heading to the front door. Who in Apollo's name was so damned insistent?

Through the glass panel in the front door, she took in two men in pale suits, the gold olive-branch pins on their shoulders holding a swag of purple fabric in place.

Officers of the government.

FAPA.

Federal Agency for Paranormal Affairs

Allegra stiffened, but since she couldn't hide now that they'd likely seen her through the glass as clearly as she had them, she was forced to open the door.

Pasting on a polite smile she greeted the men. The one closest to Allegra was a tall blond, his hair cut square on his forehead, giving his face a closed-in look. His eyes were beads of suspicion, scanning her from head to toe.

Allegra forced her face into a mask of calm, giving away nothing of her emotional turmoil. She'd heard that some of the FAPA agents had the power to read minds and to foretell the future. Probably not as strong as Allegra's power, but sufficient to know when they were apprehending a guilty party.

In this case, Allegra felt guilty despite not having done a damn thing to deserve feeling that way. She steeled herself as the blond-haired hulk spoke.

"Citizen Allegra Damascus?"

"Yes, that's me," she said, keeping her tone even. He was already putting her on edge, making her nervous.

"I'm Agent Kendall from the FAPA office in Las Suertes."

Las Suertes was the nearest large city. A visit from the city office meant something big was happening. Serious enough to bring in the big guns.

"This is Agent Ravik. We have a few questions for you."

Allegra hesitated, then gave a subdued nod before showing them inside. Something told her she was going to regret being so welcoming, but for now she wasn't about to hinder an official investigation. Even if she were the subject of said investigation.

Agent Blond, Allegra had already forgotten his name, refused to take a seat on the sofa she'd indicated, instead inspecting the rows of framed black-and-white photographs that bedecked the shelves set against the stone fireplace wall.

Allegra sat, watching him complete a circumnavigation of the simple white and gray decor of the room, his eyes roving, observant, critical. As he moved, Allegra rubbed her finger over her left wrist absently.

He came to a stop beside his partner who'd been nice enough to sit with her, his small dark face the picture of respect. He hadn't met her eyes, just gave her a fleeting glance or two.

An act maybe?

Now, Blond studied her from beneath his thick pale eyelashes, his nose slightly tilted upward, his demeanor a little too haughty, more suited to a senator than an agent. "We've received some disturbing reports."

He let the comment hang in the air, as if Allegra would magically know what he was talking about. She didn't.

She shook her head slowly, biting her lip, and sent him a questioning glance.

He shrugged one shoulder and his brows twisted in annoyance. He removed a small purple notebook from his pocket, producing the book with a flourish.

"People have been discussing your 'prediction'."

Allegra's stomach tightened. "What prediction?"

Word must have gotten around fast for the feds to get here so quickly.

Allegra's stomach tightened and she had to force herself to sit still.

"Your predictions of doom, Citizen Damascus." The second agent had finally deigned to speak. He too had removed his notebook and was staring down at the pages, his expression disapproving now. No longer neutral. "We've been informed that you are spreading tales of impending death within the community. The citizenry are unhappy with such disturbing rumors."

"*Who's* saying these things?" asked Allegra, leaning forward toward the wide stone coffee table, though she could guess easily enough.

"Our source is irrelevant in this matter."

"What? That's ridiculous. Aren't all citizens supposed to have the right to rebut against any accuser?" With effort, Allegra forced herself to retain control of her emotions, and her tongue. "The Breslins know full well what happened," she said calmly.

"Why don't *you* tell us what happened?" Blond took a step closer, his expression now hard, intense, as if his life depended on her answer.

Allegra lifted her chin, reluctant to go into detail about what she'd seen.

Blond took it as defiance.

He stormed forward, four long strides that brought him right to her feet. The threatening move forced Allegra to stand. She would not remain seated while the hulking man loomed over her, beating her into submission with his shadow and his height.

She looked at his face, refusing to lower her gaze as he studied her. She, in turn, studied him, assessing his strength, muscled shoulders, well-developed thighs. Large hands. There was a power to him that Allegra knew she'd be useless against if he threatened her bodily.

Despite her martial arts training, or perhaps because of it, she wasn't stupid enough to assume that she'd be able to take him, especially when he appeared to be almost twice her size.

Besides even if, by sheer luck, she managed to take him on, there were two of them. And they were federal agents.

Paranoid, aren't you.

Agent Ravik took a breath. "What we have heard so far can be construed as an attempt to scam your clients. An attempt that backfired on you."

"*What?*" Allegra wasn't sure whether to be shocked or amused. "Look, I would not have said anything to Breslin, except that I was so startled by such a sudden and vivid vision, that I wasn't able to hide my reaction. And, I have not the slightest idea whether what I saw was genuine or not – I *hope* it was just my vivid imagination." If only. "The accusation that I wanted to scam them is totally baseless. You'd be hard pressed to find a witness who can testify that I ever asked for money."

"That demand usually comes *after* the victims are properly frightened," Blond observed, unimpressed by her denial. "You beat it when they refused to fall for your spiel."

Allegra huffed in indignation. He was stretching the story so much that she didn't think people would actually believe him, but from the looks of his partner who was staring at her so disapprovingly, his version might actually make sense to those who had never met her.

Blond glanced at his partner who gave him a short tight nod. He looked at Allegra again, his attention focused squarely on her face. "Your prediction of death is creating unrest and undue concern amongst the citizenry. We have tried to calm that down, but felt the need to speak to you face-to-face." He paused as he watched her for a few, very long, moments. "We need to ascertain your legitimacy."

Allegra folded her arms. "And have you done so as yet?" she asked, slowly.

She should be losing her patience with his smug superiority, but instead she was a bundle of nerves, her thoughts flicking back and forth from vision to vision, her mind counting down the days until this disease ran rampant and killed everyone.

And killed the people she loved.

"Unfortunately, yes we have," Blond said, pulling her from her self-pity.

Allegra took a few steps back, putting the single sofa between herself and his threatening bulk.

He smiled. "You are not a trained or licensed seer, just an opportunistic amateur. I'm more certain now that this whole vision thing is a scam. I'm going to have to write up in my report that this visit resulted in a first warning. Any further 'prediction' activity may still be considered a nuisance, but after the third warning you will lose your license to practice physiotherapy. I doubt the Nike Agency would want anything to do with someone who scams their clients, no matter how . . . *talented* . . . they are with their hands."

Allegra was horrified. And outraged.

She swallowed hard against her fear. "How dare you come into my home and accuse me of such ridiculous things. Firstly, you've been decidedly incompetent, and had made up your mind before requesting my side of the story. And secondly, your accusations are all unjustified. To think you can summarily accuse me and write me up, when there isn't even any proof other than what others have said or imagined—"

"We have sufficient proof in the testimonials of several trusted sources." Blond's voice was sharper, and now even Ravik seemed angry at Allegra for having the gall to come to her own defense.

"Well, you two can just go to hell. The nerve of you people, barging into my home and making accusations and threats." Her voice wavered, and she knew it made it obvious that she was scared. She took a step around the sofa and walked toward the blond agent, putting bravado in her tone as she pointed at the door and said, "Leave right now."

Blond stood his ground, though his partner rose to his feet, as if to leave. But when neither man budged any further, Allegra let out a deep sigh. Without thinking, she stalked to Blond and gave him a small shove. Nothing more than a touch of her fingers to his arm to direct him to the door.

Allegra's fury fell away as the room was replaced instantly by a small enclosed space. Allegra blinked, opening her eyes slowly, staring around her in shock. She sat in the passenger seat of an automobile, the vehicle dark and gloomy, lit only by a distant street lantern.

Beside her sat Blond, his head lolling to the side, his eye staring at something beyond her shoulder.

Allegra tried to look away, but the vision didn't allow her freedom of movement.

Instead, she was forced to focus on Blond who no longer possessed the bulky shoulders and upper-body physique of a bodybuilder. Instead, his limbs and torso were emaciated, the flesh no longer filling the space between skin and bone.

He opened his mouth to speak and blood-flecked saliva dribbled down the side of his chin, dripping slowly onto his pink shirt. He seemed unable to voice his words, no sound coming from his lips.

Then Blond moved his head, turned enough to reveal the left side of his boil-infested face. The sores had eaten at his skin and here and there, flesh had rotted away leaving gaping holes through which Allegra could make out his bloodstained teeth.

She cried out, her hands shivering beyond her control. She let his arm go, taking a few steps away from him, and stared around the room, still not convinced she'd been released from the vision.

Blond frowned and dusted off his upper arm where she'd touched him, as if she was contaminated. "What in Hades name?" he said sharply.

Allegra backed away, shock filtering through her body, rendering her legs numb. Her breath left her lips in shallow puffs and the room began to tilt precariously. Convinced she was going to fall, she reached for the back of the nearest sofa.

"What happened?" Blond stepped closer, his brows furrowed. His expression was a strange mix of concerned and threatening.

Allegra shook her head, reluctant to say anything to him of what she'd seen. It would only cause further problems.

"What did you see?" His tone was insistent now.

Allegra shook her head and inhaled, the sound harsh in her throat. "It shouldn't matter anyway. You said I was a charlatan."

She gave a bitter smile.

His jaw tightened and he glared at her. Faced with his ire, Allegra forced her voice not to shake.

"What I saw isn't something people want to hear."

His eyes widened. When faced with the possibility of someone seeing into your future, people tend to see things differently.

Or so Allegra hoped.

He didn't respond, but his expression said she was out of choices. She had to speak. "You were dying. Boils all over your skin, lips bleeding, coughing up blood."

Allegra hesitated as the memory of the horror in her vision

came back to her. She shook it off and looked up at the cop, her expression sad. "You will die a . . . horrible death."

The agent's mouth dropped open. Then it closed again, whatever he'd planned on saying evaporating at the expression on her face.

Silence echoed around the room and Allegra felt a little deflated now. She was still upset at their accusations, but didn't think it was worth complaining to their superiors about her treatment.

Not now.

Allegra forced her limbs to obey and turned slowly. She walked to her front door, and opened it with a tug, her hands still shaking. She waited there, still and unmoving, until the two agents walked reluctantly toward her.

"I'd like you to leave please," she said, tired from the vision, tired of the haunting memories of all the things she'd seen in the last few days.

They exchanged a doubtful glance, a silent consideration of what to do next in light of her horrific prediction. Allegra entertained a short horrible possibility that they'd arrest her for resisting their questioning, but she was pretty sure that was illegal without a warrant.

Besides, they both looked far too unnerved.

Whatever passed between them Allegra would never know.

Then they walked past her, both men pasting on practiced, formal smiles, pausing only long enough on the threshold for Blond to say, "You will have no more trouble with us as long as you stop with your scam. We don't suffer charlatans in our jurisdiction."

The power of his threat was lost as his voice shook uncertainly. He'd taken her vision to heart. More than Allegra had expected, given his accusations and harsh attitude toward her since he'd walked in the door.

Then they were walking down the stairs, leaving Allegra furious that they still hadn't paid attention to her words.

Or her warning.

Fear tainted Allegra's thoughts, and a bubble of nausea rose within her as she slammed the door, bolted it and walked to the living room on unsteady legs.

Blood rushed through Allegra's head, her emotions a maelstrom of worry and helplessness. Feeling the need to cool off, in more than just the metaphorical sense, she hurried upstairs to her bedroom, and dragged off her clothing, not caring that she sent her skirt flying into a corner. Right now, a swim seemed to be in order.

Water always made her feel better, so maybe it would calm her down.

Allegra rummaged in her closet for her bathing dress. Justifying its astronomical price, it definitely ticked the beautiful box; swathes of draped fabric that repelled water, wrapping their way around her curves. It ended in an irregular-hem, gauzy half-skirt that reached one knee and left the other bare.

She'd chosen the swimsuit in direct opposition to the new fashion touted by the popular Vestal Virgins. There was nothing virginal about the Vestal Virgins, from the way they partied, to the men they spent time with. Despite their questionable morals, it seemed too many girls wanted to be like them, and too many men wanted to be with them.

Their idea of a swimsuit was a narrow piece of silk that covered the boobs and crotch, and not much else.

Vestal Virgins indeed.

They'd been touting the ultra-revealing swimwear range of a popular designer, but Allegra and Xenia had refused to follow in their wake. Not that she ever did anything because it happened to be popular, or touted by the press.

Allegra had never aspired to easy popularity, or to follow the latest fad. Perhaps it was because she'd grown up on the edges of society. Acceptable, but not quite rich or beautiful enough to become a part of any important circles.

Her father, Aleks Damascus, hadn't come from money. He'd made his fortune in real estate, building in a few years what many of the founding families had taken decades or even generations to accumulate.

Still, as successful as he had been, he'd never been welcomed into the fold. It hadn't mattered. Not to Allegra and her family, nor to those people who'd been their true friends.

Allegra grabbed a towel and headed outside. Her private balcony led one flight down to a marble patio, which in turn opened out onto the teal blue waters of the main swimming pool. She'd always loved the pool, had felt it quite stunning especially as it often matched the blue of the heaving ocean beyond it.

The pool had been Allegra's only extravagance after both her parents had died. Built like the ancient baths, it was tiled with pure white, gold-veined marble, its interior painted a deep teal.

Allegra dropped her towel on a lounger and strode straight to the edge. Without missing a beat, she propelled off the edge of the pool using her toes, launched into the air and curved into a swan dive, neatly slicing through the surface of the water with barely a splash.

The water swallowed her whole, taking her deeper into its womb, safe and secure. Water had always felt the safest place in her world. Beneath the surface was silence and peace, more so now that she felt bombarded by everything around her. The visions were a persecution that she wasn't sure she could endure. Not long enough to learn how to handle them and still remain sane.

She sank lower, almost sitting on the bottom of the pool, staring up at the surface above, her hair spreading around her head like a golden halo. The water caught the sunlight and sparkled, as if she was floating inside a universe of suns. Heavenly peace at last. Calm cocooned her body and mind.

She so loved the depths of the pool that over the years she'd trained herself to hold her breath longer and longer, enabling her to remain submerged for extended periods of time.

Just as she was beginning to enjoy the serenity, the sound of whispering shattered her peaceful calm. Allegra straightened, the shock making her lungs tighten. She scanned the pool around her, but she was still the only occupant.

But there, again, she heard the whispers, like a thousand voices all vying to be heard.

And then one sentence grew clearer. "It all depends on you." It seemed to call desperately to her from within the maelstrom of chattering voices.

"It all depends on you, daughter. Persevere, child."

The voice was clearer now, almost familiar. Excitement rippled through Allegra and she felt that when she turned around she'd see the owner of that voice. She spun in the water, swiping her hair away as it floated against her face. But still the pool remained as empty as it had been when she'd last checked it, clear sparkling water occupied only by Allegra herself.

And the voice echoed in her ears. "Do not fail. Do not let them discourage you, child. Stay the path. It all depends on you."

Allegra shook her head, her lungs tightening as air escaped without being replaced. But she wasn't ready to exit the water.

Not yet, not until she figured out what this voice meant.

But even as she spun around in search of the speaker, even as she strained to hear the woman speak again, Allegra knew the voice had gone.

Her lungs tightened and at last Allegra was forced to give up her wait. She kicked to the surface, breaking through in a frantic splash. She gulped in air, filled her lungs, then sank deep into the water again. But though she waited as long as she could, she heard nothing else.

Not even the strange scratching whispers.

At last, Allegra accepted the voice was gone, and rose to the surface despondently. She'd had such a sense of knowing when she'd heard the voice that she'd desperately wanted to see the speaker, and as illogical as it sounded, given that she'd been submerged, to talk to her.

She wiped water from her eyes, then swam to the edge of the pool facing the ocean and propped her elbows onto the side, aware for the first time how chilled her skin was. The intense blue of the sky had turned dull, the dark clouds now scudded overhead.

The weather seemed to reflect Allegra's inner turmoil.

The warm stone of the pool's edge sent heat deep into her skin and Allegra sighed. From her position, she could see the wide expanse of the sea, and a narrow stretch of beach below the clifftop on which her parents had built their home.

But none of that beauty had any effect on Allegra. All her mind could wrestle with was that voice.

Who was the speaker?

What could the message mean?

Coming so close on the heels of the terrible visions she'd been having, the voice made Allegra afraid now, instead of comforted.

She had the most awful sense that from here on out, things were just going to get worse.

CHAPTER 6

Knowledge is often its own special kind of torture.

Sitting at his desk, Maximus Vissarion clenched his fingers into fists, the tendons in his hands tightening dangerously. Frustration wasn't going to help the situation but at least it gave Max's restless energy an outlet.

Just enough to redirect the feeling of utter helplessness.

With the body of the Pythia Aurelia barely cold, the States' Governing Council was in an uproar, at a loss as to what to do about the prospect of the world's impending doom.

It all sounded so morbid and yet it was the frightening reality.

Max pushed to his feet, ignoring his chair as it skidded across the fake marble tiles of the FAPA office floor.

His movement drew the attention of a couple of his subordinates who turned to watch through the open doorway for his instruction. He got to his feet, headed out of his office and curled his finger, beckoning the entire team to follow him.

This kind of information was best shared in private.

He'd received the okay from his superiors to bring his team up to speed, but the situation was so precarious that they had to take precautions to avoid a countrywide panic.

Inside the meeting room, Max headed to the shallow platform and sat on one of the pairs of seats. He'd always hated the low throne-like chairs that resembled the old Roman Caesars' stools, but tradition was sacrosanct within the agency, so Max had little choice.

Unlike the boardrooms of more senior FAPA officials, Max's meeting room possessed no table. He'd always felt less official rooms like this helped to foster discussion and cooperation.

So far it had worked.

The rest of the team took seats on stone benches lining the walls, and Max studied them with a critical eye. Probably a good thing full togas weren't required here, although the swag of purple fabric over every left shoulder was showy enough.

Max raised a hand, a gesture that immediately settled the team. They all looked at him expectantly. As serious as the situation was, the urge to laugh almost got the better of him. He didn't think his team was expecting the kind of news he was about to deliver.

Max cleared his throat. "I have some . . . bad news for you. I want to warn you though. Everything I say within this room is top secret. And let me assure you that anyone who causes panic will be severely disciplined."

As if that matters, considering we'll all be dead soon.

He got to his feet and focused on the worried expressions of his team. "I've just come from a Council meeting. According to multiple and reliable predictions, we have a major epidemic coming. We've been conducting tests all around the world, hoping to identify the source, but as yet there has been no sign of its origins. Unfortunately, none of the seers were powerful enough to provide us with as specific information as we could have obtained from a Pythia."

Max began to pace as he spoke, his restless feet refusing to allow him to stand still. His words seemed to have sucked out the air in the room and he wanted to inhale deeply to rid himself of the suffocating feeling. But he refused to show his team how affected he was.

Agents in Max's senior position were meant to be resilient, unaffected by catastrophe and tragedy.

He cleared his throat. "All testing in the New Germanic States has come up negative. At least, as far as we know. But this threat is so dire that I believe it would be in everyone's best interest to share what information they have."

Max slowed his pacing to face his team. "Not everyone agrees with my view. The situation as it stands is one filled with theory and rhetoric, as well as suspicion. The Code 8 states, because of their germ warfare and biological research status, all suspect each other. The only good thing is they've agreed to suspend all experimentation and production of artificial viruses and germs for the next five years. But even so, it doesn't change what's happening right now."

Max studied the now-somber faces of his team. They weren't liking his news.

No surprise there.

A few raised their hands but Max sighed. "I know this is hard to take in, but let me get through the whole thing and then I'll answer questions."

He went back to his seat, but sitting felt too much like he was doing nothing. He faced them again. "All pharmaceutical companies and nutrient supplement production companies have had government overseers allocated, so be aware that some of you may be reassigned temporarily."

A rumble of dissatisfaction emanated from the seated agents. Max chuckled. "Makes little difference, people. As of today, everyone, every man, woman and child on this planet, has a matter of months to live. Possibly weeks - we won't know for sure until we find something concrete that will provide a more accurate timeline. If we don't locate and destroy this virus before it spreads, reassignment will be the least of our problems."

Max waved a hand, opening the floor to questions only because he knew his team would be filled with them and he could parse the rest of the details out a little at a time. Probably easier for them to absorb the bad news that way.

Jerard Bax got to his feet. "Why are we not letting the general public know?"

Max shook his head. "General Aulus thinks it would cause chaos, and I have to agree with him. Not even the senators have been told, this has to be kept within FAPA and a few other agencies who know to keep their mouths shut."

Flavius Lex, Max's Senior Locator, frowned. "The government is not aware? Not even the President?"

"Several other countries' top agencies have been briefed, and the results are not encouraging. Almost everyone in the know is abandoning their duties. A few have delved in charitable activity, others are frantically collecting wealth, as if that will help when they are dead from disease. The majority, such as Senator Gallo have taken to wine and orgies with Vestal Virgins. And other women not so virgin."

That drew a round of sober chuckles from the team. "Even preparations for the next Games have been halted, as too many countries' senators and backers have withdrawn to redirect their funds and energies elsewhere. But of course, the public is not told the real reasons."

Gallo had been a mistake. Aulus had made a judgment call, revealing the impending pandemic to the man, thinking he'd use his pull within the pharmaceutical industry to help the cause. Instead the man had gone off the rails. At least he'd kept the news to himself.

So far.

"So what else is being done?" asked Corina Brava, one of the two seers on his team. Although not of the same level of power as the late Pythia, she had made invaluable contributions to their investigations over the past five years. She did not look surprised at his news; he wondered if she too had seen something of what was coming, but he didn't ask. If she'd had anything to add, she'd have said as much.

Max sighed. "Senator Calvinius has sunk a large budget into PharmaCorp to develop a vaccine."

"How could they do that, without access to the original virus? If it even is a virus." Corina looked unimpressed.

Flavius cleared his throat. "He's been shackled by the Overseers I presume?"

Max nodded. "Exactly. It's more of a forlorn hope, and may do more harm than good." The Code 8 Overseers were extremely vigilant when it came to infringement. "But whether he submits to the rules is something else altogether. The biggest problem right now is that we are chasing our tails." Max hoped his voice wouldn't reveal how he really felt to his team.

"Especially now that the last Pythia has died," Marcus Asante said, the anger in his voice almost tangible.

Marcus was Max's second-in-command, the Senior Agent in charge whenever Max was out at meetings, visiting to the Pythia or in the field.

Max nodded. Only a few days ago, Max had sat a vigil outside a small town in rural Argentina. The last descendant of the original Pythia, Aurelia, had been dying of old age, and her humble farm had been inundated with visitors from major governments from around the world, intent on witnessing her death and hoping she'd be well enough to give them a last prophecy of their own.

Her decline and impending passing had been kept a secret from the general public in the hopes that the international press would not descend on the home and desecrate the moment of her death.

To Max it had been emotionally taxing knowing that a line that had lasted nearly three millennia would forever come to an end. From all appearances, Apollo had nothing more to say to humans. His wisdom and advice were so desperately needed, and yet he remained silent. No wonder so many people were beginning to doubt his very existence.

Max sighed and faced his team. "It's unfortunate that Aurelia died without giving us any further wisdom, or a clue that would help us save humanity from this new threat. We are on our own from here on out, and we need to behave responsibly with what we know."

He scrutinized the faces of his team, no more assured as to their intentions as he'd been of the superiors who had briefed him and a few other division heads an hour ago. People were naturally frantic, which was more harmful right now than impending worldwide destruction.

"Remember, there is nowhere to hide, nowhere to run. As terrible as it sounds, there is no escape from this disease, so packing up your family and running for the hills isn't advisable. You may do so if you wish, but you'd only be adding to the panic when it does erupt. And it will be fruitless, for they will all die anyway if we can't eradicate the disease."

"So we're supposed to stay and keep working only to die?" Corina lifted a brow.

Max nodded. "Or you could run away. And die." Max smiled sadly. "In the end, it is your choice. But if we are able to find a cure for the disease, then rest assured you will feel the full brunt of the agency's punishment for desertion."

Flavius smiled. "Well. How about we hope for a cure then. I'm not sure what's worse. FAPA punishment or living in the hills with my ex-wife and our two brats."

Everyone laughed and the levity broke the strain of the conversation. Max disbanded the meeting and headed for his office, where he paused beside his desk to stare out the window at the green rolling hills.

The trees hid villas, townhouses and marketplaces, but the sprawling city was built with such respect to the natural surroundings that you could hardly tell how large it was. It almost looked rural.

Max sank into his chair and stared at the files piled upon his desk.

As much as he'd put on a positive face for his team, the hopelessness of the situation made ordinary office work feel increasingly pointless.

CHAPTER 7

 urelia's death still weighed on Maximus's soul.

He'd known the oracle well, having been the designated FAPA representative who'd visited her every few months to hear her prophecies.

Her existence was both the best and the worst kept secret, with most governments and organizations knowing about her, but with the general public largely unaware of her importance, or of her prophecies.

Her foretellings had grown garbled and incomprehensible over the last few years, so bad that on the last two visits Max had returned without any actionable information. His frustration had only been amplified by General Aulus's impatience with the whole concept of prophecy. His boss had never been a fan of the Pythia.

Max flipped open the first file. Wasting the last remaining days of his life on dull routine was pathetic, but he remembered his words to the team and realized he was in no position to set a bad example.

He'd perused and signed off on a dozen files when he opened a report from the Las Suertes Office.

The report referenced claims that a scam artist had predicted how a rich tennis player would soon die of a terrible illness.

Max frowned. Had news of the coming catastrophe leaked out in Las Suertes, of all places?

From the report, the two agents, incompetents that they were, had brushed the story off as a crackpot trying to scam her clients. Granted that could be true, but given what Max knew, it was alarming enough to warrant further investigation instead of assuming it was merely a scam.

The young woman who had made those claims, a physical therapist in Barbarina Town, could conceivably be the real deal. Many people, like Flavius and Corina, possessed legitimate powers to foresee events.

Which was the very reason they'd been aware of the upcoming destruction. Aurelia herself had implied something a year ago, but at the time her predictions had begun to make less sense, and her cryptic utterance had been hard to unravel.

A few months back, four FAPA seers had dreamed of similar events but that had been a one-off, as none of those agents had since reported a similar vision.

Max re-read the report before him, trying to understand the woman in question and what possible motive she could have for masquerading as a seer and making such claims.

He put Citizen Allegra Damascus's name into a FAPA search program – if she had ever been interviewed or suspected in connection with a crime or trial, or if she was in the habit of making prophecies for payment, the program would reveal it.

Nothing came up.

So why had the local agents jumped to the conclusion she might be a scam artist? It did not make sense.

Nothing in her history implied that she was crooked, nor was there anything in her past that implied an ability for prophecy.

Why had she so suddenly begun to have visions that were so terrible and dire?

It was rare for seers to come into the gift in their late twenties. The power usually reared its head in the early teens and only grew stronger with age. Complete visions of a particular person's future were very rare, not at all likely for a mere beginner.

He stiffened as a thought crossed his mind.

Could it be ....?

Max held his breath as he counted back the days since Aurelia's death. It had occurred just six hours before the incident with the tennis player, as described in the report of the visions of the mysterious Citizen Allegra Damascus of Barbarina Town.

Could it possibly be . . . ?

He grabbed the phone and listened to the ticking of the rotary-dial as he dialed each number. Right now, it sounded like the ticking of a deadly clock, counting down the seconds to a horrific demise.

Click, tick. Click tick.

The agent who answered identified himself as Kendall, the same Kendall who'd filled in the report. Now that Max had had a moment to reread the file, he'd gleaned that Kendall, along with his partner Ravik, had failed to take the woman seriously at all. Hadn't even bothered to write up her version of the events.

After a quick discussion, Max put the phone down in disgust. The local agents had completely mishandled this new seer. In light of this experience, she'd hardly be inclined to help FAPA, or the government, now.

The case file also confirmed that the woman had had a vision while the two agents had visited. But Kendall had insisted the vision had been a ploy, a scam to get rid of him and his partner. His report had been restrained, but had been clear enough in his contempt of the woman.

Contempt or fear?

Max shook his head. Often people did things when afraid that made absolutely no sense in the clear light of day.

He leaned back against the soft cushion of his chair, peering out the door to where his deputy sat. "Marcus. You have a minute?"

Marcus lifted his dark head, his short dreadlocks swaying slightly as he got to his feet, hurried into Max's office and closed the door.

Marcus Asante, if he were a girl, would be called prim and proper.

His clothes were always perfectly folded, gathered or pleated, the colors of his garments well-matched and never clashing with the garish purple of the FAPA shoulder swag. His hair, always rich and glossy, looked good even in the dreadlocked style he loved, which could sometimes so easily end up looking like a cross between a bird's nest and a tangled nest of vipers.

Max knew because he'd worn the style himself for years, in his wild youth, before finally giving it up when he'd taken his new position in charge of the FAPA Capital division.

Marcus sat on the edge of Max's desk, peering at the file and accompanying paperwork, his manner no different than at any other time, despite having just learned of the threatening plague. He possessed a cool nerve as well as brains, and the man was astute, a quality Max appreciated in a second-in-command.

Moreover, Marcus was a talented investigator. Max would have been hard pressed to find anyone better suited to take on as deputy.

"What's up?" Marcus asked in an easy tone.

"I have a case in Las Suertes. I'm thinking of going in person to check it out."

"Sensitive case?"

"In a manner of speaking." Max slid the file over to Marcus and used his cobra-shaped scroll opener to point at the line that indicated Allegra's visions.

Marcus grunted, took the file and skimmed the contents. Done, he closed it and met Max's eyes. "I know where you're going with this."

Max nodded. "You usually do."

Marcus smirked, but ignored the comment. "I agree personal contact is advisable given the sensitivity of the situation. Recon only?"

Max nodded. "We can't afford to scare her off. If she's the real deal, then she herself may not know the extent of her power."

Marcus shifted to stare out the window. "You're thinking she could be the new Pythia?"

Max shrugged. "Given the timing, it's certainly possible. Either that, or she is a powerful seer that has managed to remain under the radar all her life."

"Or she's a powerful seer who has only just begun to have visions."

Max nodded. "That would explain how careless she's been."

"Agreed. According to that report," Marcus said as he pointed at the file, "she's a scam artist. But from what I've read, it looks like she's merely inexperienced. No scammer worth her salt would make such visions public without having a publicity plan in place."

Max laughed. "Excellent point." He got to his feet and grabbed a stack of files, placing them onto Marcus's already-splayed palms. "While I'm gone, you can handle the Bank of Hera heist."

Marcus lifted an eyebrow. "Hardly scintillating work in view of an end-of-the-world epidemic."

"Be careful what you wish for," warned Max, hiding a smile. Marcus was good at his job, whatever case it was. And knowing him, he'd likely have the heist case wrapped up before Max returned from Las Suertes. "Give the water contamination case to Lila. And Giorgio can take the robbery at the Sicilian Ambassador's villa."

Marcus nodded, gathered the files and headed for the door. On the threshold, he turned and met Max's eyes. "Will you be gone long?"

Max shrugged. "A day or two?"

"You flying?"

Max shuddered. "Not like I have a choice. Can't afford the delay of a road trip right now."

"Make sure you take your potion."

Max grimaced. "That stuff is poison."

"It's either poison, or throwing up all over yourself. Not a good look for the Commander of the FAPA Capital office." Marcus grinned.

With that he disappeared, chuckling when Max flipped him off.

CHAPTER 8

*L*ord Severus Langcourt stared out at the dull Londinium sky. The heavens hung low, pressing down on a city already darkened by greed, mistrust and betrayal. He'd been clenching his jaw almost without realizing, and now the dull ache forced Langcourt to rotate his jaw to ease the pressure.

He turned away from the rain-soaked scene, and focused his stony scowl on his assistant Charles Roquefort. Roquefort was the type of sycophant that would never rise within the ranks, no matter how much he simpered.

Langcourt kept him around partly because of his cowering, which in Langcourt's opinion translated neatly into supreme, humble efficiency. And it did not hurt that Roquefort persisted in addressing his master as *Sire*, an appellation generally reserved for sovereigns.

The man wore his hair in a short, straight-across-the-fore-head cut, as if he somehow believed that sporting the style of Caesar would automatically increase his standing. Langcourt inhaled sharply, making Roquefort's mouse-like nostrils twitch in response.

"I had thought that Aurelia's death would mean the last of the

Pythia line." Langcourt found it hard to speak the words, given fury filling his throat. He'd thought himself finally rid of those interfering females.

"The Pythia's death is surely a great loss to the world, Sire." Roquefort, as usual, took the wrong lead and said the wrong thing.

Langcourt clicked his tongue and glared. "Aurelia's death is no great loss. The Pythia blood should have dried up a long time ago. Several of my family's—nay, my ancestors'—plans were thwarted by untimely warnings from those cursed crones."

Langcourt glanced outside again. The bleakness of the view was a far calmer picture, reflecting none of the roiling emotions he felt deep within his core.

Suddenly the room, with its heavy tapestries and deep pile carpet, began to close in on him.

The old villa had been in his family for centuries, and was filled with treasures from around the world, from cities conquered by long-dead Roman generals of pure Langcourt blood.

Langcourt's family was well-remembered within the history annals, well respected even today in a time when warriors were no longer revered.

Such a shame that the modern world put more stock in peace and harmony than in conquering and submission. Langcourt would have been far more at home in the time of the Roman occupation, far happier being the conqueror for all the world to see, than fighting in the shadows, hiding his truth.

He cleared his throat and snapped his gaze to Roquefort, twisting his neck to glare at the small man. "I've received notification from our agents in Fornia that a possible new seer has come to light."

Roquefort frowned and Langcourt enjoyed his confusion.

"Seers reveal themselves all the time, Sire. Perhaps it would be unwise to concern ourselves too much with a new one? Our worry will likely be unfounded. Seeing as the Pythia is dead, without issue."

The man was all too confident of himself. His ability to go from sniveling underling to overconfident smart mouth, was annoying to say the least. Which was why Langcourt enjoyed verbally beating him into submission every so often.

Langcourt sneered. For all Roquefort's attempts at intelligence, he did manage to fail spectacularly all too often. Langcourt leaned over, rested his hands on the desk and stared at his assistant's face.

"My dear boy, it would be wise for you to expand your mind, think a little more outside that little box which your consciousness currently occupies."

Langcourt's cold smile widened as Roquefort's eyes grew a tiny bit larger.

"Perhaps you also need to understand the ramifications of the existence of a powerful seer. Then you would realize that the Pythia line contained many intelligent individuals. And as an intelligent individual, I myself would have put into place various contingency plans that would keep the line hidden as best as I could, keep the existence of at least some descendants hidden from the world. Particularly from people like me."

Roquefort's expression cleared as Langcourt's words sunk in. "Forgive me, Sire. It hadn't occurred to me."

"That is exactly my point, dear boy." Langcourt's lips compressed into a thin line. "I'm beginning to tire of your inability to keep up. I may have to consider a replacement should you continue to display such a pathetic lack of intelligence."

Roquefort, for all his simpering, was unable to come up with a response to that and Langcourt enjoyed the man's discomfort simply because he enjoyed seeing that flare of pain in a person's eyes.

He supposed Roquefort served his purpose. A living

pincushion that was also useful in performing menial, but necessary, tasks.

"As I was saying, a new Seer has piqued the interest of our Fornia division. Seeing as your background can be useful to this particular case, I'd like you to investigate the genealogy of the Pythia line again. See if we can get a trace on a descendant in Fornia. Or anywhere else for that matter."

On the mention of Roquefort's professional expertise, the man perked up, sat straighter. He was, of course, merely a lecturer, his qualification only at Master's level.

Langcourt would have been much happier with a doctorate but he'd had little choice. Roquefort had been the only genealogist at Cambridge acquiescent enough to do Langcourt's bidding.

He sighed inwardly.

I suppose one must persist despite the obstacles placed in one's path.

He turned to face the bleak view once more. "The last Pythia lived in Ralabia State for a time, one of those benighted Southern states settled by a mongrel mixture of immigrants. There is a possibility that she left behind a secret heir. She'd have hidden the existence of the child for its safety. And for the safety of the Pythia line."

Roquefort cleared his throat. "And perhaps given the child a different birth name?"

Langcourt nodded as he watched inky blue clouds bank on the horizon. "Check the timeline of when Aurelia lived in Ralabia, and match it up to births to anyone with the slightest connection to her. Friends, servants, employees. The gift is passed through both males and females of the Pythia bloodline, but can only manifest in a woman."

Behind Langcourt, the genealogist was scratching away in his notebook.

"That should make it easier to focus on female descendants. I expect you will be creative in your investigations."

"Yes, Sire. I don't expect it to take too long."

Langcourt sharply turned on his heel. "Again, you disappoint me, Roquefort." The man startled, unsure again, and Langcourt smiled. "Aurelia was not the only female who may have birthed a secret child. You will need to go further up the line, as far back as you possibly can, to identify possible heirs. I don't think you understand the scale of this investigation."

Roquefort's eyes hardened for a moment. As a genealogist he ought to know the intricacies involved in such a search, but sometimes the man displayed a severe lack of intelligence.

Then Roquefort nodded, his expression a little more certain. Perhaps the challenge satisfied him, but Langcourt cared little for his assistant's justifications. He slid open a drawer in his heavy pedestal desk and removed a thick, leather-bound book.

Placing the book on the desk in front of Roquefort, he said, "This is a record of all known descendants of the Pythia line going back two thousand years. It's as detailed as our investigators were able to get. Until you, of course." Roquefort smiled. "I expect you will be more thorough." It wasn't a suggestion. Langcourt's tone said he expected nothing less than perfection.

It would be easy and enjoyable to pound down the man's self-respect further, but Langcourt needed to leave him some sense of devotion if he was to function as expected.

There was a fine line between devotion and hatred.

Langcourt waited until the genealogist had finished his notations. "How long will that take?"

Startled, the man's face paled and he rose to his feet. "I'll get started on it right away, Sire. I should have the preliminary results to you in two days at most."

As he bowed and began to back out of the room, Langcourt said, "Make it one day."

Roquefort's eyes widened with shock. Langcourt suspected that the man understood now that the difficulty of his investigation had just grown exponentially with the reduction in time frame.

But, he merely blinked, nodded and bowed. "Yes, Sire," he said as he opened the door and let himself out.

Langcourt seated himself in his armchair and steepled his fingers. The deep soft cushioning of the two-hundred-year-old chair encased his body.

It had belonged to French King Louis, taken from his palace at Versailles when Langcourt's great-grandfather had helped raid the residence during the French Revolution. A bloodstain marred the old leather beneath the left arm of the chair.

King's blood.

His great-grandfather hadn't had it removed, instead reveling in the fact that he'd helped spill the blood of a monarch.

Even then, the Langcourt line had perfected the art of exacting submission. Nothing could stop a Langcourt from getting what he wanted.

Not even the gods.

CHAPTER 9

The flight to the West Coast was bumpy, uncomfortable and nauseating. Thankfully Max had heeded Marcus's advice and downed the disgustingly bitter *melissa* herb concoction he'd bought at Rhea's Herbal Store on Antonius Avenue. He'd also taken some *dittany* pills to calm his nerves in order to concentrate on his files.

The long flight should have been conducive to work, had he not been afflicted with airsickness every time he stepped aboard a plane. The Wright X720 aircraft was one of the first mass-produced planes and from all the bouncing around it did, Max was beginning to wonder if one day it would come apart in the clouds, and expire from age mid-flight.

Owned by FAPA, at least the plane was well-stocked and furnished for work. But, despite the comfortable seats and desks, Max couldn't concentrate. His mind went back to his last visit with Aurelia.

Her handmaiden had delighted in making him and the other attendees wait outside in the courtyard, with the hot sun beating down on his uncovered head.

A handmaiden who couldn't exactly be called a maiden,

considering Mara herself was all of ninety years old and more shriveled than the tray of dates she'd offered him.

When at last she'd emerged, her expression had been filled with somber sadness as she'd informed them of the Pythia's death.

Max had asked to have a moment with her remains, and while he'd paid his final respects he'd expressed his deep sadness at the old woman's lack of descendants.

At the time, he'd thought the handmaiden's sudden bark of laughter just a bitter reaction to her mistress's death, but now, with the possibility of another Pythia coming into power, Max began to wonder if that laugh had indicated she'd known something he didn't.

He shook the memory off, ignoring the cold chill that settled in his chest. He'd grown fond of Aurelia, and the Oracle had taken a liking to him. He wondered now what FAPA would do without her visions to help guide them.

She'd saved entire cities with advance warnings of volcanic activity, effluent poisoning, and once even a mass reaction to a government-led leprosy immunization project that had killed two percent of the people who'd received the vaccine. Not that Max's boss had ever properly appreciated the Pythia's priceless help. There had even been occasional grumbles about the duration and cost of Max's visits.

That vaccination disaster had needed weeks of cleanup and tons of paperwork. It had been very difficult to keep the truth from the press and public. Max suspected the authorities would have preferred it if the Pythia had kept that particular insight to herself.

Odd that the old woman had never mentioned a secret Pythia descendant who could take her place. Did she even know about Allegra?

Or was Max now grasping at straws in the hope that a new

Oracle existed, because a future without the Pythia's guidance was indeed a hopeless and dire situation?

He glanced out of the nearest window, staring out at the vineyards, villas and vast forests covering the land. Perhaps this visit would prove fruitful.

Perhaps Allegra Damascus would offer a hope he'd thought lost to the people of the world.

CHAPTER 10

*A*llegra paced along the kitchen floor, staring down at the gold-veined tiles, yet seeing nothing.

The heat of the morning was intense, and the back of her thin shirt clung to her skin. She'd thrown on a pair of blue cotton shorts and a singlet, the weather demanding the lightest, and as little clothing as possible.

She'd been tempted to swim, the cool waters calling her. But the voice from the pool haunted her, whispering in her ears, repeating the words over and over.

It all depends on you, daughter. Persevere, child. Do not fail. Do not let them discourage you, child. Stay the path. It all depends on you.

She stopped in her tracks, her bare feet slapping against the marble. She dragged her fingers through her hair, pulled it into a coil at the top of her head and spun toward the kitchen. But before she could lose herself in preparing breakfast, even though she wasn't in the least bit hungry, the phone rang.

The loud jangling echoed inside the house and jarred Allegra's nerves even more.

She rushed to the phone, irritated at the intrusion onto her peace. Then she paused, wanting to laugh. What peace?

She lifted the receiver off the cradle. "Allegra Damascus." She'd dropped automatically into professional client mode and was grateful she hadn't barked at the caller the way she'd wanted to.

"Hello, honey. It's Gladys."

"Gladys. Hi." Allegra suppressed a tired sigh.

Allegra had told the agency not to call her and yet here they were still calling. But she wasn't the type of person who could easily decline to help others in need. It was one of the reasons she'd avoided speaking to anyone from Nike. Allegra knew she'd give in eventually.

The exhaustion must have fed into her tone as Gladys said, "I'm truly sorry Allegra, but we've received a call from a particularly insistent patient. I'm really not certain what to do with him. He is relentless." Gladys spoke in a rush, her words tumbling out as if she was afraid Allegra would put the phone down on her before she finished.

Not that Allegra would do such a thing.

When Allegra didn't respond, Gladys continued, her voice lilting the tiniest bit. "It's a Mr Vissarion. He wants to see you. And only you. I told him you were not taking clients at the moment, but he asked that you make an exception just this once."

"Can't take no for an answer?"

"Apparently not." Allegra could picture Gladys rolling her eyes.

Allegra sighed. "I'm sorry, Gladys. He's just going to have to deal with it like the rest of my clients. I just can't see anyone right now. It's best if he seeks treatment elsewhere."

Gladys sighed too, and Allegra felt sorry for her.

"I'm sorry to put you in this position Gladys, but really it is for the best. I have a personal emergency that I need to deal with. I have to figure this out before I can devote my full attention to our clients."

"I understand, honey." Gladys did sound as if she understood.

Her tone was calming, soothing, something Allegra needed very badly. "I'll make him understand. He'll be upset, I think."

"I feel bad having to refuse, Gladys. But I just can't."

"It's okay, honey. You take care of yourself," said Gladys. Allegra could picture her smiling, the dimples in her rounded cheeks deepening.

Allegra rang off and headed back to her computer, impatient that it was taking so long to wake up. She bit her lip as she listened to it clank and whir, the base vibrating as the fan worked to keep its electronic innards cool.

Allegra knew little about the device, just enough to be grateful she could afford one. They'd been out for a few years, constantly upgraded, new ones already outdated the moment you bought them.

As clanky as they were, the latest introduction of elektroweb search engines and the constantly expanding documentation and information they provided, had made their bulk and ugliness worth it.

Now, she stared at the screen as she brought up lists of contagious diseases and began to write down symptoms in order to cross check them yet again against her visions.

An hour passed and Allegra found she couldn't concentrate any longer. She'd ended up with pages of research on diseases, lists of symptoms; coughing, sneezing, rashes, boils, skin infection, fevers, sweats.

Too bad that there was no clue to the likely geographic origins – these symptoms had occurred in some combination so often, on all continents, that she needed to find some other line of research, if only she could think of one.

Allegra's neck hurt from bending over, her fingers were cramped from writing and her ink was about to run out on her.

She wiped her quill-pen on a piece of paper and rested it on its cradle before heading to wash her hands. The ink in the device had begun to leak and always stained her fingers but it was unavoidable. She'd have loved to have used the text document on the computer, but it was inconvenient to shut the browser down each time she wanted to make a note.

The new technology was impressive, but it still needed work.

She wiped her hands on a kitchen towel, folded it neatly and hung it on the handle of the oven door. Her investigation was taking too long. She'd made so little progress that she felt like tearing her hair out.

A ball of frustrated energy was building inside her, slowly increasing in intensity, and Allegra was afraid that it would soon explode and she'd lose her mind. As it was, she remained afraid of touching anyone.

She was so afraid that she'd entertained, for a brief moment, the fear that at some point touching her own body would provide a vision of her own death.

Thankfully, as yet, she hadn't had that experience.

She'd prefer never to see her own fate.

She shuddered, pushing the thought away as she grabbed her running shoes and socks which had been sitting beside the threshold to the patio. Slipping them on, she headed out across the garden toward the rickety wooden staircase her father had erected. The stairs ran down the cliffside, providing direct access to the private beach below.

A run would do her good.

CHAPTER 11

As soon as Allegra's toes touched the warm ground, she set off in a sprint, her feet flying as she kicked up the sand and sent it spraying behind her. Running had always helped her to think. It did well to maintain her health and her figure too, so she wasn't complaining.

It was mid-afternoon; the worst of the heat was gone, but here on the beach there was always a refreshing breeze. She gulped in the sea air greedily.

She felt the burn in her lungs, in her calves, as she ran and reveled in the heat of it.

At Allegra's left, the waves crested and hit the shore, teasing her feet as they came ever closer. The wet sand would have been cool beneath her bare soles, and she wished she'd run barefooted. But this wasn't a saunter down the beach.

Allegra meant business.

Lost in the run, her mind was at peace. If only for a few precious minutes.

The beach ended up ahead as the shore curved into a rocky headland. Allegra's beach was more a cove than anything, but the length was sufficient for a good run.

At the rocky outcropping, she stopped and caught her breath, running in place as she cooled off. She extended her right foot, then bent low, feeling the warm pull of her hamstring.

As she stretched the various muscles, she turned her head to look at the beach, her eyes settling on the figure of the man walking toward her.

Broad-shouldered, tall and muscular, his skin glowed a rich gold. From a distance he was Herakles, striding forth with a purpose.

Dressed in dark slacks, a light blue long sleeved shirt open at the neck, he exuded an energy that Allegra felt even from so many feet away.

She continued to stretch as he drew closer and she liked what she saw even more, now that she could appreciate the strength of his jawline, the breadth of his shoulders, and the intensity in his gray eyes. Eyes not too many shades different from Allegra's own almost-silver ones.

He gave her a quick smile as he came to a stop in front of her, but all Allegra did was watch him warily. No matter how good he looked, he could still be a creep, or a killer.

Or both.

"Citizen Allegra Damascus?"

Allegra's expression closed even more. This was no random run-in. "Who's asking?" she asked carefully.

His returning smile was rueful. "I've been trying to get an appointment with you."

"Mr Vissarion?" Allegra's stomach tightened.

This client had wanted to see her that badly he'd come looking for her at her home? Far too stalker for her. She was beginning to reconsider her opinion on his attractiveness.

He looked about to speak, but Allegra cut him off, her tone wary. "How did you find out where I lived? The agency isn't supposed to give out that information."

Gladys was going to get an earful.

Vissarion shook his head. "The agency was extremely protective of your privacy. They refused to provide me with any information. I obtained your home address from the local FAPA division."

"They gave you my details?" This was going from bad to worse. The federal agents were giving her information out to all and sundry now?

He smiled again and despite her distrust Allegra felt heat coil deep within her core. It wasn't a good sign to be so attracted to a potential stalker.

Especially when he'd used subterfuge and lies to get to her. Not to mention accosting her without prior warning.

He cleared his throat. "I'm afraid Agent Kendall had little choice. There isn't much any officer can do when a superior asks him for information. Though, in this case, all the details were in the case file."

"Superior officer?" Heat bloomed in Allegra's head. Mr Hot-and-Sexy was a damned fed.

He pulled a wallet from his pocket and flipped it open to reveal a FAPA ID card. Maximus Vissarion, FAPA Commander Adamstown Capital Division of FAPA.

Okay, so he really was the boss man. He seemed remarkably genial for someone with such a senior position, and all the way from the capital at that. Still didn't change the fact that he'd tracked her down like a stalker, going so far as to lie to her agency.

Allegra shook her head, her nerves a discordant bundle in her gut. "I'm sorry, Commander Vissarion. I have nothing to say. As you mentioned, everything is already in that report of yours, and since you've read that you already know all the details."

She gave him a polite smile, then set off down the beach at a slow jog. She'd wanted to sprint off at top speed, but she suspected the man was athletic enough considering all those well-placed muscles.

There would be no reason to run off like a frightened female.

Footsteps thudded beside her. Allegra looked right and found herself staring into stone-gray eyes again. He kept pace with her smoothly, looking at ease, even in his most inappropriate pants and shirt and leather shoes.

"Please, Citizen Damascus. It's vitally important that I speak with you."

Allegra stopped in her tracks so suddenly that she had to stiffen her leg muscles so she didn't fall over her feet. "Do you not get it? I said I don't want to speak to anyone. Not you, not FAPA, not anyone. Can you people not respect that?"

Having so recently encountered the arrogant FAPA agents, Allegra suspected that Maximus Vissarion would be more of the same once he got to his interrogation.

Vissarion stopped beside her and simply shook his head. "I'm afraid I can't leave. This is far more important than you or me, or our personal needs."

Now that he was looming over her, Allegra took in his size, realizing for the first time how big he really was. Allegra wasn't a small woman but this man rose way over six feet.

She took a step back, glanced at the long stretch of beach, her peripheral vision shifting over the clifftop houses, the residents too far away to respond to a cry for help.

She had her training, and could probably do him some well-placed damage, but FAPA agents were known for their military training. He'd be hard to fight off no matter how talented she was.

"I have nothing to say to you. So please leave me alone." She made a last-ditch effort to get rid of him, even while knowing it was unlikely to work.

As she backed away, Vissarion closed in on her, not allowing her to put any distance between them. Her heart hammered against her ribs now, no longer with attraction for the man.

Fear rippled through her limbs as he advanced on her.

When Vissarion reached out to grab hold of her hand she instinctively cried out. A low thud echoed beside her as if something heavy had landed on the sand to her left.

When she turned to check if Vissarion had brought backup with him, she let out a terrified shriek.

A huge boar, all bristles and tusks and stamping hooves, shuddered beside her, living flames flaring within great obsidian eyes.

He lowered his head, stamping his foot, giving every sign that he was about to charge the commander.

"What in Hades is going on?" whispered Allegra, staring in shock from the boar to the man, and then back again. She was too terrified to take her eyes off the creature in case he decided that *she'd* be his next meal.

But the gigantic beast seemed far more interested in the commander than Allegra. Strangely enough, she wasn't exactly enthusiastic about seeing Vissarion torn to shreds, despite his would-be stalker status.

She screamed as the creature charged Vissarion, watching in horror as the man sidestepped the animal with inches to spare.

The boar's tusks were honed to deadly points and had missed Vissarion's sternum by an inch, leaving a clean rip in his pristine blue shirt.

The boar galloped off then turned to face them again, great rushing snorts emanating from its glistening nostrils. A gold ring hung from its nose, glinting in the sunlight.

"What is that thing?" yelled Allegra as she edged behind the commander.

But Vissarion stepped around Allegra, putting her in direct line of the approaching beast.

What a craven thing to do.

"What in Hades are you doing?" she shrieked, craning her neck to look at him, stunned that he'd use a woman as a shield.

"He won't hurt you. Stay where you are," he whispered in her ear, holding her shoulders tightly.

She let out a low strangled scream. "You're trying to kill me. Why are you doing this?" Tears blinded Allegra but she blinked them away, furious with herself for allowing her emotions to weaken her in front of this stranger.

The waves crashed on the shore, sounding louder to her ears now that she was caught within a maelstrom of fear and anger.

"You have nothing to fear," he said against her ear. His voice was filled with elation, as if the sight of the charging boar filled him with joy.

The man was demented. That much was certain.

Allegra sagged against him as she watched the beast gallop closer. The edges of her vision dimmed but Vissarion squeezed her arms again and gave her a slight shake. "You'll be fine. He'll never harm you."

Allegra shivered, barely listening to him as she stared into the fiery eyes of the oncoming boar.

What evil had she done to deserve such a death? Perhaps her visions were a curse on her for some crime she'd committed?

Or had she done something wrong with her knowledge to anger the gods?

Unable to face such a painful fate, Allegra closed her eyes, holding them shut so hard they hurt.

The hoofbeats came to a sudden stop and a rush of warm air blanketed her face as the animal huffed against her skin.

He is sniffing me.

The idea galled her so much that she cracked open an eye and peeked at the creature. Shock froze her in place as she stared into the boar's fire-lit eyes. His body shimmered with sparks of blue electricity, but he didn't attack her.

In fact, it looked like he was about to nudge her, as if he wanted to be petted.

Eyes wide, Allegra glanced over her shoulder at a smiling Maximus. "It is confirmed, then," he muttered, as though to himself.

"What's confirmed?" asked Allegra out of the side of her mouth. She refused to move her head and lose sight of the boar, regardless of how compliant he appeared to be.

At the sound of Vissarion's voice the boar lifted its head and sniffed at him. A strong hand settled on her left shoulder, and the boar inched closer and inhaled.

It huffed and snorted, backing away and giving its head a swaying shake. Then it reared up on its hindquarters and disintegrated into nothing.

Allegra sucked in a breath, forcing air into her lungs.

She was *not* going to faint.

She refused to faint.

Not in front of Maximus, the demented-hot-agent-man.

She leaned forward, hands on her knees and breathed deeply. Vissarion seemed to understand and let her catch her breath. Thankfully she didn't keel over and kiss the sand.

She straightened after a while, schooled her features and met the commander's eyes.

"Coward." She spat the word at him.

He only chuckled, his gray eyes sparkling.

"Not at all. You felt threatened, which is why he came. But he knows me, so it's unlikely he would have killed me." Then Vissarion paused. "Okay. Maybe he would have hurt me to begin with, before he recognized me. By then, perhaps it would have been too late."

Allegra shook her head and waved her hands in his face. "Enough." She stared at him, clenching her fists to stop them from shaking. "What the hell was that thing?"

Vissarion straightened, still amused, but slightly more sober. "His name is Xales. He's a gift from Aries."

"He's *yours?*"

"Not mine."

"Huh?" asked Allegra, finally cottoning on to what Commander Vissarion was saying. *"He's mine?"*

He nodded, looking like he was bursting to say more.

"That makes no sense. It . . . he . . . just disappeared into thin air."

"That's what familiars do."

"Familiars?" Allegra frowned, backing away from him, now wary again. "I am not involved in witchcraft."

"I wasn't saying you were. And besides, this type of familiar isn't connected to witchcraft. The boar is directly connected to one particular line of seers. It follows and protects each Oracle throughout her lifetime of service, and then he is passed on to the next in line."

Allegra shook her head again, unable to process the words he spoke. "What are you talking about?" she asked slowly, backing away and jogging toward the house.

She didn't really want to hear his words, her action effectively dismissing him. But she should have known that this agent wasn't easily dissuaded.

"Your visions."

She stopped at the bottom of the stairs and turned slowly to face him, one hand on the wooden banister for support.

"How long have they been going on?"

He waited as Allegra scowled. "Five days."

Vissarion nodded. "Six days ago I was in Argentina, at the deathbed of a powerful seer."

Allegra shrugged. None of what he had just said made any sense to her. "What seer?" she asked. Her stomach was already clenching when he answered.

"The Oracle of Pythia."

Allegra laughed. "She is just a myth."

"As mythical as the Seer's Boar?"

Allegra shuddered. "Okay." She folded her arms. "I admit you have a point, but I'm still not clear what this has to do with me."

Allegra was lying.

She had a vague sense of where this was going, but she refused to accept the possibility.

Not yet.

CHAPTER 12

The sun was warm on Allegra's skin, but beneath she was cold to the bone.

Commander Vissarion had trailed her up to the house, his silence following her like a living thing. He'd allowed her to take the lead, had even said she was the one in charge. That he'd take it at whatever pace she wanted.

It had sounded very much like a proposition to her, and she'd wanted to laugh out loud. But the rising hysteria within her center warned that should she lift the lid to her inner turmoil, she would, like Pandora, be in for a lifetime of trouble.

Allegra had suggested coffee at Khan's Koffee in Barbarina Town, a few minutes' drive away from the house. She'd wanted to remove the agent from her home, to take him to a public place where she would feel safer.

And now they sat on the outside terrace of the coffee house, at her usual table, waiting for the waitress to set down their cups of espresso. As tiny as the cups were, they contained a good kick in the pants.

Which Allegra certainly needed at this point.

She picked at the bowl of figs, grapes and dates that she'd

ordered, pushing the fruit around on her plate. Her appetite had disappeared along with the boar. Which she was trying to convince herself she'd hallucinated. Maybe right now she was hallucinating again and she was still asleep, safely back home in her bed.

Because only a bad dream would make sense of this morning's events.

Commander Vissarion looked uncomfortable as he studied the crowd, searching the faces of passers-by as if looking for someone.

"What's wrong?" Allegra asked, sipping her coffee. The bitter bite was an instant hit to her palate, and went down smooth.

"I don't like sitting out here. It's too exposed." His eyes scanned the surroundings again, then paused as he watched a couple across the road who glanced over at the coffee shop one too many times.

"You really need to calm down, Commander Vissarion. You're going to draw attention to us with your suspicious behavior."

He snorted. "That's a bit of a mouthful. Call me Max." When she merely nodded, he said, "We need to talk about this in a more private place. We must not be overhead. The information we have to discuss is important. Top-secret."

Allegra's eyes widened but she didn't object. Besides, she was not keen on advertising the strange, barely believable details of her recent days.

They drank their coffees and left the table to move further inside the coffee house, finding seats at a rear alcove shrouded in shadows. This time Allegra ordered a milk coffee and a coffee cake.

She was going all out.

"Thanks for agreeing to move tables."

Allegra shrugged as if it was nothing. But it had taken every ounce of willpower to clamp her jaw shut and let Vissarion have his way. She'd done so only to placate him, her entire purpose being to get him to tell her the truth.

He sat back, comfortable at last with the cowl of shadows enveloping them. "Your visions . . . they focus on a terrible worldwide plague. One in which people suffer from fevers, coughs and chills, followed by boils, sores and an intense thirst. One that seems to dehydrate them from the inside out."

Allegra stared at him in horror. "How did you know that? I never told anyone all the details."

Vissarion leaned forward. "We have seers who have confirmed this."

"And this Pythia … the one you know . . . did she predict this plague?"

"Once, a year ago, she mentioned something. Only vaguely. Aurelia had been ailing for a few years now. Her powers of prophecy, her sight . . . they had been fading with her."

"She told you about this a whole year ago and you did nothing?" Allegra was unable to keep the judgment out of her voice, but she didn't care. If he'd ignored the original warning, then he was guilty of being supremely irresponsible.

Vissarion sighed and leaned his elbows on the table. "Her visions, or at least what she'd mentioned to me of what she'd seen . . . they were vague. At the time, she'd been hysterical, terrified. Almost unable to speak of it. She'd already begun to lose the power of speech. Her handmaiden helped translate her hand signs, but there just wasn't enough information at the time."

"And now? How do you know these things if your Pythia is dead?"

"FAPA has numerous agents who also have the sight. It's one of the reasons we recruit them."

Allegra stiffened. Was Vissarion trying to recruit her? Was this whole thing, including the boar, a ruse to get her to comply? She shook her head, shutting off that train of thought.

"And their visions are the same?"

"As yours? In a sense, yes. All the senior seers in the agency, anyone with enough power to be considered trustworthy, are seeing visions of people dying. Through a collaborative effort we've managed to put details together that have given us a picture of what we are looking at. A mass epidemic a few months from now. Although they can't expect total accuracy, they're estimating three months at best."

Three months.

Xenia's purple flower.

Though it was a blow to hear her visions confirmed, in another way it was a strange relief that she was not the only one to carry this burden. Allegra shook her head, trying to clear her mind. To focus on the essential information.

"How do their visions work?"

"Mainly through touch. Similar to yours, only much less powerful, more shadowy. And sometimes through dreams. Our seers have visions but they aren't expansive enough, detailed enough. They aren't telling us what we need to know, only the worst of the epidemic symptoms and the aftermath. But the Pythia's powers are much stronger, they extend much further."

"Aftermath?"

The agent's face went a little gray. "Total annihilation of the human race. The seers cannot see people in their visions. Or at least not enough people to make a solid survival estimate or even a guesstimate."

"I see."

Allegra sat back, turning over Vissarion's revelations in her mind. It was a lot to take in. Had she not already seen much of what he'd described, she would have passed *him* off as a crazed lunatic.

At least now, she could confirm that she herself was neither crazed, nor a lunatic.

"What does the Pythia have to do with me? Why did the Boar come to me?"

Maximus sighed and his shoulders hunched. "Have you not pieced it together for yourself?" He smiled sadly.

Allegra shook her head. "I'm piecing well enough, thank you. The only problem is, I can't see how I could possibly be related to her, or be descended from the Pythian line—which I can't even believe I've accepted as anything but a myth. My parents had no powers, and neither did my grandparents."

Not that I knew of.

"Allegra, *you* are the Pythia. Aurelia died six days ago. When did you get your first vision?"

"Five days ago," she said softly, looking away from his keen steely eyes. Allegra refrained from adding that she did occasionally have strong premonitions and warning dreams. Still, she had to admit that the current level of conscious visions took mere premonition to a whole new level.

"I know it's a lot to process, but you need to accept it. Fast. We don't have the time to wait for anything. Humanity's days are numbered and *you* are our best hope of stopping our imminent doom."

Allegra shook her head and sat back. "This is insane."

"The end of the world is pretty insane, don't you think?" Vissarion said, his tone now cutting.

She could tell he was losing patience and she didn't blame him. She didn't want all this craziness to be true.

And yet his words meant that her visions had not just been a product of her wild imagination, that she'd really seen the terrible future ahead of everyone.

In that moment, she felt the pull of grief. She'd seen Xenia's death.

It had been real, not just some random dream.

Tears formed a hard knot in her throat.

She had to pull herself out of her thoughts to concentrate on Vissarion's words as he spoke again. "Tell us what you want. Whatever it is, we will make it happen. Money? Travel? You need only ask and we will provide it, as long as you cooperate and help us prevent the mass extinction of our species."

Despite the weight of his words Allegra stiffened. "I'm not for sale."

"I apologize. I don't mean to insult you." He had the grace to look regretful of his words.

She shrugged and then sighed, defeated, exhausted. "I don't need money in order to do the right thing for our world and our survival as a species. It's just that I don't see how *I'm* supposed to help you do anything about it?"

"Your powers are hidden inside you, Allegra. All you need to do is to bring them to the surface."

Allegra shook her head. "What powers, Commander Vissarion? All I get are visions."

He smiled. "Please call me, Max." Only after she nodded, did he say, "I know how some of the Pythia's visions work. I spent a fair amount of time traveling to Argentina over the last few years to meet with her. In her time, Aurelia was a valuable asset to FAPA as well as to international investigation teams."

"You became friends?"

"I don't think the previous Pythia knew what it was to have friends. She was a very lonely person. Her power kept her apart from everyone." He sighed.

"Perhaps she kept herself apart from everyone *because* of her powers." Allegra's voice hitched and though Maximus studied her face, she didn't turn away. "I understand what it's like to know things about those you care for."

She knew her fear was openly displayed on her face but she didn't care that he saw it. Somehow, knowing that he too was afraid of what was coming, made his company bearable, agent or not.

Max nodded, his shadowed features telling Allegra that he understood what she felt. He cleared his throat. "We'd all lost hope. We thought that Aurelia had died, that the last Pythia had died, without any known relatives. But it's obvious that you must be her descendant."

Allegra shook her head. "Without investigating my ancestry, I wouldn't jump to any conclusions."

Max smiled. "Can I show you something?" When she nodded, he reached for a plump date and a fig and set them in front of her. "The date is 'yes' and the fig is 'no'."

Allegra frowned. What was this man up to?

She was beginning to think he was a little strange in the head. Still, she nodded with a tilt of her head, uncertain but curious to see where he was going with this strange demonstration.

Max turned to look across the restaurant and out the giant glass windows. The street outside was sunny and bright, filled with passersby hurrying off, determined to get somewhere. "See the man in the red suit, the one with the blue hat?"

Allegra nodded. The man looked like an Indus peacock with those colors, but with fashion what it was in this day and age, Allegra had seen much worse.

"When he reaches the end of the street will he turn left?"

Allegra's brow scrunched as she stared at Max. She hesitated.

Max shook his head. "Don't overthink it. Before he gets there, just touch the applicable fruit."

Allegra took a deep breath, watched the man closely then reached for the date. Max turned to watch as the man reached the corner and turned left.

Feeling a light lilt of exhilaration, Allegra looked at Max who was smiling very widely indeed. "Right. A few more tests?" When she nodded, he proceeded to ask her a number of random questions about the people outside, the waitstaff in the restaurant, and the patrons.

Every time Allegra was right in her prediction, however insignificant it was.

Max leaned close. "Is there a way to prevent the coming epidemic?" Without hesitation, Allegra's hand moved to the date.

Max grinned.

"It proves nothing, Max." She gave him a sad smile. "I was hoping for that outcome so naturally I chose *yes*."

Max sighed and sat back. "Would you be willing to enter a trance? Trance states are quite pure in that they don't allow interference from the conscious mind."

Despite her misgivings, Allegra gave a tiny nod. "I'll think about it." Max's jaw tightened just the tiniest bit. "I'm sorry, Max. This is moving a little too fast for me."

"I know it is. But you must also understand that we don't have the time left to squander on uncertainty and hesitation."

Allegra swallowed. Max was right.

She was being selfish.

There was more to the situation than just Allegra's own indecision.

When she didn't reply, Max leaned forward and rested his elbow on the table. "You need FAPA's protection, Allegra. As the most powerful Seer in the world, you'll be sought after, a prize to be taken."

"By who?" Allegra laughed. Her head was beginning to heat up with Max's latest revelation.

Abducted?

Could this get any more insane?

Max smiled. "Various governments, some of which find nefarious conduct acceptable, crime syndicates. Honestly, the list goes on. Which is the reason you need our protection."

"I'm a martial arts champion, Max. I can take care of myself," she scoffed. "And besides, according to you I have a gigantic, hairy and scary familiar, remember. I'm pretty sure he's going to be enough to protect me."

Allegra got to her feet. She could see the disappointment in Max's face, the war inside him; wanting to convince her but not wanting to force her.

Yes, she respected him for that, but right now she needed space.

"I'll be at my villa if you need me." With that she left him sitting alone at the table, watching her as she disappeared into the street.

CHAPTER 13

$\mathcal{S}$urveillance Report:
            Agent 2481-K, Level 7 International
Location:
Khan's Koffee, Barbarina Town, Fornia, New Germanic States
Target:
Citizen Allegra Damascus - Age 24. Physiotherapist. Parents deceased. Possibly the new Pythia
Description: blonde, gray eyes, tall.
Surveillance:
Observed target residence. Target subsequently acquired by FAPA agent, identity unknown.

Followed agent and target to Khan's Koffee. Acquired table beside them. Agent changed plans, concerned with being over-heard. Target and agent obtained table inside.

Decision made not to follow inside as agent would have been alerted. Unable to listen in on conversation but visual observation sufficient to determine general content of discussion.

Agent performed standard Negative-Affirmative Seer Test. Target passed.

Target may be the new Pythia. Surveillance continues until Priority 1 enabled.

Priority 0: Identify FAPA Agent

Priority 1: Acquire Target

Caveats: Any means necessary. Target required alive.

Max strode down the corridor to General Cornelius Aulus's office, still slightly nauseous from his four-hour flight from Las Suertes.

Despite his feeling of urgency, of time passing inexorably, Max had forced himself to gather all available evidence and write up a detailed report while on the plane.

Cornelius was cold, pedantic and old-fashioned, stuck in the old ways of doing things. He often made it difficult to push through cases that needed a little more than the cursory touch.

And he'd never been sympathetic to FAPA relations with the Pythia.

Max was grateful Aulus had never interfered with Max's ongoing relationship with Aurelia. Now, as he reached the General's domain, he wondered what Aulus was going to say about the existence of a new Pythia.

On entering his boss's office, Max performed the standard military greeting. And waited for Aulus to lift his eyes from his reading material. The man had always impressed Max with his bearing.

Tall, slim, his balded head giving him an imposing air, Aulus was of Moor-slave stock, his prominent family tracing their lineage all the way back to servitude in the house of Julius Caesar himself.

But there was nothing humble about this man.

A few moments later, Aulus sat back and waved Max to one of the two wooden chairs in front of his desk. The General liked his decor à la ancient Roman military, and the two stools were more serviceable army than comfortable office furniture. They proclaimed 'say your piece and leave' rather than 'come in and let's talk'.

Max set the folder in front of Aulus and took his seat. "I do believe we have located the next Pythia, Sir." He waited as the general's eyes skimmed down the report's contents.

"Convenient that she's living in our own nation." Aulus spoke almost under his breath and Max stiffened at the sarcasm layered within those words.

He ignored the tone. "I'd like to return to Las Suertes and remain until I can persuade Citizen Damascus to tell us something more helpful about the source of the coming epidemic."

Aulus merely grunted and Max took that as encouragement to continue.

"She has refused a security detail but I'm confident I can change her mind. She'll realize soon enough how vulnerable she is."

The general leaned away from the file and lifted his dark eyes to Max's face. One could almost forget Aulus's African ancestry. Until he narrowed his eyes and stared at Max like a Kemet king.

"On the off-chance that you are onto something, I'll supply two non-seer agents. That should be sufficient while only *we* know of her existence. At this point, I can't afford to spread the resources of our Sighted Force too thin."

Max sat forward. "But sir, that would be a mistake. We're leaving her wide open in case someone hostile realizes who she is."

"I'm sorry, Commander Vissarion." Aulus closed the file and got to his feet. "But that's as much as I'm able to give you right now. My hands are tied. Unless there is a more substantiated threat to her safety than your vague fears, I cannot justify additional reinforcements for this unknown woman's security."

Max sat back, knowing any further argument with his boss would just make things worse. The man disliked being pestered.

Yet Max couldn't help but ask, "So, only if someone tries to abduct or kill her will we give her a decent security detail?"

Aulus gave Max a sharp nod, then took an irritated breath. "You may attend to the new . . . the *alleged* . . . Pythia personally as long as you have your department's affairs in order."

He waved Max off, leaving him with little choice than to salute and head to the door. As Max reached the threshold, Aulus called out. "Vissarion?"

Max stopped and glanced over his shoulder.

"Do whatever is necessary to retrieve as much useful intelligence on the epidemic from this . . . oracle."

Max nodded and headed back to his office, wondering what exactly Aulus had meant about 'doing whatever was necessary.'

MAX WAS FINALIZING the last of the files for close-off before he left for the airport when his office phone rang.

"Hi, Max?" Her voice was soft, tentative and hesitant.

"Allegra." He smiled at the mere sound of her voice. "I'm glad you called. Are you alright?"

She let out a soft laugh, then cleared her throat. "I wanted to let you know . . . I'll try the trance you mentioned."

Max let out a sigh of relief. "Thank you, Allegra—"

She cut him off. "On one condition."

"Name it."

"I want a friend of mine to be present."

Max nodded to himself. Allegra certainly had a good head on her shoulders. "That's absolutely no problem."

Allegra paused for a moment and the crackling of air came down the telephone line.

Max smiled.

Allegra wouldn't know that Aurelia's voice often set off electrical charges when she spoke on the phone or used a microphone. Max focused on Allegra now.

"Can I suggest tomorrow afternoon? At the old ruins of the Apollo Temple in the Daryan Hills?" suggested Max. "It should provide us with the right vibes."

"That's not far from my villa," Allegra said. "I'll meet you there at sunset?"

"I can pick you up," Max replied.

"Thank you. I would appreciate that."

"And Allegra?"

"Yes?" she asked, a little wary now.

"Watch your back."

CHAPTER 15

General Aulus surveyed the room.

The morning was warm in the Capital and the sun streamed into the President's boardroom. On walking into this hall, one would be forgiven for wondering if one had been transported into the days of Caesar and Antony.

A large stone table took center stage inside a sunken meeting area, which was surrounded by dozens of columns and statues of white marble.

All that was missing to complete the illusion were the obedient slaves, tongues conveniently removed in order to keep the proceedings secret.

The eight most powerful Senators running the New Germanic States were gathered, along with the President, as well as the directors of the Internal Security and the Military.

Aulus wanted to laugh at the pretentious lot of them. Still in their purple togas, having come straight from a Senate session, the senators were a perfect example of ostentatious, old-fashioned foppery.

But Aulus understood their need to cling to tradition. The purple togas, forbidden to lesser functionaries, announced their importance at first sight. Something the Senators enjoyed very much.

Yet despite their positions of power, these politicians were as ignorant as blind sheep. If they knew the truth about the coming end of days, they would continue to behave in an irresponsible and unworthy fashion. No need to scare them, especially when considering their unpredictability.

Still, it was a little difficult to take their plans to make war on several other countries seriously, when Aulus knew the likelihood of any one of them living to see those plans realized, were slim to none.

Not unless they found a way to stop the impending plague.

The buzz of conversation settled into a smooth rhythm of reports and responses, first from the senators and then from the President.

The man was a mere figurehead. A puppet seated at the head of the States, whose strings were pulled as and when the Senate saw fit.

The fool was far too self-centered to even realize it. And if he ever did, he'd never admit to such a blasphemy.

The President shifted his watery gaze to Aulus and gave him a solemn nod. With his height, and slim physique, and all that gray hair, the man came across as distinguished. Until you looked into his eyes.

"General Aulus, do you have good news?"

Aulus nodded as the room turned its attention to him. "Bear in mind that I still require proper verification from my field-operatives, but it does look increasingly likely that the new Pythia has been found. And for the very first time in history, she is a citizen of the New Germanic States."

A chorus of muted clapping echoed around the room as the gathering voiced their approval.

One of the Senators grinned and slapped the table. "Excellent! This will give us a serious advantage over the rest of the world.

The new Pythia can do well to advise us if our war plans are going to prosper."

Imperial Councillor Brutus, the Director of Internal Security, leaned forward. Aulus hid a smile. The man was a trained lawyer and never failed to provide his unwanted opinion on the legality of any proposal being tabled.

"We should consider the ancient International Treaty of the Oracle of Pythia. It still binds us all, including the New Germanic States. The Pythia is, and always will be, free to move and live wherever she so chooses. Not to mention the fact that access to her power is never ever to be restricted. We do not want to be found in breach of this Treaty. The penalty is being banned from access to her visions."

There was reluctant assent, although many of the senators were scowling. Then Senator Nikolos leaned forward. "*We* may know all that, but the treaty is very old and obscure. Neither the new Pythia nor any of her friends or advisers will be aware of its existence or provisions."

Nikolos glanced at Aulus. "Can we verify if she is trained or educated in any way with regard to the Pythia's lore and her rights?"

Aulus shook his head. "I believe she grew up isolated from the traditions of her ancestors."

Nikolos sent a triumphant smile to the gathered senators. More mumbles of assent, although Director Brutus didn't look all that happy.

The President nodded. "If she could be . . . convinced . . . to sign up with FAPA before she learns of these rights, then I'm sure we can keep her under our control. We need to remain ahead of the rest of the world in this battle for supremacy. We ought to do whatever it takes."

He smiled, looking very pleased with himself. Amazing how the man had missed entirely how well he'd been manipulated into making the suggestion.

Senator Nikolos sat back with a smile.

The meeting broke up soon after and Aulus walked off, still feeling the thrum in the spot on his shoulder where Senator Nikolos had slapped him happily, eager to know what Aulus was doing to ensure the new Pythia would remain compliant.

While he'd reassured the Senator that all was in hand, Aulus was beginning to wonder if Vissarion was the best agent to bring the Pythia under FAPA's control.

Vissarion was not the most cynical of men, and might feel reluctant to manipulate or trap the girl. On the other hand, there was no guarantee that another agent would even get along with her.

And unfortunately, Vissarion had a lengthy term of experience with the last Oracle. Which made him the best, and likely the only, man for the job.

Before he left the building, Aulus decided to leave Vissarion in the dark regarding the Senate's decision to control the Pythia.

Perhaps it would be best to encourage Vissarion to foster a more personal relationship with her.

If she lost her heart to the agent, like most women she'd be more inclined to be loyal to her lover and, by extension, tied to her native country and its rulers.

A convoluted plan, but Aulus could not replace Vissarion now. He could end up losing the cooperation of the Pythia entirely, and he couldn't afford that.

Besides, it was all moot until they were able to identify and avert the coming epidemic.

Treaties and senate decisions were worth nothing, if the world was truly about to come to an end.

$\mathcal{X}$enia, Allegra, and Max stood basking in the glory of a red-gold sunset. The temple of Apollo dominated a clifftop that looked out at the Endless Sea.

The majesty of the view and temple would have been the architects' original focus when they had designed their masterpiece nearly a thousand years ago, but now the temple complex was sadly dilapidated and crumbling, a testament to the diminished status of religion in these decadent times.

Nobody had bothered to remove the rubble heaps scattered inside the temple grounds. Allegra stepped gingerly around them, glad of her choice of footwear - sturdy, low-heeled pumps - as she kept a wary eye out for rattlesnakes.

The temple still retained its classical proportions and sense of beauty though, reminding her of the majesty of the ancient Greek and Roman dominion over the world.

Now, Allegra picked her way closer toward the main building to the stone altar in front of the temple steps. When had the derelict priests last conducted sacrifices on it?

"Here?" she asked Max as Xenia tottered closer on her high

heels. Trust Xenia to dress totally inappropriately for outdoor activities.

Max studied Allegra's face. "What do *you* think?" He meant for her to tell him.

With a hesitant nod, Allegra acknowledged his meaning, and scanned the grounds of the temple, taking a deep breath. She exhaled and calmed herself, sensing more than asking, for the right spot.

From within the center of her calm, something drew her to the peace and tranquility of the temple itself. She moved as though in a dream, stepped across a broken column, picking her way between the shattered remains of the once-stunning ceiling.

The inner sanctum of the temple lay open to the sky, and Allegra stood on the cracked mosaic stone floor, staring up at the already rising sliver of the moon.

A large portion of the presiding god's statue, Apollo's chest and waist, lay on its side. Allegra used it as a seat, not trusting that her legs would hold her. Hopefully the God would not mind, if he existed . . . but then, if there was a Pythia, surely he had to. The Pythia's power was supposed to come from him.

Her mind was still wrestling with the implications.

Xenia, her head wrapped in a pale blue turban, eyes covered in gigantic sunglasses, headed over to the edge of the temple building with Pepper at her heels. The dog watched Allegra with a worried expression as Xenia carefully dusted the stone before sitting down. She smoothed down her ankle-length silk wrap skirt, giving Max a wary glance.

With her friend's eyes hidden by those glasses, Allegra wasn't sure if she was scoping the commander out, or watching him in case he made any sudden moves.

Allegra would have bet on the latter.

The commander in question strode closer and crouched beside Allegra. "Probably easier said than done, but try to relax and remain calm." When she nodded, Max said, "I suggest you lie down for this."

Allegra raised an eyebrow, a little suspicious now.

"I'd prefer not to have to clean up the mess if you pass out and crack your head open on the stones." He gave her a half smile.

Allegra laughed, feeling a little bit of her tension dissipate. She shook out her hands in an attempt to relax her stiff arms. She was wound up far too tight for this.

After carefully testing the remnant of carved stone, Allegra lay back and stared up at the darkening sky.

Deep magenta swirled and mixed with rose pink and burnt orange, an amalgamation of color that was exhilarating and calming at the same time.

Max sat beside her and gently placed his fingers at her temples.

"Are you going to zap her into her trance or something?" Xenia's cool voice echoed from across the floor.

Allegra grinned and so did Max. "Unfortunately, I don't have *that* power."

He ignored her friend then, and proceeded to trace small circles at Allegra's temples, the tips of his fingers gently massaging her sensitive skin.

Heat simmered where he touched her, and Allegra briefly entertained the thought that he was coming on to her, but when she looked up at him, his eyes were shut and his forehead creased with concentration.

She refused to acknowledge that she'd been tempted to reach out and rub away those lines. Before she could think further about it, she sank into a different space and time.

Here, she watched the scene from somewhere beyond herself.

Max still sat beside her on the stone column, Xenia, across the way, cloaked in shadow. Nothing was different except all color had been sucked out of this strange version of Allegra's world.

The sky above was an icky mess of black and gray with not a touch of citrus or rose in sight.

Max shifted. Probably sensing that he'd succeeded. When he spoke, his words echoed around Allegra as if they were cocooned within a metal cell, the sound vibrating off the stone around her.

Max moved away, then knelt beside her, giving her space. "Allegra, are you ready to answer some questions?"

She gave a slight nod.

"Do you need the fig and the date to indicate yes or no?"

Allegra shook her head. "I'll be fine," she said then gasped. No sound emanated from her throat, and Allegra felt a shiver of fear run down her spine.

Where had Max sent her?

"Allegra, you must concentrate. You can't remain in the trance state for too long. It will drain your energy and your life force."

She nodded, sticking to physical movement more because the thought of not having a voice was little too traumatizing.

Max cleared his throat, diverting Allegra's attention from her emotional upheaval. "I'll ask you a series of questions. Take your time to answer them, and only answer if you are sure. No answer, means you cannot tell me yet. For whatever reason."

Allegra nodded again and waited as Max removed a device from his pocket. A dictaphone.

Good thinking, Commander Max.

Max cleared his throat. "Will the epidemic start in a governmental facility?"

Allegra shook her head.

"In a non-governmental facility?"

Again, she shook her head.

"In the New Germanic States?"

"No." Allegra said without thinking. Max sat back, staring at her, shocked.

Had he heard her answer? Surely not.

But before Max could say anything else, a dull thud echoed

through the temple complex. Something hit the ground. A male voice swore, his low baritone carrying inside the temple. More scrabbling sounds were audible as someone got to their feet, kicking aside stones and rocks. Then a man's head popped out from between the columns behind Xenia.

The newcomer wore a bright red shirt printed with blue macaws, and a heavy camera hung around his neck.

Allegra blinked.

Bright red?

She'd exited the trance almost instantly.

"Is everything alright?" the stranger asked, giving Allegra a worried glance.

Max got to his feet. "Yes. Everything is ok. Just, my wife keeps fainting on me." He gave Allegra a warning look, which was entirely unnecessary.

"Ah. In the family way, I take it," said the man, his pink cheeks blooming. "Can I get a picture?"

"No." Three voices spoke simultaneously and the man took a step back in the face of such a unanimous rejection. Even Pepper offered a short growl in support of his mistress against the intruder.

"The light," Allegra spoke. "It hurts my eyes."

Recovering quickly from the rebuff, the tourist nodded. "I see. Yes. Not a problem at all. Well, do take care." Then he was off ambling among the ruins, snapping photos of the pillars and broken rocks, setting off bright blasts of light in the encroaching darkness.

"Are you feeling alright?" asked Max, concern darkening features already shadowed by the approaching night.

"I'm fine. Let's try again." She took a deep breath and lay back down.

But this time, Max's fingers at her temples did absolutely nothing for her.

Not in terms of the trance anyway.

In terms of firing the blood in her veins, his touch achieved a lot.

She sat up after a couple of minutes and pressed her fingers to her forehead. "I'm sorry. I think the first time around must have drained my energy. I can't focus at all. Not enough to go through that again."

"Are you sure?" asked Max, a little distressed.

Xenia was already beside her. "Did you not hear what she said?" she snapped. She pushed her glasses back onto her head and glared at Max.

"I'm fine, Zee. Look. I just need to go lie down for a bit. That was a little too much like getting drunk."

Xenia nodded and helped her climb to her feet. "Hopefully you can handle it better next time around." She spoke curtly, and Allegra knew that her friend was having a hard time accepting the whole vision/trance aspect that now came with being around Allegra.

Allegra took a breath and calmed her nerves. Perhaps next time she went into a trance, it would be easier.

The same could not be said for the next time Commander Max touched her.

They left the temple grounds and hurried down the steep path to the parking lot below. Allegra had thought she'd been so smart wearing low-heeled pumps, but the ragged path was littered with stones and debris. The lingering weakness from the trance contributed to her unsteadiness, and when she finally did slip she wasn't surprised.

Max reached for her, coming to her aid from Apollo knew where. They'd descended the cliff-side together, but Allegra didn't recall him walking close enough to her to save her stupid ass.

His fingers touched bare skin, and her vision clouded, her skin going cold, sharp sparks of electricity flaring.

She must have made a sound, probably a scared whimper from the expression on Max's face. "Are you okay?" he asked, steadying her again.

This time she managed to control her features. "I'm fine. Really." She gave him a neutral smile. "You really have to stop asking me that question, Max."

"Allegra?" Max stopped and faced her, totally ignoring her words. "What did you see?"

She shook her head. "Nothing. I didn't see anything," Allegra shrugged off his hand and hurried toward the car.

Stones skittered on the ground as Max strode after her, closing the door mere seconds after she opened it. Allegra spun around, forced now to face him head on.

"What?" she snapped.

She was annoyed but more with herself and her inability to handle these terrible visions. Wasn't she supposed to be some great oracle?

And now, added to it all were electric shocks when she touched Max.

"Tell me."

She stared at him, shaking her head.

"Tell me what you saw." His voice shuddered, filled with emotion, and Allegra hesitated. After all he'd done to help her, she owed it to him to be honest.

She took a deep breath and waited for her heart to slow down. "I didn't see anything. The electricity when we touched…it scared me." She paused, searching his face as if waiting for him to say it was okay, that everything was going to be okay.

Instead, he gave an encouraging nod. "It's okay. Go on."

Faced with his trust, Allegra couldn't lie to, or evade him. She sighed. "I saw nothing. Your touch…I expected to see something horrible, maybe you'd be emaciated, as if your body was eating itself from the inside out. Maybe you'd be struggling to breathe, sweating, near death. That maybe—" she stopped. "That maybe I'd see you dying, Max."

Her voice broke.

Allegra was overwhelmed by all the death in her visions. Too many people she cared about were dying. Nobody deserved to see such a thing and still be helpless to stop it. And yet with Max she'd seen nothing. Just blank bare nothing.

"Allegra. Listen to me. It's okay."

Max gripped her shoulders where his skin wouldn't touch

hers—was that a mix of fear that she may still see his death, or was he just avoiding electrocution? Xenia hovered behind him, frowning with worry, holding onto Pepper's leash so tight the dog whined softly.

Max paid her no attention.

"We're going to stop this. It's why I'm doing all of this. It's why I worked with Aurelia. Her visions? They helped so many people. Do you have any idea how often we were able to save lives because of Aurelia's visions?"

Allegra swallowed, unable to answer with more than a nod.

"I know what you saw…all those people…but I'd very much like to change that future if I can."

Allegra smiled stiffly.

The fact that she hadn't had a vision of Max dying in front her, made her wonder what was so different about him that she'd been unable to access his destiny. It didn't make any sense.

She hid a shudder as she slid into the back seat of the car with Xenia and Pepper, leaving Max alone up front to drive in silence.

Now, she was more sure than ever that it was better not to know your own fate.

CHAPTER 18

Driving away from the Apollo Temple ruins, Max kept his expression neutral. Not that Allegra was paying him any attention. She and her flamboyant friend were discussing something in hushed tones, and he'd heard mention of a purple flower and Pepper, whatever they were.

He'd been impressed with Xenia's protective attitude with her friend, which only served to assure him that Allegra had a solid foundation of support.

Just as well that they'd been occupied. It had given him the opportunity to assert a modicum of control over his emotions.

Max had had to force himself to remain calm when he'd first touched Allegra up at the temple. The electricity that had traveled through his body as a single touch was unusual for Max.

He was certainly no monk, but he had to be honest with himself. No woman had ever had that effect on him.

He couldn't deny how attracted he was to her, but he had to remain professional. He couldn't afford to lose her cooperation now by making any unwanted passes.

The job was the top priority.

Saving the world was top priority.
Anything else would simply have to wait.

CHAPTER 19

*D*espite the late hour, Xenia was pacing the floor of Allegra's kitchen, insisting that it was an excellent idea to take her yacht, the *Qurux*, out on the water.

"It's a beautiful calm night, and you need a distraction after all that trance business." Xenia stood with one hip against the kitchen counter, tapping her nails on the marble surface.

"Fine," said Allegra, "just let me get my wrap."

She left Xenia mumbling about wraps on nights like these and headed for a change of clothes. Before too long, they were sailing out onto the midnight blue waters of the Endless Sea.

Allegra lounged under the stars while Xenia fixed them drinks at the bar. They were alone on the boat, except for Captain Flecht. The old sailor had been happy enough, despite being unexpectedly roused from his sleep. He'd smiled, his weatherbeaten sun-browned skin crinkling at his eyes and had cheerfully taken them out on the yacht.

The sleek white vessel belonged to Xenia's parents who were never around, and never really cared what their daughter did with their money. It seemed a game for them to spend it as lavishly as possible, keeping their yacht hanging around the harbor for months on end.

Allegra's family had also been wealthy, her father having run a prominent real estate conglomerate, but they hadn't thrown it around the way the Silanyos did.

Not that Xenia's frivolity with money meant she was vacuous or uncaring. She'd just never needed to worry about it running out.

Xenia handed her something red and opaque in a tall, frosted glass. Xenia's Blood Vodka. For Allegra, as long as it contained alcohol, it would do. Here, out on the water, she felt calmer.

"Thanks." She took the drink and waited as Xenia wriggled onto the lounger beside her.

Xenia raised her glass. "To the end of the world as we know it."

Allegra stared at her friend. "Zee. How can you be so callous?"

Xenia smiled, already a bit tipsy. "Not callous, Allie. Just realistic. You're going to try to prevent this epidemic, right? You and Max and whoever else is involved. But on the off-chance that you fail, you should probably see to your cute agent friend before it's too late."

Allegra sipped her drink. She tasted alcohol and not much else. "What do you mean?"

"I saw the way he looked at you, and you simply cannot deny that he is one damned fine specimen of adult maleness." Xenia giggled and sipped her own Electric Blue concoction.

"You're drunk."

Xenia gave a high-pitched sigh. "Maybe. But I'm not stupid, and you shouldn't be either." She poked Allegra's shoulder with one manicured fingernail. "Grab that sexy agent for a booty call. Have some hot sex to tide you over. Before it's too late."

Allegra snorted. "I'm not going to jump into bed with some guy, no matter how cute he is, just because we think the world is doomed."

Grumbling, Xenia sat upright, swaying a little. Allegra kept an eye on her in case she tipped off the lounger and fell flat on her pretty face.

Xenia pointed a finger at Allegra now. "You can waste away your last days if you want, but I'm going to take advantage of this opportunity."

"What's that supposed to mean?"

"I'm thinking now would be a good time to hook up with Evan for a night or two." Xenia sipped and giggled. "He had a great ass, that one. Maybe it's time to make up."

Allegra snorted again. "Yeah. I wonder how his *boyfriend* - whom Evan left *you* for - will take that."

Xenia pouted. "Oh. Right." She looked up at the dark star-studded sky and squinted. "Maybe Jean-Baptiste?"

"Married."

Xenia gasped as something occurred to her. "We could have a threesome."

"Xenia," Allegra scolded her very much inebriated friend.

The girls burst into laughter, but a sudden lurch of the deck cut their amusement short. Both got to their feet and scanned the heavy skies.

Wind gusted from the west, tossing the yacht up and down.

"Where did this squall come from?" yelled Xenia, the wind plucking up the sound of her voice and tossing it into the gusting air.

"Squall? This is a freaking storm."

A wall of waves hit the boat broadside, tipping it over. The girls clung to the rails as the boat began to crack apart, as if a great angry god was squeezing it within his fists.

"This makes no sense. There wasn't any warning on the weather channel, and the captain would have refused if he knew a storm was coming."

"You can't always predict the weather," yelled Allegra, but she was sure her friend hadn't heard her.

Another wave smashed against the boat, flinging both the girls into the dark sea. Allegra dove cleanly into the water, then surfaced beside Xenia who'd had the air knocked out of her and looked about to pass out.

Allegra slipped an arm around her friend's waist and swam to a piece of wood floating on the water a few feet away. Only after transferring Xenia to it, did she recognize the wreckage as a part of the bow of the yacht.

The broken boat floated on the heaving surface of the ocean in a scattering of broken wood and furniture. No sign of the captain. Allegra felt sick to her stomach.

Had the man gone down with the yacht?

As much as she was tempted to dive down to look for him, she knew it would be foolhardy. In the middle of the night, the ocean would be pitch black. She'd only end up killing herself.

For now, Allegra hung onto the piece of wood, remaining at Xenia's side. They'd been tossed overboard so fast that neither of them had had time to don their life vests. All their emergency procedure training, and none of it had been worth a damn in an actual emergency.

Before long, both the girls began to tire; arm muscles spent, legs losing strength as well as feeling. Cold waves barraged them constantly, and Xenia began to slip from the bow.

"Hang on," yelled Allegra, wiping her wet hair from her face. The storm raged so loud she could barely hear her own voice.

"I can't," shouted Xenia. "No strength." She slipped again, her fingers scrambling, her fancy manicure now all broken and bleeding.

Allegra grabbed for her, but her fingers met dead air. "Xenia?" she screamed, scanning the water around her, frantic, terrified.

With no Xenia in sight, Allegra had no choice. She dove beneath the crashing waves, reaching blindly into the water for anything, clothing, a hand.

Hair.

Allegra's fingers twisted around Xenia's long hair and she pulled, using a steady strength. No sense in tugging too hard and scalping her friend.

Xenia would never forgive her.

She pulled until Xenia began to rise, then changed direction and pushed her friend to the surface. Relieved that Xenia's body was floating upward, Allegra began to kick more strongly.

When Xenia's foot connected with her head, Allegra wasn't sure if she should laugh or cry.

Submerged as she was, the force of the kick sent her deeper, pushing her down beneath the powerful waves.

Allegra held her breath, struggling frantically to get to the surface. Her lungs burned as her body convulsed with the lack of air.

Allegra thought of Max.

She was never going to get to tell him that she wanted to kiss him.

She'd never get the chance to tell him that she really did want to help save the world, that she'd do anything to use her power to help people.

Her vision darkened and she smiled to herself.

Maybe it was for the best. What would they have been able to do anyway, two people against an unseen enemy?

Just as blackness began to claim her, something nudged hard against her elbow. Grabbing for it, her fingers sank deep into a bristly carpet.

More flotsam from the yacht?

She grabbed hold as it rose, lifting her higher.

Not wreckage. An animal.

Though Allegra was blind in the water, she knew it was Xales, come to save her.

The boar lifted her to the surface where she spent a few moments, coughing up water, Xenia frantic beside her.

Allegra wasn't sure what had frightened her friend more. The fact that Allegra had almost drowned, or that she'd been saved by a giant boar.

"Allegra? What in Apollo's name is that?" Xenia shivered and pointed her slim finger, a cracked nail hanging by a strip of bloody skin.

"I'll explain later. Grab on tight. He's going to get us to safety."

Xenia hesitated, staring in horror at the creature who seemed to float serenely while the girls were in danger of being swallowed whole by the black sea.

"Zee," Allegra screamed.

Xenia blinked, stared at Allegra, then grabbed onto Xales's side.

The girls held onto each other, shivering, trying to share their own dwindling warmth, as well as absorb some of Xales's body heat. What seemed like forever later, they crawled up onto the beach, completely exhausted.

They lay against the wet sand shivering, relieved, and in shock.

Allegra was in the middle of a fit of coughing when a voice whispered in her mind. Female again, but a different voice entirely.

"Stay out of the water, my child. The seas are unfavorable to your quest."

Then the voice was gone, lost in the roar of the waves.

Allegra frowned, lifting her head to look out at the dark roiling ocean. A strange light glowed from beneath the surface and a low rumbling echoed deep into her bones.

"What in Apollo's name is that?" asked Xenia, through chattering teeth.

Allegra shook her head. She didn't want to voice the truth. She knew exactly what it meant.

It was a threat. Stay out of the sea.

Stay out or die.

CHAPTER 20

*A*llegra closed the blinds that looked out onto her drive, suppressing a soft sigh.

After the near-drowning incident, Max had insisted on placing guards around the property, claiming that until FAPA ascertained the cause of the sinking of Xenia's yacht, they had to regard it as an attempt on Allegra's life.

Little did they know that it probably was.

But not by anyone that they could possibly keep her safe from. What power could mere human guards pit against the ill-will of a god?

Everyone knew that Poseidon's wrath rose from the depths of the oceans, culminating in tsunamis and volcanic eruptions and deep-sea earthquakes that rocked countries all over the world.

Death, destruction and mayhem in the wake of a god who saw humanity as a curse on the Earth. Until now, Allegra had always thought such fears were foolish superstition based on a dire lack of education.

Now, she knew better.

The guards had positioned themselves discreetly around her home. Max had taken up residence within the house, insisting he needed to ensure her safety more than ever. Allegra hadn't had the energy, or the inclination, to deny him.

She envied Xenia, who'd simply hired a top-notch security company to provide her with around-the-clock protection. The Silanyos had taken the destruction of the *Qurux* in their stride, and Xenia had calmly narrated a story of insurance payouts and a hunt for a new, and bigger, yacht.

Captain Flecht's death weighed heavily on both girls though, and Allegra made a note to ask if he'd left family behind.

Being that close to death would certainly put things into perspective for anyone. More so for Allegra, considering the responsibility she bore on her shoulders.

The door shut as Max finally left the house. Allegra had managed to convince him to go out and buy groceries for lunch. They had plenty of additional mouths to feed.

She had no intention of starving the men who were protecting her, even though Max had declared it wasn't her problem what, or when, they ate.

Allegra returned to the computer and browsed through the elektroweb while the machine continued its humming. The constant noise and vibration against the table had given her a mild headache, but she forced herself to ignore it as she researched the histories of the previous Pythias.

One article she found had claimed that the Pythias could sometimes hear the voices of their predecessors, dispensing advice.

Another hinted at mystic links to the Pythias of the past. Both claims were considered to have been debunked, but Allegra sat back and gave the idea careful consideration.

She'd heard voices twice now, and they had been undeniably female.

Was that who she'd heard when she'd been submerged in her pool? And when she'd escaped the fury of the ocean?

Had they been the voices of her ancestors?

She closed her eyes. *"Help me,"* she whispered, leaving her computer and closing her eyes wearily as she leaned against the window. *"How do I do this?"*

Not that she truly expected a response, but Allegra was disappointed when no voices came to her.

Shutting the computer down, Allegra paced restlessly before deciding fresh air was in order. She moved slowly through the silent house. She'd forgone her music these past few days. Even the classical symphonies she loved couldn't help calm her tumultuous thoughts.

Allegra entered the back garden and nodded at the shadow that was one of her guards. The roses were blooming so beautifully this time of year, and she'd been shamefully neglecting them.

Allegra grabbed a set of pruning-shears from the basket on the patio and strolled along, snipping off a few deadheads, picking off dried leaves.

A row of red and orange roses had been planted near the cliff's edge. Her mother had complained they were too close and were a danger, but Allegra's father had laughed her worries off and insisted the bushes were barrier enough.

As Allegra bent to prune the first one, the sound of someone crashing through the tree-line had her spinning around, shears at the ready.

Four armed men, dressed head-to-toe in black, faces masked, dashed across the garden. One shot at the guard stationed near the edge of the garden, and Allegra's stomach twinged as she heard her protector hit the ground.

A second intruder headed straight for Allegra, while the third pointed a machine gun at the guard in the bushes beside her. They'd come so fast the FAPA agent hadn't had time to raise his own, smaller weapon.

The thug heading for Allegra reached for her waist but she feinted right, kicking hard at his shin. He howled as a loud crack echoed across the garden. Allegra sped off toward the house, but a second thug crashed into her, taking her down.

They hit the ground hard but Allegra rolled over and was on her feet within seconds. Her martial arts training had not been for naught.

Jujitsu, Capoeira and Jeet Kun Do. Three of the most effective forms of martial arts known to the modern world.

She was as light as a cat on her feet as she spun and kicked. But her size was, and always had been, her disadvantage and since there were three brutes left who were intent on taking her down, she had no illusions about her odds.

One thug grabbed at her and Allegra saw her opening. She landed a solid kick to his balls, taking him down in a squealing mess, but it didn't last. A second thug shoved her to the ground and pressed his knee between her shoulders. His weight held her down and there was nothing she could do but struggle.

It seemed like it was all hopeless, when Xales finally decided to show up.

Hoofbeats resounded on the ground and then her captor went flying across the garden. The boar hadn't done more than stun the thug, because the man landed and rolled and was on his feet, his beady eyes staring through the slit in his mask. His confused expression told Allegra he was wondering what had hit him.

When he caught sight of the huge boar at Allegra's side, he took a wary step back. Xales then ran at the thug who was holding a gun on the bodyguard, taking him down within seconds. The guard finally pulled his gun free and began to shoot.

The thugs left in a mass exodus of blood, broken bones and bullet wounds. As much as her guards wished to follow the attackers, they chose instead to stay with Allegra.

In her opinion, it was a mistake since she had Xales for protection, but they must have had strict orders because they refused to leave her.

Just as she entered the kitchen, Max walked through the front door, bags bulging with shopping weighing both his hands down. He took one look at Allegra's face and dropped the groceries on the counter, running to her side.

"Are you okay? What happened?"

When Allegra gave him a quick rundown he grunted. "I knew I shouldn't have left you alone."

"What could you have done against a band of armed thugs?" asked Allegra. "I only escaped because I had Xales with me."

Max shook his head and grabbed the phone, calling the attack in and requesting reinforcements.

Ignacio Felix, the security detail team leader entered the house with a wallet one of the thugs had dropped during the attack. "Definitely unprofessional to have his identification on him. Rachel managed to grab it while they fought. At least *she* was thinking smart." He handed the wallet to Max who relayed the information to headquarters. Max waited while they searched the man's details then rang off.

At last, he said, "He's a local thug-for-hire."

"Which explains his stupidity." Ignacio's voice was cold.

Max grunted, then glanced at Allegra. She'd taken a seat by the window. Xales had disappeared and her heartbeat had at last returned to normal.

"The local police are on their way. It's their jurisdiction, so let's just let them do their thing and keep the details to a minimum. As far as they need to know, we're just protecting Allegra because we heard chatter that implied she was on a target-list for abduction."

Ignacio nodded and left to take up his post again.

Allegra didn't speak. She watched in silence as Max made himself at home in her kitchen and prepared beef patties, got the grill out on the patio fired and proceeded to serve them with freshly barbecued burgers.

There were no complaints, either about the menu or to the quality of the meal.

CHAPTER 21

*L*ord Langcourt could barely contain his fury. "What do you mean you failed?"

"I apologize, my Lord. Everything went according to plan. We were well prepared, my Lord."

"If you were so well prepared then why did you fail?" Langcourt spat the words out, his fingers gripping the phone so tight he could hear his knuckles pop.

"It was the boar, my Lord," whined his agent. What was his name again . . . Pedro or something. Not that it mattered. Failures had no future in their organization.

"A boar?" Langcourt spoke so softly that the agent would have barely heard him.

The Pythia's familiar had arrived. So it was confirmed that the girl *was* the new Pythia. Langcourt slammed his fist into the wall beside him.

"Indeed, a boar, my Lord. A giant boar appearing out of nowhere, standing up on its hind legs for Hades' sake. I was sure the men were hallucinating, but they all swore to it."

Langcourt smiled, all teeth, no humor. "Don't worry. Sit tight. I'm sending a specialist out to direct your next attempt." Langcourt was already paging through his Rolodex. "He knows a way to deal with such creatures."

Langcourt stabbed the cradle to disconnect the call, then pressed the button for his secretary. Roquefort answered a second later. "Get in here."

He dropped the phone and began to pace in front of the window. When Roquefort entered Langcourt faced the taller man, to see a grin spreading across his face.

"Good news, my Lord?"

"Yes and no, my boy. We were on the right trail after all. The team in Las Suertes came close to capturing the one and only Pythia in the world, only to be foiled by her *familiar*. Eternal wealth may be the reward of success and no mangy animal, no matter how ancient or sacred, is going to stop us."

Langcourt shook his fist, making Roquefort flinch, though the man remained where he stood.

His master paid little attention. "Call Citizen Norris immediately. We have need of his expertise."

Roquefort quit the room leaving Langcourt alone to enjoy the thrill of the chase.

They were so close.

He'd have the Pythia at all costs.

Whatever it took.

CHAPTER 22

*A*fter leaving her to recuperate for a few hours, Max suggested Allegra attempt the trance again. They were going to run out of time if her visions didn't reveal something helpful very soon.

She was sitting out in the sunshine, enjoying the view of the ocean. After her near-drowning yesterday she'd been a little pre-occupied—not surprising considering her life seemed to be in permanent jeopardy these days.

The attacker this morning had made things even worse and Max had asked if she was having second thoughts.

If she were, how could he blame her?

But none of them could afford to waste time feeling sorry for themselves. Despite his facade of unaffected calm, Allegra knew that the suffering of humanity—which seemed so inevitable—must have hit him hard.

But facing the confirmation of one's death must be trying, and Allegra hoped that the sudden distance he'd put between them would only be temporary.

She looked away from the view and smiled at him as he

walked out onto the patio, the sun blazing down on his dark head. "If you want to try the trance, I'm ready when you are."

Max nodded and paused beside her. "Here or inside?"

"Under the shade if you don't mind. I'd prefer not to get burned in the sun if we go on too long." She got off the chair and headed to the covered patio, taking a seat on one of the loungers.

While she settled, Max disappeared inside, returning quickly with his auto-quill - one that came with an inbuilt well of ink - and notebook. He placed them on a small stone table beside the lounger and sat beside Allegra.

Reaching out, he placed his fingers on her temples and repeated the process he'd used at the Apollo temple. Once again, she fell into a trance with ease.

Allegra inhaled slowly and blinked, staring at her patio, at the sea before her. Everything had lost color, the view composed entirely of shades of gray.

Max's voice filtered through to her and he began to run through random questions that made no sense to her, about robberies and assassination attempts, even a bar-fight gone wrong.

Just as Allegra was beginning to grow tired of what sounded like unrelated, inane questions, Max asked, "Will the pathogen arise spontaneously?"

Allegra felt a bubbling of energy within her and she nodded.

"From natural causes?"

Another nod.

Max paused. "Will the disease arise in Brittania?"

No.

"Latin Continent?"

Allegra shook her head this time.

"Now we're getting something." Max leaned closer. "What about—"

But before he could voice the question, the doorbell rang,

pulling Allegra out of her trance in an instant. Her ears rang, pain licking at her eardrums as she blinked against the noon sunlight.

Max looked disappointed but they both knew what had happened the last time. He wasn't about to pressure Allegra for a second trance.

She wasn't sure if she was relieved or frustrated.

CHAPTER 23

Max grabbed his cell phone from his case, while Allegra went to answer the door. He often wished the phone wasn't as heavy as a damned gold brick, or as large as a milk carton. But he shouldn't complain.

Only his position as head of a governmental department allowed him to use the device when he was out on missions. It was more than the normal population had.

The general answered on the third ring. "Maximus. What do you have for me?"

Max bristled at the question. It made it sound as if the general had a personal stake in Allegra's visions. "Sir, we've made progress. The Pythia has confirmed that the pathogen will not arise within the New Germanic States."

The general took a breath. "Excellent, Maximus." Max was dismayed at his superior's reaction. Before Max could respond, the General said, "This means I can authorize the Bioweapons Program to be resumed, effective immediately. The other partners to the agreement will still remain in suspension, so it gives us a comfortable head start."

"Sir." Max shook his head as he attempted to respond but the general didn't allow him to get a word in.

"Vissarion. The time is ripe for you to make your move."

"Make my move, Sir?"

"Your mission, Vissarion. Convince the Pythia that she needs to remain loyal to us. Seduce her. Tie her to you, body, mind and heart. I care little what you do, how you go about it, just that you do whatever it takes to ensure the girl remains loyal to the States and nobody else. The quickest route will be to satisfy her in bed, whatever kinks she may prefer. I trust you'll be up to the challenge."

Maximus could hardly believe his ears. This took crudeness to a new level. With effort, he kept his voice calm. "Sir. I don't believe I can come up with anything more counterproductive than that."

The general grunted, but only paused for a second. "You have your orders, Vissarion." There was a dangerous edge to his voice.

Tread lightly, Maximus.

But Max refused to be used. "I apologize, Sir. But I'll be damned before I whore myself out as a means to an end that would only benefit the government and FAPA."

"Vissar—"

"Neither will I use a young woman in such a manner, regardless of her value to our country."

Furious, he would have flung the phone over the edge of the cliff if he didn't know how expensive the damned thing was. And of course, government property.

Max switched it off, listening to the sound of high-pitched voices and soft barking.

It would be no great personal sacrifice to get close to Allegra. In fact, he'd known all along that he'd wanted to.

She was smart, intelligent, beautiful and tough. His men had given him a detailed report on how she'd taken down two of the thugs all by herself. They'd been impressed and so was Maximus.

But as much as he'd love to draw her closer, woo her heart, now that General Aulus had made it part of his mission, any closer relationship with her would feel tainted.

Acting on his feelings for her on his superior's orders would be wrong, dirty.

Max tightened his jaw, deciding there and then that he would maintain a strictly professional relationship with Allegra, much as he'd done with Aurelia.

Even if his heart didn't like it.

CHAPTER 24

*A*llegra had thought that a new day would bring a clearer head.

How naive she was.

Max was making breakfast when Xenia had arrived on her doorstep, waving the Las Suertes Tribune morning edition in her face. Pepper rushed in, racing around and around Allegra's legs until she bent and patted his head fondly.

Her fingers stilled as she glanced at the headline.

NEW PYTHIA DISCOVERED IN FORNIA

"Bloody reporters make you sound like oil or gold, or something." Xenia scrunched up her face and stared up at the ceiling. "To be honest, you're the only one in existence, and most people believe that the line had died out long ago. So the furor is understandable."

"Are you validating this insanity?" Allegra snapped as she turned the page.

The front page article was surrounded by a number of smaller articles scattered throughout the pages of the edition, detailing

Allegra's life, her education and career and even her economic status. They had managed to omit only two crucial details; her name and her face.

Small mercies.

Max had left the stove and come to stand at Allegra's shoulder, scanning the paper as she herself read through the details of her own life.

"Damn it. We were supposed to keep you safe from discovery. This just puts you in the international spotlight. Not to mention making you a target."

Max was halfway to his strange cordless phone when it rang so stridently it managed to shut Pepper's incessant yapping up.

A few minutes passed with Max's responses limited to *yes, no* and *I'm sorry, Sir*. When he shut off the device, Max's face looked gray.

"I have to return to the Capital urgently. My superiors are furious and I've been assigned to find the leak or else."

Allegra hurried to his side, worried now. "Are they blaming you?"

Max shook his head, but his expression remained closed.

"When do you leave?" she asked softly.

"You mean, when do *we* leave."

That brought Xenia to her feet, her eyes watching the interplay between Max and Allegra closely.

Allegra ignored her. "What do you mean?" she stared at Max.

"They feel it's safest for you."

Max reached for her, holding her upper arm. She shook him off. "No, I'm not going." As she spoke her vision shifted, her eyes opening to a scene she least expected.

Allegra stood in the middle of a room, bars on the doors and windows, bright fluorescent light stripping the scene bare of all color. Was this what awaited her, if she went to the capital with him?

Allegra wanted no part of that prison.

The vision vanished and Allegra let out a soft breath, glad her shock could be so easily suppressed. Clearing her throat, she said firmly, "I'm not coming with you."

Max stared at her and for a moment, his annoyance was clear in his eyes. But then he tilted his head and watched her face. "Very well," he said slowly, still studying her features.

Hopefully she'd given nothing away. Smiling softly, she said, "You've allocated eight guards to the house, Max. Surely that's enough. And I have Xales in case things go sideways."

"And she has me," piped Xenia from beside the sofa. Even Pepper felt the need to add a yip, though Allegra doubted he'd be of any use against determined attackers.

Allegra rested her palm on Max's arm, feeling the muscles bunching beneath her fingers. "I'll be fine, Max. Go and do what you need to do. Find out who leaked the story and if it's going to jeopardize my safety and the safety of our mission."

The mention of the mission seemed to steady Max and he gave her a firm nod. "Fine. I'll come back on the earliest flight."

He took a step toward her, hesitated for a moment as though on the verge of kissing her, then only gave her a small smile.

He turned on his heel and headed for the table where he gathered his files and case and phone. He left within minutes, saying little else, but instructing her to be careful and giving the guards a morale-boosting talking to.

They seemed to respect him, which gave Allegra both a sense of safety and a sense of pride in him - which was ridiculous, because she wasn't anyone special to Max.

Soon after he left, Xenia decided that they needed fresh air. "They didn't release your identity, Allegra, so a walk along the Claudian Boulevard will be safe enough."

"Just because they didn't reveal my name doesn't mean someone out there doesn't already know who I am." Allegra was thinking more in terms of the safety of her guard unit, but they took her field trip in their stride, got themselves ready and followed the girls as they trundled down the mountain to the town in Xenia's new automobile.

As they headed for Khan's Koffee and the girls chose a table and made their order, Ignacio took a seat beside Allegra. He had a small notepad and an auto-quill ready on his knee.

Allegra gave him and his stationery a pointed glare. "What is that for?"

"Commander Vissarion said if anything happened I needed to make notes. Your prophecies are too important to go by unrecorded."

"Will you shut up," growled Xenia, leaning forward with her eyes flashing. "Do you want the whole bloody world finding out what we are trying to keep under wraps?"

The man had the grace to look a little abashed. He apologized and took his leave once Xenia assured him that she was very capable with pen and paper if the need arose.

Allegra watched as he crossed the street and leaned against a streetlight, from where he continued to keep a close eye on them.

"If he thinks he's going unnoticed then he's dreaming."

"If you keep glaring at him like that, anyone watching will know immediately that he's there." Allegra's voice was soft as she sipped her milk coffee. "Besides, do you see any paparazzi? They'd be here already if they'd gotten our scent."

Xenia merely rolled her eyes and sipped her latte. Pepper sat beside Allegra, his head on her lap, and she let him be. The warmth from his chin gave her comfort, something she hadn't known she'd needed.

Everything was spinning out of control around her and she was powerless to stop it.

The sun in Fornia was warm this time of year and it beat down on the top of her blonde head. Soon her strawberry blonde locks would be bleached white, a color she hated with a particular passion.

She promised herself that if it got any whiter she'd have it colored. Something dramatic would be good. A deep purple sounded just about right.

But the thought of that color brought her mind back to the giant purple flower she'd seen in her vision of Xenia.

Allegra stared at her friend and sent prayers to every god she knew to keep Xenia safe. Allegra would do everything in her power to help avert the pandemic, if only to save the life of one person.

Xenia.

Then she smiled to herself. And maybe also to save Max.

She had to admit that the commander had gotten under her skin with his sexy baritone and his impressive body.

No. His body wasn't truly the deciding factor. It was that look in his eyes. The one he had when he thought she wasn't looking.

Allegra realized that she missed Max. Which was ridiculous considering they'd only met a few days ago, and barely knew each other. And besides he was merely doing his job under the orders of his superiors.

But Allegra had gotten used to having the sexy fed around. Not only was he good to look at, he certainly made a mean chicken-and-mushroom risotto.

Her heart thudded.

Both her body, and that strange intuition of hers, told her he was a keeper. He certainly wasn't the wham-bam-thank-you-ma'am type of guy.

Maybe what Xenia had said on the yacht made sense, and she *should* enjoy his attentions while she could. Allegra wondered if he'd rebuff her if she came onto him.

What did she have to lose anyway, when they were all staring death in the face?

After coffee Xenia headed off to meet her parents for lunch and Allegra had the guards take her to the Nike clinic for a while.

She had some paperwork to complete and she'd also decided it was time to tender her resignation. Fully and finally. There really was no point to waiting and hesitating - no amount of time would change her mind.

Physical therapy was no longer something she was capable of performing, not when every time she touched someone's bare skin she saw visions of their demise.

She had a terrible fear that she'd always see visions of death when she touched someone, even if she and Max somehow managed to prevent the coming plague. Her fear was probably completely irrational, but Allegra felt it all the same.

Three guards took up watch at the entrance while three of them entered to check the place out before Allegra went inside. Two of the agents stayed with her in the car.

It seemed a little like overkill, but Allegra left them to it. Better safe than sorry.

The recon team returned, happily reporting the clinic

premises were all clear. Allegra left them in the car and went inside, escaping the heat and enjoying the cool conditioned air of the facility.

She was in her tiny office - more of a cubicle than anything - retrieving the printout of her resignation from her printer when someone walked into the room.

With her back to the door, Allegra felt immediately threatened. As she spun on her heel, she held up the single sheet of paper as if it was a deadly dagger.

"Tox," she snapped. "You scared me."

Allegra's ex, Doctor Toxinius Cassian, smiled, his professionally-whitened teeth gleaming like one of those billboard posters for toothpaste. He was the last person that Allegra wanted to see.

"You've been scarce, Allegra." He grinned, his tone condescending. "Moping around at home isn't a good look, you know."

"Moping?" His words brought her head up.

He heaved a long sigh. "Allegra, it's pretty obvious to everyone here that you're taking our breakup badly." When she shook her head, stunned by the accusation, he smiled sadly. "I know it must have been a shock to you to see Vanessa and me at the Gala dinner this weekend."

"Huh?" she frowned.

Vanessa? Allegra hadn't kept up with Tox's women simply because he usually had a long line of them waiting. It was hard to remember who he was dating, or whose heart he'd recently broken.

Their breakup some weeks earlier had been more a blow to her ego than a knife to her heart, and yet Tox had never accepted that she'd gotten over him so fast. His oversized ego wouldn't let him.

"I'm sorry you have to find out about our engagement in the society pages, but it couldn't be helped. Vanessa is a Brookfield and her parents are old money. The press is always waiting for juicy details."

Allegra smiled. "I'm happy for you, Tox. If you are happy, that's all I need to hear."

In fact, Allegra was more than glad to hand Tox and his enlarged sense of self over to Vanessa-from-old-money. Let the socialite deal with Dr Toxinius.

She stuck out her hand, smiling happily at him. He looked at her hand perplexed as she waited, forcing him to shake it and accept her good wishes.

As soon as his palm touched hers, the vision slammed into Allegra's mind.

Tox lay on pink satin sheets, struggling to breathe.

Raw, open pustules around his mouth and eyes leaked yellowish-pink liquid while Tox's body convulsed.

His eyes bulged as his torso lifted off the bed. Then he stilled, the life draining from his eyes as she watched. Allegra blinked, looking around the room, almost gasping as she caught sight of a woman sitting on the floor beside the bed.

She was strawberry blonde, much like Allegra, and wore a pale pink babydoll nightie, the delicate color marred by the profuse stains of blood covering the front of the negligee.

Her hand lay in her lap, one finger curled around the trigger of a gun. Her arms were covered in open sores and Allegra's eyes traveled up her hands, her gaze drawn toward a horror she knew she'd see.

Only the left half of the woman's face remained, ragged pieces of flesh pressed inside her skull, bits of brain and bone plastered against the wall behind her. Her single remaining eye stared sightlessly at her dead fiancé.

As blue as the sky, as dead as night.

The shock sent Allegra back to consciousness and she had to force herself to remain calm and control her reaction.

She gave Tox's hand one final shake, recognizing the knowing look in his eyes. He'd assumed she'd held onto his hand that much longer because she couldn't bear to drag herself from him.

Self-centered asshole.

"It was nice seeing you, Tox. Congratulations." She extracted her hand from his grip and waved her document in front of him. "I've got work to do, so don't let me keep you."

He stared at her for a long moment, and Allegra smiled pleasantly and waited him out. Tox liked stretching things out.

He'd learned a long time ago that making people uncomfortable forced them into action, whether to agree with him, or to get away from him. He'd been proud of that technique.

Allegra had called it bullying.

So, she waited him out, keeping her shaking hands as still as she could. At last his lips twisted.

He'd lost the game. He gave her a cursory scan, head to toe, his lip curling as if in distaste.

Then he turned and left without a word. He hadn't asked her how she was, hadn't inquired as to the reason for her absence. Not that she'd expected it, but the fact was glaring.

She sighed and headed over to the director's office to hand in her resignation.

She'd meant to complete all her paperwork, but right now she didn't give a damn.

She just wanted to get out of there.

Now.

CHAPTER 26

Allegra and her retinue—that's what she'd taken to calling them because it sounded less depressing than *bodyguards*—had to pass through the town on the way back home.

Reason enough to stop off at Sweet Passion, her favorite bakery, for a batch of muffins. Allegra had never been any good at baking, often creating brownies and muffins that could double as deadly missiles. The carbon content in them would be enough to supply a pencil factory, or so her mom Julia had always said.

The guards followed her inside. They'd all dressed in different garb, workman's coveralls, a suit, golf attire, a toga. From looking at them, you'd never tell they were part of the same team, so perfectly did they blend in with passersby and tourists.

The coffee shop was so full she could barely find a place to stand. The guards were forced to lag behind, with only one of them—Ignacio—remaining at her side.

Allegra had been waiting patiently in the line for the selection of the day's muffins when a shot went off, sending the patrons and the staff into a mass panic.

The smartest of them hit the ground, no doubt hoping to keep clear of any bullets.

Allegra followed suit, touching down beside Ignacio. When she glanced over her shoulder at the entrance, her heart sank. The doors were shut, guarded by two large men in masks, sub-machine guns in hand. The rest of her team was still outside, staring into the shop looking helpless and angry.

Panic simmered within Allegra's chest and she shifted to scan the rest of the shop.

A dark-haired, pinch-faced woman lay beside her, staring straight at Allegra's face, a strange look in her eyes. "It's going be okay. Don't be afraid," she said, hoping to allay the woman's fears.

But the brunette just stared at her, a hard expression furrowing her brow. Allegra felt the jab in her thigh just as the woman's lips curved into a cold smile.

"What?" Allegra gasped.

She reached for her thigh, touched the spot that now throbbed. Panic sent her heartbeat thrumming. When Allegra heard the loud screams, she knew that Xales had arrived.

The crowd scrambled away from the giant boar, although some still had the presence of mind to stay down. People screamed and bumped into Allegra as they stampeded toward the back of the store, sending racks of fresh-baked breads and crois-sants tumbling every which way.

Their fear of the men with guns was no doubt compounded by their terror at a gigantic creature making a sudden appearance.

Allegra twisted around, the movement oddly difficult, as if she were swimming through molasses. Her lids were heavy and she forced herself to open her eyes, only to see Xales charge one of the men with guns.

Two of them fired, but the bullets sank inside the boar's hide and had no effect on him.

Xales ran one of the gunmen down and was turning to deliver the same treatment to the second masked thug, when a man walked in from the back room behind the counter.

Dressed in a black toga with a black cloak thrown over his shoulders, he glided inside, his expression as dark as his attire. His black hair encased his skull like a layer of ink, giving off an oily gleam.

Something told Allegra that this man was bad news, but even though she tried to cry out, to warn Xales, she was unable to say a word.

Allegra could barely hold her head up to watch the unfolding scene. As Xales charged his enemy, the man in black flicked his wrist.

Allegra watched, unable to breath as a shimmering golden net appeared above the boar, growing larger as it landed on the animal's head and shoulders.

Amid the shocked cries and moans of the terrified patrons, Allegra couldn't hear her own gasp of horror.

Xales was her protector, but someone had found a way to subdue him.

What kind of magic was this?

She grunted as she desperately fought to get to her feet. She couldn't stand by and watch these men capture or hurt Xales.

Inherited familiar or not, he still belonged to her.

Allegra looked around for Ignacio, hoping he'd be able to offer her a hand to get to her feet. To do something about Xales.

But when Allegra looked to her right, where he'd been just moments before, she choked on her shock.

Ignacio lay on his side, staring at her blankly, the hilt of a dagger protruding from his neck. Tears filled her eyes as she reached for him.

Even though she could see he was gone she still felt the need to shake him, had the odd sense that maybe if he heard her voice he'd wake up.

But she couldn't move her hand.

She glanced back up at Xales, unable to do a thing as the net closed around him, expanding to cover him from snout to tail.

And then, in a shimmering of gold that was too beautiful to be appropriate for this horror, Xales and the magical net disappeared into thin air.

Frantic now, Allegra tried to struggle but she felt worse than numb. It was as if her head floated in a sea of nothingness.

A movement beside her drew her attention, but she was helpless to defend herself, couldn't even turn her head.

Something dark covered her face, blocking off all light.

A bag?

Or had whatever the woman injected into her thigh begun to affect her brain?

Allegra felt rough hands wrap around her, lift her off the ground. She tried to kick and struggle, to elbow them away, but despite her panicked angry efforts, she remained immobile and helpless.

Blackness took her before she could devise an escape plan.

CHAPTER 27

The flight was bumpy this time, strong winds tossing the plane left and right among the gathering storm clouds, while lightning played havoc with the electronics.

From the barely subdued terror on the faces of the flight attendants, Max wondered if they'd reach the capital alive. It seemed that the gods were unhappy with him.

Or maybe with FAPA.

Whatever the reason for the bad weather, he was supremely glad when they touched down at last, relief easing the tense muscles in his thighs and neck as he gathered his things and left the small plane.

Despite the nausea and the bumpy ride, the privilege of using the agency's private plane was a luxury he'd prefer not to trade in anytime soon.

As he entered the FAPA headquarters building, his deputy Marcus caught up with him, raising an eyebrow in mute question when Max did not even stop.

"Boardroom," said Max, striding to his office.

He had nearly an hour until the meeting scheduled with General Aulus, and he planned to put it to good use.

After rifling through the reports on his desk, he was happy to note that Marcus had taken good care of the daily workload, leaving Max only the most important papers to sign. He did so quickly and threw the stack in the out-tray before hurrying to the meeting room.

His team was attentive and curious when he entered, and he got down to business right away.

"I'm sure you're all aware that we've found the new Pythia."

A chorus of assent rippled around the room, underpinned by curious murmurs. Max waved them to silence. "You have questions?" he asked before he continued.

Marcus sat forward, clearly the mouthpiece for the whole group. "We're very eager to meet her, sir."

Max nodded. "I'll arrange it as soon as I can. I do believe you will like her."

"She's agreed to cooperate?" asked Corina, wiping her platinum hair out of her face.

Max smiled. "Yes, she has. We did obtain a little more information. She's confirmed that the pathogen will originate outside of the New Germanic States."

"Does that mean we're going to lock the borders down?" Jerard asked.

Max shook his head. "It's unlikely that anything we do will stop this virus. It's far too virulent for that and increasing border biosecurity would merely delay the inevitable. What we need is to cut it off at the head."

Marcus rubbed his chin, his brows scrunched. "It shouldn't be too much longer, now. The Pythia will help us stop this before it's too late."

Max clapped his deputy on the back. "I'm glad we agree on that Marcus. Now, we just have to help her train a little faster."

Max asked for a quick rundown of the team's recently closed cases, and what they currently had on their plate. While he listened, he felt pride in his people for managing their daily tasks so well, despite knowing that in a few weeks all their work could have been a total waste of their time.

Leaving the team to continue the meeting under Marcus's guidance, Max headed to meet General Aulus. He'd requested Max's presence at a meeting of department heads.

Despite his own seniority, Max preferred to miss these meetings as much as possible.

At such meetings, heads were likely to roll, and Max hoped he wouldn't be pulled off the case. Aulus could be unpredictable at the best of times.

The moment Max walked into the room he knew he was in for a trying hour. "Commander Vissarion, so glad you could make it."

Max smiled and bowed his greetings, then took his empty chair at the foot of the table. He waited as the general discussion was completed and they began to discuss the Pythia.

Aulus said, "I'm happy to say that there's a very high likelihood that this Pythia is the key to averting the impending pandemic."

Aulus crooked his finger at Max who rose and stepped to the general's side, waiting.

"Our only problem is that despite every effort to keep her existence under wraps, the papers have gotten wind of it." Aulus looked up at Max. "Have you seen them?"

Max nodded. "This morning's papers. Splattered all over the front pages. They know a lot about her. They've withheld her name so far, but there's enough information within those articles for anyone smart enough to follow the dotted lines and figure her identity out. Not to mention that people who know her well will immediately guess it's her." Max tightened his jaw. "I'd like to know who could have leaked this information, considering this was a top-secret project."

Aulus's eyes narrowed, but he didn't overreact. Instead, he nodded slightly. "I have my suspicions."

A heated debate followed, and the departmental heads demanded to know more about the situation, and who the traitor might be.

General Aulus got to his feet. "I have a strong feeling it's one of the Senators. I briefed some of them on the emergence of the new Pythia, but the papers have details I never gave them. They have enough fingers in different pies to have obtained such inside information by nefarious means."

"That sounds a bit dramatic," someone called out from the end of the table.

Aulus glared at the speaker. "Nevertheless, we know all too well that information has a way of leaking past even our own security protocols. The Senator involved likely has a mole on his payroll. Someone well-placed and trusted enough to know this much about the new Pythia. It's still odd that her identity wasn't revealed outright, so perhaps they don't know exactly who she is."

"Yet?" asked Max, knowing the path Aulus's mind was taking.

After the last attack, the bodyguards knew she was more than just an ordinary seer. But Max hoped he could give them the benefit of the doubt.

Aulus faced Max. "There is only one thing we can do, Vissarion. Have her sign an ironclad contract that ties her gift and her personal services solely to FAPA. Make her an official agent if you have to. Have her sign a non-disclosure agreement as well."

Max's jaw dropped.

They wanted to trap Allegra into serving the NGS exclusively.

And they wanted to use Max to do it.

CHAPTER 28

Max tried to contain his fury.

He was appalled that they were treating Allegra like a commodity. But he could hardly voice his disagreement. Not here in front of all these people.

Aulus must have read his expression correctly because he clicked his tongue, irritated. "There is no time for scruples, young man. You're doing what could be considered the most important thing you will ever do for your country. For mankind."

Max hesitated and Aulus took a step closer to him.

"The news is out, Commander Vissarion. Time is of the essence. Governments around the world will be vying for the Pythia's ear. Hundreds, if not thousands of petitioners will descend upon Las Suertes within days. Do you even understand the ramifications of that? For the benefit of the New Germanic states we must deny everyone her Sight. She's far too vital a resource to lend out to all and sundry. You must move fast, Vissarion."

Max frowned at Aulus's tone, but was unable to ask him anything further as a commotion ensued at the threshold. A man entered, pushing his shaggy hair out of his face as he tried to explain who he was.

"Let him pass," yelled Aulus. To Max, it looked like the general was losing his patience.

Max remained silent and watched as the thin, tall man stalked forward like a praying mantis, head held high, eyes large and nervous.

Aulus addressed the meeting. "Dr Kenji here has some vital information to share. He told me the barest details on the phone, so let's hear what he has to say before we make any further decisions."

The doctor dropped his papers on the table beside Aulus and gave Max a stiff smile. "I'm a virologist attached to the government's biosecurity division. We've studied the coming pandemic with the help of the strongest seers in our employ. We've verified that it's based on a spontaneous mutation, which could occur in either human or animal. The species isn't as important as the pathogen's virulence. It's extremely contagious."

"So what's the incubation period?" Max heard himself asking.

Kenji glanced at him, sending him a respectful nod. "It would have to be at least three weeks for it to spread so widely, so fast, as the seers are predicting. The scale of this pandemic is astronomical. It's like nothing we've ever seen before."

"And you used different seers to provide this information?"

The doctor nodded. "Including input from allied nations. They are all agreed."

Someone stood up, but Max couldn't see his face. "So what good is a Pythia who can't see any of these details in order to help us eliminate the disease?"

Max leaned forward to identify the speaker. Commander Garson Laine, Head of Research and Development. Max wasn't surprised.

Max sighed. "You have to understand that the new Pythia is like a baby learning to walk and speak. She's never deliberately used her Sight before. And if we push her too hard she'll self-destruct."

Laine snorted. "We're wasting time sitting around waiting for her to . . ." he sneered, "walk."

Aulus fixed him with a basilisk stare. "Have you not heard of the Pythia Sofia?"

The man sat back and shook his head.

Max's voice held a touch of ice as he spoke. "Sofia was a new, but extremely powerful Pythia. Robur the Great used her Sight to amass his conquests, but his generals became greedy. Wanting to impress Robur, they forced Sofia to use her sight too often. She went mad."

"As a result, almost eighty years passed without a Pythia. That is not what we need in this emergency." Max spoke, keeping his tone even. "What's of greater importance right now is this new knowledge."

Laine grunted. "Personally I think the best move we can make is to bring the Pythia in and figure out how she works."

Max's head began to heat up. "Are you suggesting we experiment on the Oracle of Pythia?" he asked in horror.

Laine smiled thinly. "I'm not suggesting anything. I'm saying it's the smart, prudent decision. The Pythias are so rare that it's only smart to study how they work and what they can do."

Max quelled the desire to go over to the man and wring his sorry neck. Best to remain on point before he spoiled everything by ending up incarcerated for murder.

Max cleared his throat and waved a hand at the doctor. "We don't have time for this inanity. We need to listen to Dr Kenji." Max shifted his attention to the doctor and asked, "The incubation period you estimate is far longer than we had initially surmised. Which means we have even less time than we thought to find and stop this pandemic before it can spread. I should not even be here. I've lost a lot of time away from her side. Time in which she could have told me something more valuable to go on."

Aulus nodded, his expression grave. "Go, Vissarion, and let us know—"

Before Aulus could complete his instructions, Marcus burst into the room. "You have to take this, sir." He sounded frantic enough even for Max to feel his stomach tighten with fear.

Aulus glared at Marcus, but the expression of consternation on the younger man's face must have held him back because he said nothing.

Marcus handed the phone to Max. "One of your men from the Pythia's protection detail agent is calling from Barbarina Town. The seer has been kidnapped. From a bakery . . . in broad daylight." The words spilled from his mouth, but he kept his volume low enough for only Max and Aulus to hear.

The departmental heads at the table leaned closer and despite Marcus's discretion, within seconds the entire room was abuzz. Several agents rose to their feet in their consternation.

"How did this happen when we were so close?"

"We have to retrieve her."

"Was she taken alive? Do we know if she's still alive?"

Aulus faced the table, waving at the gathering to relax and to sit down. "We will get to the bottom of this."

"Maybe if we hadn't pulled Commander Vissarion off her detail we'd still have her in hand," cut in the head of Bio-Weapons. Max bristled, even though the man was saying what he'd said himself.

The problem was he was referring to Allegra as if she was a mere object, a possession.

Aulus was nodding. "Perhaps you are right. But we can't change what's happened." He turned to Max. "You will return immediately."

Max snapped his gaze to Aulus. "The storm, Sir. All the airports are closed. Not even our planes will be allowed to take off."

Aulus raised his eyebrows. "We'll get you there. Even if we have to requisition a fighter-jet from the army."

Max nodded, though his stomach turned queasy at the prospect. But he would face any risk if it meant he would be able to hunt for Allegra more quickly.

Aulus looked at Max. "Any resource you need . . . ask and it's yours. No questions asked."

Max had to force himself not to tell the man that it was a little too late for such a show of support, but he shut his mouth.

Aulus shook his head. "This doesn't look good for us. The new Pythia goes missing the very day the press reports on her existence? The Senate is definitely going to hold us responsible for this."

"Even though it's likely one of them who leaked the information?" said the Bio-Security chief.

"Even more, because of that," said Aulus.

Max took his leave then, tired of the back-and-forth and the worthless discussion. He needed to get back to Barbarina Town and find out what had happened. His stomach was a tightly-clenched ball of fear.

The reality of having Allegra ripped away from him, the pain of not being there to protect her, left him feeling raw. He was afraid.

The fear of what might happen to her in the time it would take for them to find her and rescue her, made him feel cold, and sick inside.

Max didn't want to think about it. As much as he'd been trying to convince Allegra that she was in danger, he'd hoped at the back of his mind that he was wrong.

Leaving her side had been a mistake of epic proportions.

CHAPTER 29

Max had left the Capital so quickly he'd barely had time to talk to Marcus. He'd grabbed Corina Brava, his top seer, and Flavius Lex, his most experienced locator and taken the first flight out using one of the army's newly-commissioned supersonic jets.

Max had had no clue the army had converted a jet meant for fighting wars and flying under radar, into a vessel to carry senior staff across the world. He wasn't about to question the privilege, not when every minute counted and they needed to get Allegra back, not when the jet got him faster to the scene of her abduction.

The four-hour flight to the West Coast had been completed in under an hour and Max swore to himself he'd never fly supersonic again. Not if he could help it. He felt like he'd left his stomach and all his bones back in the capital.

From the dazed expression on Corina's and Flavius's faces, they were in absolute agreement.

A car was waiting for them on the tarmac and sped them off into the Fornia hills to Barbarina Town. Max paid little attention to the weather or the news as his mind filtered through the possibilities—which groups could be responsible for Allegra's abduction?

Max had obtained more detailed information on the abduction, and couldn't quell his rising anger and sadness that Ignacio, his most trusted man on Allegra's detail, had been killed by her captors – and not only him. Aside from the casualties within his team, two innocent bystanders were also dead, and several wounded.

It was evidence that Allegra's abductors were absolutely ruthless. They had been better armed than his men, and how on earth had they neutralized Xales?

As they turned into the driveway of Allegra's house, Max felt his fear and anger rise. He jumped from the car even before it rumbled to a halt near the front door.

Xenia was already at the opened doorway, glaring at him with reddened, accusing eyes. She was holding onto her dog's leash so tight the animal had to lift his head to avoid being strangled.

"Can you get her back?" she snapped angrily as her eyes glistened again.

"I'm going to do everything I can, Xenia."

His voice was low as he tried to ensure his own raw emotions didn't leak into his tone. He must have failed because Xenia gave him an odd look, then a short nod.

She turned on her heel and disappeared into the kitchen where—shockingly—she set about preparing tea and coffee, and piling plates with muffins and pastries.

From this pampered princess, it was no less surprising than if she'd prepared an entire meal.

Max wasn't about to complain.

Four of the surviving guards were gathered in the living room, the bright sun streaming onto them making a mockery of their emotions.

One of the men, Allen, looked up, his expression dark. He didn't wait for Max to ask for an update.

Allen took a deep breath and looked straight at Max. "Carlos is in the hospital with a concussion. He'd been watching from his car across the road. Bashed over the head with something hard. Kassim is still in a coma. Stabbed close to the heart with what looked like an icepick. Doctors are not confident that he'll wake up. Ignacio was also stabbed, but in the neck. Nobody saw who did it. He died instantly. Rachel was watching the back door. We found her with a bullet in the middle of her forehead. We thought you'd want to deal with notifying the families."

Max was glad the man hadn't drawn out the update. Quick, short, but no less painful.

Flavius and Corina had remained standing, watching from the kitchen, their expressions contained. Unlike the rest of the team, the two were Max's personal staff, and remained on the sidelines, observing.

Flavius cleared his throat. "If I may, could I be directed to some of the oracle's personal items? It would help a great deal in my attempt to locate her." The locator had a tendency toward the formal, but Max and the team were quite used to it.

Xenia had been paying close attention and hurried over to deliver her tray of cups, beverages and cakes. She hovered, waiting to hear what was happening.

The team frowned collectively at Flavius's request and Max had to hide his smile at their protectiveness of the Pythia. He glanced at Xenia. "Show Flavius to Allegra's bedroom, please? A toothbrush or comb would do nicely, thank you." He spoke gently, and it must have been different from his normal manner, because both Corina and Flavius stared at his face.

Xenia nodded and led the locator away while Max talked to the agents, going over in detail what each of the survivors had seen. They'd been taken by surprise in the ambush, and none of them were particularly proud of that.

And they had been seriously outgunned. In retrospect, it had been a mistake to allow Allegra to enter a crowded place like that bakery. And each of the survivors from his team were regretting it a great deal.

Xenia returned with Flavius, who had chosen a bronze-handled hairbrush. The guards watched as Flavius took his prize to the stone dining room table and carefully laid it down.

Flavius was a quiet man who went about his task with an unassuming air. And yet the man had been the deciding factor in many a difficult case, putting Max and the team on the right path, sometimes with just one scrying attempt.

He leaned closer, picking out a single hair from the tangle within the bristles. Pulling one of the heavy chairs up, he sat and rested his elbows on the table before closing his eyes.

The man needed little more than touch to help him sense a person's location. Though unable to give exact coordinates, his predictions were always vastly useful.

Such a talent was rare, and FAPA was always eager to recruit people like him.

Another huff of air passed through Flavius's wide nostrils, and he opened his eyes to look at Max. "I'm not getting much other than she is moving eastward."

A murmur of dissatisfaction rose within the team and Max quickly shushed them. Flavius either didn't hear them, or ignored them. He sighed. "Moving east and doing so fast."

"How fast?" asked Max.

"A train. Possibly, or more likely a plane."

Max nodded. Means of transport was always a great help in understanding the methods of one's foe.

Paper crinkled as Corina withdrew a large map scroll from her case and began to roll it open on the table beside Flavius.

Corina would get visions of the person they tracked, but she was rarely able to provide a location. Her expertise was seeing and experiencing her target's current environment.

Flavius got to his feet, vacating his seat for the seer. The two worked together, moving in harmony like the partners they were.

Their self-assured movements provided a sense of calm for the exhausted agents and they relaxed a little as they watched the pair.

Corina took another strand in her fingers and then laid it in her palm before sitting back. Her eyes glazed over as the vision filled her mind, as she accessed Allegra.

"She is too strong. I cannot obtain access to her thoughts. Only her surroundings."

It would be sufficient but Max didn't speak. Once Corina entered the trance, she couldn't hear anything around her. In Max's experience, each seer functioned differently, within different parameters and personal skill barriers.

Corina had this permanent inability to hear people while she remained within the trance.

The seers adjusted to their handicaps. Corina usually made a list of things she was looking for, and memorized them before she entered the trance.

"She's sequestered in a separate area so she can't hear what her captors are saying." Corina tilted her head listening. "It sounds like an airline announcement . . . no . . . the captain, announcing a flight time. He's saying six hours to landing – something about refueling. He has an Anglian accent."

Max stiffened.

Londinium.

CHAPTER 30

"If it's a private plane, as we must assume, could it be that they are taking her to Londinium?" Max wondered. "It's a large enough city, and significant financial center. Whoever arranged her capture is rich and influential. It might fit."

"The direction is right," Flavius said, "though from what I sense, she's not over the Atlantis Sea as yet. We might just catch her with the jet, if only we knew where they'll come down to refuel. There are several possible airfields on the East Coast."

Corina came out of her trance. "Sorry, that's all I could get. The Pythia is drugged, only dimly aware of what goes on around her."

Max made a quick calculation – without a more exact location, they would not catch the abductors before they left the States' airspace. Better to go straight to Londinium, if Flavius confirmed that destination when they got to Nova Roma.

"The Anglian Isles are a fairly large territory though. It's not going to be easy to find her." Allen shook his head as he began to pace.

"We can get transport there easy enough. Between Flavius and

Corina we will find her." Max doubted he'd be able to commission the jet he'd arrived on. Not for a trans-Atlantis flight for their whole team.

Max called Aulus who assured him their flight would be arranged and ready as soon as they got to the airport.

Max felt the fatigue in his bones, in his mind. He was weary, but of what exactly?

Allegra's disappearance had put many aspects of his life into perspective. Max could now admit to himself that he'd grown weary of his job. Whether it was answering to Aulus or the role itself, and he suspected it was mostly the former. Max longed for work with more autonomy, something that gave him true satisfaction.

And yet this attachment to the Pythia was something he'd never give up. And without his job, even with all its drawbacks, he would never have met her.

The new Pythia was intriguing, attractive, intelligent. He could not possibly request a transfer if it meant never seeing her again.

Before Max headed for the airport, Xenia handed him a small leather bag, insisting he take it for Allegra. Max had been impressed at Xenia's strength and her thoughtfulness.

They left the guards at Allegra's house on the off-chance that she'd return. It was an excuse to get them to rest, and to check on Carlos, and to be there in case Kassim failed to awaken from the coma.

A second supersonic flight was not what Max had wanted and Corina had only made it worse by reminding him that the flight across the Atlantis Sea was technically supersonic too. At least the bigger Icarus 700 planes should be a little easier on the stomach.

They arrived on the tarmac at Nova Roma Airport and headed inside to check in. The waiting lounge was buzzing as people huddled in groups, free drinks and snacks forgotten as they whispered to each other.

"What's going on?" asked Corina, keeping her voice down.

Max nudged her and tipped his head toward two men in business suits poring over the afternoon edition of the local paper. Everyone was discussing how their government had failed to properly protect the new Pythia, and wondering where she could be, and who would dare abduct her. Would there be a ransom demand?

Max and his team grabbed something to eat and remained on the sidelines listening in where they were able, after getting hold of their own copies of the available national and international papers.

Apparently, the world was deeply critical of the New Germanic States' inability to keep Allegra safe. There were many suggesting that Allegra be moved away from the clear dangers within the borders of the States, calling for international funding and manning of her protection detail, because clearly the States had fallen down on the job.

More importantly, many international governments and corporations were up in arms because they had not known about her existence until now.

A few were accusing the States, justified accusations in Max's opinion, of attempting to keep Allegra all to themselves to gain an unfair advantage. They were calling for an international summit to discuss the situation and establish firm rules of access.

Max scanned all the articles regarding the Pythia with growing dismay.

"Did you know about this?" asked Corina, her voice holding the distinct edge of accusation.

"Know what?" asked Max, struggling to focus on the blurring words. He was too tired to function anymore.

She and Flavius had taken seats with Max at a small seating arrangement of four single sofas and a glass coffee table. They were beside the floor-to-ceiling window that faced the tarmac and the planes as they took off. They could see their plane, the gigantic jet, waiting for them outside.

Corina shifted to face him, stabbing a copy of the Nova Roma Herald with her forefinger. "Did you know about this?" she repeated, her tone angry.

"What in particular?"

"That there is an International Treaty governing access to the Pythia."

When Aulus had mentioned keeping Allegra's abilities for FAPA alone, Max hadn't agreed. Now that the world had begun to talk about it, the General's plan was definitely not going to go forward.

Max was supremely grateful to the gods that he hadn't attempted to seduce Allegra on behalf of Aulus. He nodded gravely. "Yes, I knew. I've been working with Aurelia for most of my career. For the interim, I assumed we were ignoring the Treaty because we were thinking of Allegra's safety first. The fact that she'd been attacked more than once already, meant someone was out to either kill her, or abduct her. We thought it best to wait until she was safe and secure, before announcing her identity and availability to the world."

Corina leaned closer. "I can understand that, but Allegra's life is in serious danger right now."

Flavius shook his head. "Surely nobody would want to kill or hurt such an invaluable source of information? Especially now, with the looming extinction event?"

Max knew what Flavius was feeling, that disbelief that someone would target Allegra who was likely their only key to saving human existence.

"The attempts on her life so far say otherwise." Max spoke quietly. "And perhaps her captors are ignorant of the impending epidemic."

"Which makes it all the more imperative for us to find her and bring her to safety."

"There is a possibility that they aren't going to hurt her," suggested Flavius.

Corina snorted, drawing both men's attention. "If that's the case, then why did they go so far as to kill our agents? Seems to me that a tranquilizer dart to get her guards out of the way would have been enough."

Max nodded. "The excess violence they used may merely indicate how important she is to them." Even though Max spoke the words, he didn't believe it for an instant.

Corina was right. The circumstances of Allegra's abduction didn't bode well for her life expectancy.

CHAPTER 31

Blackness blanketed Allegra as she slowly became aware of her surroundings.

A soft mattress beneath her body, cool air against her cheek, light shining against the lids of her closed eyes.

At some point her captors had injected her with a sedative, and the spot in her neck throbbed like a warning to behave in case they decided it was necessary to calm her again.

She'd given them a hard time, and didn't regret it one bit, relishing the memory of kicking one of her captors in the balls. He'd squealed like a girl and had been so furious that he'd punched Allegra hard in the head. She'd seen stars, but it had been so worth it.

Not long after that, they'd drugged her.

Now, she cracked open her eyes, thankful for the light in the room, however meager and cold. She'd grown weary of the constant darkness around her head.

The hood had slowly begun to suffocate her.

Vague shapes formed around her; a dull fluorescent light shone from the ceiling, safely hidden behind a recessed panel, covered in solid metal bars. The room lacked windows too, and

Allegra began to feel somewhat claustrophobic. She'd never been afraid of enclosed spaces. And yet now a rising panic began to take over her senses.

Breathing deeply, she forced herself into a sitting position. She remained still for a moment while the spinning in her head settled. Gripping the edge of the bed, she boosted herself to her feet, steadying her swaying body with a hand on the wall.

A few stretches, a handful of jumping jacks, and some walking helped Allegra feel a little steadier on her feet, and she turned her attention to the room.

She couldn't help the cold laugh that escaped her lips.

A hotel room?

What a joke.

Dull patterned carpeting covered the floor, a double-bed sat against the right-hand wall, flanked by two nightstands. On the wall opposite the bed sat a dresser, a metal sheet recessed into the brick behind it pretending to be a mirror.

A small arrangement of a tiny, two-person dining table and two metal chairs occupied the back wall. The table and chairs were all securely bolted to the floor.

After checking the bed, nightstands and dresser, she confirmed that all the furniture was equally fixed and immovable.

Smart.

As with most hotel rooms, a small passage led to the exit, with the entrance to the bathroom to the right. Allegra rushed to the door, grabbing hold of the handle and trying to open it, desperate to get out.

The door wouldn't budge.

She cried out in frustration, turning around and slamming her back against the door. She rested her head on the cold metal and stared up at the ceiling, hope threatening to disappear.

But she couldn't give up now.

Straightening she took a deep breath and focused on the bathroom door at her elbow. The tiny bathroom was meager, tiled in white, the toilet missing its lid, and the toilet paper - that they had thought to provide it was a surprise - was stacked on the floor, no holder in sight.

Another smart move, because anything rod-like and pointy could be used to kill a person.

Even the towel rails were missing.

The sink had separate hot and cold water faucets, but the wrong way around from home. Which made Allegra suspect that she was somewhere on the Latin Continent.

With her curiosity sated and her frustration levels far too high, Allegra paced the room. She ran out of breath too soon, her throat scratchy, as dry as the Nubian desert.

A polystyrene water jug and two paper cups sat on the dresser.

No glass.

Pity.

Coughing slightly, Allegra reached for the jug and poured herself a cupful. She drank deeply, figuring if her captors had wanted to drug her, they'd likely just stab her with a needle to get the job done.

No need for subterfuge, considering they had subjected her to such jabbing already.

Feeling a little better after the drink, Allegra took stock. Her spine and limbs were stiff, muscles tight, clothing wrinkled beyond belief even for the easy-wear fabric, and stained with sweat too.

Allegra needed a shower.

She scanned the drawers in the dresser and came up empty. No change of clothes; maybe they weren't so considerate after all. She recalled seeing a towel folded on the basin and headed for the bathroom. The towel was far too short, hardly larger than a face towel.

With a sigh, she used the toilet, but wasn't confident enough to fully disrobe and shower. Instead, she washed at the sink, cleaning up as best as she could with the tiny sliver of soap sitting beside the taps. She felt fresher, but without clean clothes she remained uncomfortable.

Back in the room, she used the next hour to stretch, and perform a few martial arts routines. She refused to panic or become hysterical, even though it felt like the room was closing in on her. Even though she was terrified of what her captors wanted from her.

Had it been rape, she'd have known by now.

Sex-trade market, maybe? She'd have to wait to find out.

But Allegra strongly suspected that her abduction had more to do with her mind than with her body.

They'd captured Xales. More importantly, they'd known *how* to capture her boar familiar.

That, in itself, told her that her captors wanted her for her power.

And the fake hotel room was her prison.

She didn't want to dwell on how long she could remain in here. For all its hotel-like appearance, it was still uncomfortable and restrictive.

Allegra had only just sat down to take a breath after exercising when the door clicked open, its soft hush confirming it had a pneumatic door; most likely one that didn't take keys.

Wonderful.

Not that Allegra could pick a lock to save her life.

A tall, dour-looking man entered the room, his lanky, almost emaciated, frame oddly corpse-like. His deep-set black eyes stared at her, unblinking, yet for a fleeting instant, Allegra could have sworn she'd seen a quickly hidden smile. A gloating smile of satisfaction.

"I see you are up."

"Your perception skills are clearly outstanding," said Allegra, giving him a cold glare.

He stood beside the door and she figured she'd never make it to knock his lights out in time. He was smart.

He ignored the insult.

"You are being held at the headquarters of the Order of Hermes. We are a very exclusive brotherhood. I suggest you make good use of your last few days. I'd also recommend you take this time to access your gifts and reveal any prophecies that may be of use to the world. Very soon, you will no longer have that privilege." He smiled openly now, and started to turn away.

"Wait. What do you need me for? Why did you take me? And what did you do with my boar?"

He didn't answer, and in fact grinned wider at the mention of Xales. He was going to leave without giving her a response. Allegra decided he'd only come to unsettle her. Probably some kind of strange torture technique.

She tried another tack. "Why would you want to die with the rest of the population of the planet?"

He paused, studying her face through the crack in the door.

"We only have a few weeks left." Allegra spoke louder. "Three months at the most. And I can help prevent it. Help *you* and your family survive?"

He'd opened the door a little wider and was looking at Allegra with such a cool expression that she couldn't even fathom what he was thinking.

Excellent poker face.

She folded her arms. "I guess if you do kill me, then I should be satisfied knowing you doomed yourself by your own actions. Fair warning though, your death will be horribly painful. And not in the least quick."

He watched her now, his eyes widening, startled at her confidence in her words. Perhaps he knew she wasn't lying, but he remained a little uncertain, beady black eyes shifting away from her face for the briefest second.

"If you don't believe me, then any fairly competent seer

should be able to confirm what I've said. Or perhaps, speak to your government," she suggested with a calm smile.

He hovered in the doorway, still looking like he couldn't decide whether to stay or go.

Allegra shook her head, watching him coldly. "I suggest you do it fast?" She looked down at her wristwatch and drew what seemed like an appropriate number from the air. "Twenty-two days and counting."

This time he paled and took a quick step back. The door shushed closed, leaving Allegra in utter silence.

Without the contentious presence of her captor, Allegra felt a little calmer. Still, she had nothing to do with her time and it made no sense to hurt herself by overdoing her exercises.

She lay on the bed, staring up at the stone ceiling. It was time to ask for help.

Allegra shut her eyes and concentrated, trying to regain the sense of peace she'd experienced when the voices of her ancestors had spoken to her.

By now she was convinced the voices belonged to some of the previous Pythias who watched over her through the timeline.

She'd grown accustomed to that particular myth all too easily. Possibly because she liked the idea that someone, somewhere was keeping an eye on her.

Looking out for her.

She lay there for almost thirty minutes until at last, when she was about to give up, she heard the first voice.

"Dear child." The voice from the beach echoed in her mind, and the sound of it trilled through Allegra's blood.

"Thank you for hearing my call," whispered Allegra. "I need your help. I don't know what to do."

"Allegra, child. Do not lose hope, but I must warn you that the situation is very dangerous. You must have courage. Fortitude. You must be resilient and resourceful too."

Before Allegra could ask her what she meant, the voice faded leaving her alone again.

Frustrated, she got to her feet and began to pace again, going through everything she could recall, all the visions she'd had, everything she'd been told by the Pythias, everything she'd read in her research.

The hours dragged, and though she had no idea what time it was, her body clock implied it was nighttime. A meal arrived, delivered by the corpse man, but Allegra didn't trust the food - what if they drugged her again?

She stared at the plate; a pasta dish, marinara she guessed.

Then she laughed. What good was foresight if she didn't use it? She wouldn't be able to tell if the food had been drugged, but she sure as Hades would be able to see if she ended up dead or unconscious *after* the meal.

She touched the plate and slipped into a peaceful state.

And saw herself doing nothing other than walking up and down the room and talking to herself. Deeming the dish safe, Allegra consumed the meal, and drank the accompanying cup of lukewarm, way-too-sweet tea.

Fatigued after an awful day, she lay on the bed, allowing her muscles to relax. But sleep wouldn't come.

There was nothing in her prison that encouraged peace.

CHAPTER 32

*L*ord Langcourt was furious.

He glared out at the black night sky with such anger that his body vibrated and his fists clenched of their own accord.

The plan had been simple enough. Capture the last Pythia, sacrifice her to Hermes, just as they'd been doing with all those young children in his monthly rituals, and be rewarded with yet more untold wealth.

And as an added bonus, she would not be around to give away his plans and crimes to his enemies.

Langcourt had put the extraction plan in place in the hopes of getting rid of the one obstacle to their greater plan.

But unfortunately, she was still alive.

Technically, he could remedy that easily enough. Just sacrifice the girl and be done with it. But, he'd encountered a problem he hadn't expected.

A deadly epidemic foretold by the Pythia, a foretelling that many influential people around the world were aware of, and believed.

The elite members of his society were up in arms, divided down the middle into two factions. One that didn't give a damn that the Pythia had such powers or that she could see the future, and the other that wanted to take advantage of that power.

The latter group believed it shortsighted to kill her as she might be the only person to offer the world salvation. Especially if the epidemic was as bad as their sources had implied.

Either way, both groups had insisted that Langcourt stay the woman's execution until they could agree.

And so his hands were tied. Foolishly, they had insisted on playing the waiting game with her.

They seemed to think that if they kept her under control until after the epidemic's danger point had passed, it would afford them some form of safety.

But Langcourt had his doubts about that plan. It was dangerous to keep such a high-profile prisoner right in the middle of Londinium, especially when hundreds of operatives from all around the world would be looking for her.

Yes, they had the resources to keep her hidden. And yes, they even had strategically placed agents to keep them informed if official investigations got anywhere close to them.

But Langcourt had learned long ago that spies existed everywhere. Had that not been the case, *he* would have been unable to infiltrate so many international organizations so easily.

He slammed a fist into the wall beside the window frame, glad that it was made of stone despite his knuckles bearing the brunt of the impact. He enjoyed the feel of the pain as it coursed through his hand.

Never let it be said that Lord Langcourt was afraid of pain.

He glared out the window at the moonless sky and the sight of the dark night calmed him somewhat.

A sacrificial ritual was scheduled for tonight. A special child had been selected for the Reaping.

At only three years old, his age had made some of the

members of the order a little reluctant to use him for the ritual.

But Langcourt had been adamant.

The child, despite his age, was extremely powerful. As the offspring of two extremely gifted telepaths, he'd been born with concentrated telepathic power.

Such abilities would definitely have been encouraged and nurtured by his parents, something Langcourt had refused to allow. Better that the boy and his power be used for the Order's purposes than for him to be out in the world, using such abominable abilities to learn secrets that should better remain buried.

Langcourt rounded his desk and headed to the wood-paneled wall on his right. He'd installed a row of hidden floor-to-ceiling closets, built to resemble wall-paneling. A slight press of the door in the right place, and it opened with an almost imperceptible click.

He liked to have secretive things like that around him, hiding places that nobody knew he had. A row of cloaks hung on a rail, different colored for different purposes.

He withdrew a white cloak, the weave fine, the thread cashmere and llama. He swung it around his shoulders, knotting the thin silk ropes at his neck.

Before leaving his office, he pulled the hood of the cloak over his head, shadowing his face. Although the pure white of his cloak would announce to anyone he passed who he was, Langcourt still enjoyed the fact that nobody could see his face. The cloak would act like a mask, allowing him to observe things that he usually wouldn't.

He'd noticed a long time ago that when people couldn't see one's face, they tended to be more relaxed, revealing details one didn't witness when holding a face-to-face conversation.

He descended into the depths of the building, noting the change in air temperature and humidity as he walked down the three levels into the mansion's ancient dungeons.

For most of his prisoners, Lord Langcourt never made much of an effort, since they rarely lasted all that long.

But he'd made a special effort for the Pythia. He wasn't exactly sure why, perhaps he had been impressed by thousands of years of historical tradition. Perhaps he wanted to toy with her.

So many people grew up listening to how powerful the Pythia was and what incredible skills she possessed. Langcourt could hardly blame himself for half-believing the stories. It was hard, sometimes, to change one's unconscious biases.

Now, he passed the prison cells and headed for the secret exit that led out into a thirty-acre piece of forested land.

Heavily guarded, Langcourt's land sat just on the edge of the city and was extremely private. This made it the ideal location for the rituals. There were no surrounding buildings that overlooked his property. The Order required privacy to complete their deadly rituals, an absence of nosy neighbors who could bear witness to murder in the eyes of the law.

Outside, Lord Langcourt walked onto the stage of a large amphitheater. Stone steps curved around the stage, providing sufficient seating for a full five hundred strong audience.

Large Grecian columns bracketed the top levels of the amphitheater, harking to a more ancient era. It was the only time that Langcourt had allowed himself the frivolity of building a structure which resembled ancient Greek and Roman architecture. Mostly he stuck to French Renaissance and early Brittanic.

As he took his place center-stage, he turned to scan the left-hand corner of the platform. There, in a small half-walled cubicle, the Pythia was in place as he'd commanded, two guards flanking her. It would be particularly enjoyable to watch her expression during the evening's sacrificial ritual.

He had a slight suspicion that she wouldn't be too happy with it.

And somehow that knowledge excited him.

A low drumbeat echoed around the amphitheater as it began to fill with cloaked acolytes. The dark night hung like a black ceiling above them, low and heavy. The disciples took their seats in complete silence, only the sound of fabric swishing and feet scuffing the stone echoing toward Langcourt as he waited patiently.

Two guards brought the sacrifice in and led him to stand beside the Oracle. Langcourt hid a smile. The Seer's eyes had gone from the boy to the sacrificial table, widening in horror.

Carved in the shape of a rectangular basin, the white stone was dotted with holes, providing drainage to the bath below.

A faucet, embedded into the table's base, made the job of extracting the sacrificial liquid easier. Beside the sacrificial table there sat a very short, narrow trestle.

Covered in a black velvet cloth, it bore a small collection of items, among them a single gleaming dagger, a small bronze bowl and a golden goblet. The seer required no explanation as to what was going to happen. Even the child appeared to understand, though his telepathy had probably helped fill in the blanks.

Given his ability, he would no doubt have already seen some of it through Langcourt's mind, not to mention the minds of his guards.

The drumbeat increased its pace, kicking the drama factor up a notch. From the expression on the Pythia's face, Langcourt knew that her heartbeat would be rising too, urged on by her fear and the music.

There was a beautiful power in music, the way it could agitate or calm a listener.

And now, the seer was powerless to do anything but watch. Langcourt had given the guards strict orders for her to be chained using a special set of bronze shackles.

He'd been working on its development over the last decade, initially intending it for Aurelia. But the old woman had faded faster than he'd expected, and in the end, he hadn't needed to stop her himself.

A pity though, that his quest would have to continue. He felt a little sorry for the new Oracle. From what he'd seen, the girl was clueless, naive, and far too spineless to ever become as powerful as was predicted.

She barely knew the extent of her powers, even now after having been trained by that agent. Langcourt was glad he'd been able to take her so efficiently.

And right now, he enjoyed a distinct pleasure in the horror in her eyes as she stared from the sacrificial table to the angelic little boy sitting beside her.

She'd see him, with his silky blond hair, cut short just below his ears, the little fringe beneath which peeked two great blue eyes, the tiny pixie nose and the little mouth. She'd see an adorable child, not the danger that Langcourt himself saw.

Though young, the abomination was far too intelligent for his own good. One of the reasons Langcourt wanted to get rid of him. A gifted child, showing so much intelligence at such a young age, was a genuine concern.

Combine such intelligence with his telepathic abilities, and a desire to help innocents, and you were guaranteed trouble.

Langcourt had made it his life's work to ensure that no abomination of any sort would have an overly-strong influence on the world.

The time had come to eliminate one of those influences altogether.

And tonight, he would rid the world of what might well have turned into destruction for them all.

Before he began the ceremony proper, Langcourt beckoned one of his acolytes. When the young man hurried over, Langcourt whispered in his ear. "Make sure that the Seer's guards hold onto her tightly. I suspect she might struggle and attempt to save the child."

Langcourt smiled as he turned to face the acolytes, who had by now filled all the levels of the amphitheater.

The girl could struggle all she wanted. There was only one end in sight for her.

She too would have to die soon.

CHAPTER 33

After bearing witness to the sacrifice tonight, the new Pythia could not be allowed to live. Langcourt's cowardly associates would be forced to agree soon enough.

He addressed the members of the society in the ritual words. "We are gathered here beneath the dark night. We come together to give thanks to the universe. We are fulfilling a divine purpose in cleansing the world of abominations. No abomination shall be allowed to live. Now, or ever."

A ripple of murmurs ran through the audience as the acolytes of the Order of Hermes whispered agreement and encouragement to their High Priest. They were an extremely passionate lot, and Langcourt was glad they'd followed him with minimal fuss.

Until recently, both recruitment and maintenance of the membership had been simple enough. The members supported each other socially and financially, and the reward for joining their number lay in plum appointments, rich sinecures, guaranteed wealth and protection from the law.

But now, the prospect of the end of the world, of a pandemic that would wipe humanity off the planet, would frighten anyone.

Langcourt hoped he'd be able to retain control of them for as long as was necessary, and for that very reason had refrained from revealing their impending doom.

Lord Langcourt lifted his hands to the dark sky and began to chant, singing in his low, deep voice the words of the Order's blessings.

He sang in Gaelic, the timbre in his voice thick and strong. The chant was rhythmic, almost lulling the acolytes into a trance.

As he recited the lyrical words, the drumbeats increased in pace, in intensity, transforming his words into something much more powerful. Soon, the acolytes were swaying from left to right, echoing his chants with rising passion.

The effect was quite eerie, and Langcourt had to admit he enjoyed the power he held over all these souls.

At last, when he'd worked them into a frenzy, Langcourt signaled the boy's guards to bring him over.

The seer struggled against her shackles, trying to shrug off her guards, trying to grab onto the boy's arm to prevent the two men from taking him away.

Of course, her attempt at stopping them was useless. Yet she still fought and struggled anyway.

Langcourt could see it in her eyes, that she knew how impotent she was. That she knew however hard she fought, she'd be unable to do anything to stop the sacrifice.

As the guards led the 'lamb' to the slaughter, the boy paused and turned to look over his shoulder at Allegra.

From this distance, Langcourt was unable to hear the words he uttered. He made a mental note to check with the guards later. Whatever the boy had said to the seer had made her skin go ashen.

She stared at the child, a strange expression on her face. She allowed her hands to fall, ceasing her battle with her guards. He spoke for a little too long, and Langcourt became impatient.

He was about to wave at the guard when the boy nodded at

the Pythia, then faced the stage. The Oracle did nothing to stop the boy as he turned away from her and walked toward Langcourt.

There was no longer a need for the guards to guide him.

The child was tiny for his age, his stature barely that of the average two-year-old. A short life with so much potential, soon to be a sacrifice beneath Langcourt's eager hands.

But it was necessary. Langcourt was fed up with the recent rise in mutations. The abominations appearing over the last few decades had reached unacceptable numbers.

The skills these mutants possessed were unnatural. They did not belong in the world. Those abilities gave them far too much power over the rest of the population, placing normal humans at their mercy.

And Langcourt was determined to ensure that such a situation never came to pass.

The child, a perfect example of such unnatural, abominable power, came to a stop in front of him, lifting his chin and meeting Langcourt's eyes, solemnly defiant. They'd dressed him in a little white cloak, a tiny version of Langcourt's own majestic one.

In a sea of black, and in the darkness of night, the two of them would appear as beacons of hope.

Langcourt turned to the table and reached for a bronze bowl. He lifted it, careful not to spill the holy water within. The water, blessed under a full moon within the temple of Hermes, would sanctify the sacrifice.

He dipped a finger into the water and ran it across the boy's forehead. The child didn't flinch, merely stared at him with those strange blue eyes.

Langcourt waved at two of the acolytes standing by to take the boy and lay him on the table. He didn't need to speak.

They'd all been here before, performed the same ritual so many times over that it wasn't really necessary for him to give direction. And yet he did it anyway, steps to the ritual which provided him with calm, and provided the brotherhood with peace and confidence.

The guards laid the boy on the table, belted his thin arms down—the straps located at the elbow, leaving his wrists free.

The purpose of the ritual was to obtain the power of the one sacrificed through access to their blood.

Langcourt would have much preferred a more gory ritual, perhaps the removal of the still-beating heart; something more macabre than a minimalist bloodletting ceremony, but it wasn't necessary.

Besides, Langcourt suspected at least half of the members of the brotherhood would be too squeamish for such a display.

Many of the acolytes now seated along the rows of the amphitheater would be relatively new to the brotherhood. As green as they were, shocking their sensibilities might backfire on their master.

Not yet ready to enjoy a more ghoulish ritual, they might rethink their decision to join, thus endangering the secrecy of the brotherhood.

So Langcourt would have to keep the most dramatic cere-monies for the inner circle.

He wondered what the seer would think, should she discover Langcourt's more macabre inclinations. With any luck, she herself would soon experience them herself.

Langcourt almost licked his lips at the thought of the power contained within the Pythia's heart.

He shook his head and concentrated on the boy. He knew how he'd appear to his acolytes, the sad, reluctant father figure. They'd remember him that way far longer than they'd recall the boy's death.

The child lay on the table, completely still. He didn't struggle, he didn't fidget. Just lay there staring at the dark sky, his small face a picture of serenity, his chest rising and falling as he took his last breaths.

Langcourt ruffled the boy's hair, smiled and then turned to the trestle table. He made a fuss over the dagger, picking it up with great care, turning it just so for the light to reflect back into the watching audience.

With a somber expression he returned to the boy's side, listening as the gathered brotherhood took a simultaneous breath of eager anticipation.

Long ago, Langcourt had learned the best places in which to make his incision, the best spot to encourage strongest blood-flow.

He proceeded to make incisions into the boy's wrists and ankles, cutting neat slices into veins and arteries.

The child didn't even flinch.

Langcourt was reluctantly impressed. He himself knew the pain that such an incision could cause, especially without any form of painkillers.

The child shifted his gaze and looked directly at Langcourt. He knew the child was likely listening in on his thoughts. But Langcourt didn't care. The victim's death was a foregone conclusion, and his telepathic ability would tell him so.

Probably why he was so acquiescent. There was absolutely nothing he could do to stop his fate.

His death was inevitable.

From behind him, Langcourt could hear the Pythia's renewed struggles. One of her guards held a knife to her neck, likely the only reason she didn't scream or shout in protest. When Langcourt looked over his shoulder, he met her tear-filled, furious gaze.

Dismissing her, he returned his attention to the child and watched with glee as the blood drained out of his body. This was the part of the ritual which infused Langcourt with excitement, where he grew high on the power of the ritual.

And on the anticipation of what was to come.

The Seer's presence had served only to dampen that excitement, contrary to his expectation, but he wouldn't allow her to spoil his fun.

The boy's eyelashes fluttered as life drained out of him. Langcourt waited impatiently for the moment when death would claim him.

The pale golden glow of the child's skin slowly faded. The blue eyes, staring out above him, faded to a dull gray. The slow rise and fall of his chest ceased.

Langcourt's fingers had formed into fists of their own accord. His entire body was strung tight. It was crucial that he partook of the blood at the right time. Too early and the power transfer wouldn't happen. Too late and he wouldn't receive enough of that power.

He beckoned and one of his acolytes brought a pure white stone chalice to him.

Just as he was about to kneel and release the faucet, a commotion behind him drew his attention.

Glancing over his shoulder, he scowled at the sight of the seer collapsing. She lay half on her chair and half off, supported by her two guards. Her eyes were wide open, and Langcourt suspected she wasn't looking at anything that he could see with his human eyes.

Her voice echoed around the now strangely silent amphitheater. It had a gritty power to it, almost ghostly, and the sound of it seemed to entrance his acolytes. Langcourt was furious at the influence this woman exerted over his brotherhood, but at this point he was more curious as to what she was about to say.

"You have a month in which to prepare. There will be nowhere that you can hide. Nowhere that you can run. The child will be avenged."

She paused to take a struggling breath, and Langcourt could

almost feel the gathered acolytes lean forward to hear if she had anything else to say.

"Your end will be horrible, for you will suffer a worse death than the pandemic even now drawing near. Prepare yourselves, for retribution is coming."

A ripple of unease filtered through the gathered acolytes and some even got to their feet. Their brothers pulled them back down, and Langcourt was glad he could see all their faces. He'd have them dead before they rebelled against a High Priest.

It infuriated him that the Oracle wielded such power over his acolytes, but he refused to allow his growing anger to control him. Langcourt expelled a long breath and turned on his heel to face his brethren.

He waved at the seer's two guards, indicating they should take her away and do it fast. Dutifully, they hauled her off the stage, ensuring she remained out of sight of the seated brothers.

He lifted his hands urging his followers to calm down.

"There is no need to panic. By doing so you are giving in to the power that these mutants hold over us. These abominations should not be allowed to have any influence over disciples under Hermes' protection. Steel your spine, harden your heart, and do not give them the power."

His words rang out around the amphitheater, and the rumble of discontent steadily faded away.

Still furious, Langcourt returned his attention to the dead child. The window in which he'd needed to consume the child's blood was quickly closing. The longer he waited, the weaker the transfer of power would be.

And what a waste it would be, to have the boy's burgeoning power be lost to the ether.

He strode back to the table, realizing only then that he still held the stone goblet in this grip, his knuckles so tight he'd have to peel them off the stem one at a time.

Langcourt knelt on one knee, throwing his cloak around him

in a dramatic flourish. He leaned forward slowly and opened the faucet, allowing the rich red liquid to slowly fill the goblet.

He took extra care not to spill a single drop.

The gathered acolytes watched in awe as he bent slowly and placed his lips on the rim of the stone goblet. A great sigh ran over the amphitheater as he sipped from the goblet, gorging on that power that was almost a tangible thing.

Langcourt was infinitely glad that his acolytes, even his fellow priests, had little idea of the true intention behind the ritual. He'd long ago managed to convince them that the ritual was necessary. For each and every one of them. That understanding, that the ritual imbued them all with divine energy, kept them glued to their seats.

That belief kept them silent and in awe as they watched child after child being sacrificed.

It had been Langcourt's most enjoyable part of the indoctrination process. He wasn't ashamed to see the similarities the brotherhood bore to a cult.

If it got him success it was enough.

And so they all watched closely, believing their presence at the ritual would empower them, imbue them with the strength to continue the fight.

Little did they know that in reality, they received none of its power. That the sweet reward of the ritual was concentrated solely on Langcourt himself.

He tilted the goblet, emptying the last of the blood into his mouth, slightly annoyed that much of the warmth in the liquid had already dissipated. But he couldn't complain. He'd already begun to feel the power of the child coursing through his veins.

Energy sang through his limbs as Langcourt reveled in the process of the energy transfer. It not only gave him strength, it also bestowed a longer life upon him.

A part of him had begun to tire of the need to participate in this ritual, but absorbing that power was essential if he was to continue his mission.

Without him, the abominations would take over the world.

He'd already spent two thousand years fighting the fight, and he would spend that long again if he had to.

llegra shivered with fury and horror as the door shut behind her.

She'd never in her life thought there would be a moment in which she'd be glad to be locked up inside a cell.

Her hands shook, and her stomach churned. *That poor child.* He'd known what was going to happen. And yet he'd allowed the high priest to complete the ritual without a hint of resistance.

Allegra hated that she'd been restrained and unable to stop the horror. She'd have gladly broken the old man's neck.

What benefit would killing a little child get them?

The high priest had possessed an air of power and arrogance. But Allegra had found, in her experience, that often those who appeared to be powerful were the ones who felt the most powerless.

She swallowed hard, trying to keep the contents of her stomach down. She was so riled up, so angry that she could not keep still. Pacing back-and-forth along the carpet helped, very slightly, to help keep both her anger and her dinner at bay.

Who were they, these men of the Order of Hermes? Allegra knew enough to know that cults existed in every country, pandering to every god, or non-god. She doubted very much that Hermes would be impressed with that vicious high priest and his infanticide.

What did they expect to achieve by murdering an innocent child?

Considering the depravity of people like the high priest and his followers, Allegra had to wonder why she and Max should even bother to save humanity. The coming epidemic would sweep away all such horrors.

Granted, most people were not like the high priest and his heartless acolytes. But humanity would be much better off without monsters like them.

Still, the little boy and other infants all over the world did not deserve to die. But there'd been something extraordinary about that child. Had the Order of Hermes seen that quality in him and deemed him dangerous?

In fact, when he'd spoken to her, there had not been one word of revenge. Instead, he'd tried to inspire her with a new passion for saving humanity.

But his words warred with the actions of the high priest, and Allegra's grief at the child's murder overshadowed his advice.

She wasn't ready.

Not yet.

The tears began to flow and Allegra did not even try to hold them back. She'd never seen anything so horrible in her life. Even visions of the pain-filled, bloody deaths of the people closest to her had not come close to seeing an innocent life deliberately snuffed out in front of her.

But the more she thought about it, the more the boy's words made sense.

He'd told her to remain calm, his voice sweet and gentle. He'd said he knew her powers and the struggle she had with them. He'd told her that there was nothing she could do to stop what going to happen to him.

He'd said if she got a chance to leave she should take it. And he'd told her that once she was free she needed to do everything in her power to stop the end of the world.

Allegra had been shocked, and a little dazed. The boy had spoken quickly, and with such maturity that she was a little bit confused, listening to him, while looking at the face of a three-year-old.

Just before he left, he'd met her eyes again and given her a gentle but sad smile. "I am not afraid. You should not be, either. Everything we do is destined, but destiny can be changed if you are willing to do what it takes."

Allegra shook her head, scraping tears from her eyes. Agitated now, she settled into her exercise routine, pushing her muscles until they burned.

~

TWO HOURS LATER, just as Allegra was wiping her neck and forehead with the miniature towel, the door shushed open and the high priest entered her room.

As her eyes met his face, her vision blurred. Only for a moment, but it was enough.

He stood over her, his face purple with fury, perspiration dotting his brow. In his raised hand he wielded a whip.

Had Allegra's powers increased, so that she could now see future scenarios without touching? Or maybe that was just a part of her wild imagination.

Allegra wasn't certain that she was strong enough to withstand any form of torture. Still, she'd endure whatever was coming, do whatever it took to survive this, because if she didn't live through it humanity would die.

That the little boy had displayed such strength in the face of certain death, only fueled Allegra's determination to survive and avenge him.

The high priest stood in the doorway, watching her with his beady eyes, his hands folded at his back. The muscles in his neck were bunched tight.

His face was the picture of supreme Zen, a total lie considering the tale his body told. Fury simmered beneath his affected calm. Perhaps fury at Allegra for what she'd said in front of his followers.

Allegra didn't care. It was about time they knew the truth. If she'd had the chance, she would've told them much more.

The high priest drew closer, followed closely by a burly guard. He held a small silver case, the sight of which turned Allegra's stomach.

The high priest folded back the sleeves of his cloak, revealing pale arms, his skin wrinkled and papery.

For all his public oration a few hours ago, the man certainly didn't waste time with words now, standing still and fuming while the guard dropped the case on the dresser beside Allegra and turned on his heel.

He unclipped a gun from his belt and aimed it at Allegra. She'd contemplated an escape; subdue the two men and run, but doing so with a gun pointed at her head was impossible.

"Hands," said the guard briskly.

Allegra lifted her hands and wasn't surprised when the older man bound them tightly with zip ties.

Satisfied she was securely bound, he disappeared out of the door and returned within a few minutes, a metal foldout chair in his hand.

After settling the chair in a position facing the dresser, the guard gripped Allegra by her shoulder and pushed her toward the seat. When she resisted, he gave her a light shove, the message hidden in the movement that he wouldn't be averse to shoving her harder.

Propelled forward while facing the chair, Allegra had little choice but to straddle the seat, facing the backrest.

Removing a jagged knife from his pocket, the high priest walked around Allegra. She shifted in her seat, wondering what he intended on doing when he gripped her neck.

"Face front," he said, his hot breath trailing across her ear.

She shivered and straightened, half ready for him to plunge the blade into her spine.

Without warning, he ripped open the back of her shirt with a hard upward thrust. The shirt flapped to each side, hanging limp, still moist with perspiration after her workout.

Allegra was unable to hold back the shudder of disgust when the High priest lifted the strap of her brassiere and cut through it.

She steeled her body against revealing the fear that now coursed through it. What was he going to do?

Allegra shivered with fear and revulsion. But he didn't touch her skin again. Instead, he went to the silver case and flicked open the locks. Bent over the contents, he took his time, his flair for the dramatic continuing even without a proper audience.

If he thought he was scaring her, or impressing her, he'd be wrong on both counts.

Even when he withdrew the cat o' nine tails from the case, Allegra wasn't afraid. Perhaps having had a vision of what her future looked like, she knew she couldn't avoid it.

The thing with seeing the future is there was no point in fighting what one knew was completely unchangeable.

Just as the child had said.

CHAPTER 35

Apart from transforming into a Minotaur and blasting her way through the walls of her cell, Allegra had no choice but to strengthen herself against whatever the high priest had in store for her.

He shook out the cat o' nine tails, allowing the six individual whips to drop with gravity. Each separate whip contained six small knots, of varying sizes. Allegra didn't need to look at it to know that it was going to hurt like Hades.

The high priest looked at her and smiled. "My dear, it's time you told us what we need to know."

Allegra raised her eyebrows and glared at him. "I've already told you what you need to know."

Her voice was frigid and the high priest shook his head, his smile disappearing, anger blazing in his eyes. "It's in your best interest to help us. I need to know more about this epidemic you mentioned. How do we prevent it? Where will it start?"

Allegra laughed. "I hate to break it to you, but we've been trying to find that out for the last week. I'm new to this whole Seer business. My ability isn't under control yet. I can't access my sight just because you want me to."

The look of frustration on the high priest's face was almost comical.

He exhaled harshly. "There's no point in stalling, dear girl. Give me the information I want and save yourself the pain. I promise you will not be leaving this room without telling me what I want to know."

Allegra wanted to laugh. She knew very well that she wasn't going to leave this room at all, not if the high priest had anything to say about it.

When she glared at him and refused to speak, he sighed and walked around her, spinning the whip around and around.

He didn't give any warning. Just struck, using all the power behind his upper body.

The pain was incredible.

She let out a scream as the knots on the leather scraped and cut into the soft skin of her back. A part of Allegra was curious; what would her body look like after he was done? The skin that high on her back had always been pale and smooth. She'd never even suffered from acne the way Xenia had.

Allegra's vanity was only a small part of her horror.

After the wave of pain from the first blow had faded, the high priest asked her again, "You going to tell me what I need to know? How do we stop this epidemic? How do we avoid contracting the disease?"

Allegra shook her head. "There is nothing that I can tell you. Nothing except that the epidemic will not start in the New Germanic States."

There was no point in keeping *that* information from him, especially since Allegra had already begun to suspect that this man would already know about it. If he didn't know now, he'd find out soon enough.

Not satisfied with her response, the priest struck her again. Another wave of pain hit her. She tried to protect herself, tried to close her mind against the agony.

As she sobbed through the pain, her consciousness shifted elsewhere, her mind freezing. She watched from above as the high priest struck her again.

She'd shut out the pain so well that every blow struck her without eliciting a response. She simply endured the whipping. She couldn't bear the sight of her tortured body anymore, and she looked away.

Allegra blinked, startled.

She was no longer in the cell.

She stood at the bottom of a valley, surrounded by fig and olive trees. Above her, on a hill, sat a beautiful temple of Apollo. Allegra suspected she'd gone back in time because she knew there wasn't a single Apollo Temple in existence that remained undamaged.

There'd been a time in the past, when followers of Apollo had been persecuted to such an extent that every single temple built in the god's name had been destroyed, and almost every confessed worshipper sentenced to a horrible death.

That had been almost four hundred years ago, and proof of that horror still remained in the destruction to be seen at every temple complex around the world.

Allegra stood in front of this beautifully-intact temple and felt more empty than she'd ever felt in her life. She walked up the hill and entered the cool confines of the building, staring around her, her heart heavy.

"Please. If you are here, please hear me. You've chosen me to be your voice. Why then do you allow me to experience such torture? My body cannot withstand such pain. Help me to survive so I can serve humanity. Please put an end to this torture."

As Allegra prayed she wondered about the high priest and his Order of Hermes. Surely Hermes himself would not tolerate the actions of the evil man and his followers.

Hermes was not a God known for accepting torture and

bloodshed in his name. Nor as one who would turn a blind eye to such horror.

Allegra repeated her plea, praying that Apollo would hear her. But her voice just echoed against the walls and pillars and no god appeared, no divine voice spoke in her ear.

Tears of frustration slid from her eyes, burning heated paths to her chin.

Just as Allegra let out a cry of frustration, she was flung back into her body so hard she suspected whiplash was inevitable.

A wall of fire surrounded her with heat, burning into her skin. Allegra's heart ached as she swallowed a sob. Apollo had refused to answer her call.

What good was it being a priestess of Apollo when he didn't listen, didn't help when she needed him?

And what in Hades was with the fire burning around her like a living cage?

It raged in a column, surrounding her body, and although the heat offered her some comfort, the pain in her back had returned with full force.

She hung over the back of the chair, hands dangling, wrung of all her strength, unable to hold herself upright any longer.

Voices echoed around her, hollow as if she was underwater.

"We must be overdoing it," said her guard. He sounded disappointed. "She looks like she is unconscious."

The high priest snorted, and Allegra could feel the anger rolling off him. "Very well. She is much weaker than I thought she would be. So much for being such a powerful priestess."

The guard bent and sliced through her zip ties with a short knife, and the two men departed, leaving Allegra seated on the chair, unable to move.

Beneath the pain humming through her limbs, fury simmered like a living thing. She felt fury at Apollo for failing to protect her, fury at having been given a gift and yet being unable to do anything to help people with it.

Fury that there was no way she could save herself from future torture.

Allegra had never believed in ancient deities in the first place. It made absolutely no sense that *she* would be the one given these powers.

Why hadn't the gods seen fit to bestow such an ability on someone more deserving? Someone who still believed in the old deities, who cared about them?

Because she, at this point, certainly did not.

The pain seared into her back, throbbing lines of broken skin. She rested her forehead on the cool metal of the chair and mentally followed each strip of blood as it snaked its way down her back, counting them the way she used to count sheep as a child.

Right now, she didn't have the strength to do more, and she sat there fading in and out of consciousness, waiting for the pain to go away.

Part of her knew she was almost ready to give up hope. They'd injured her so badly that there was little chance of her escaping from the cell.

Even if she could find a way out.

CHAPTER 36

*D*espite the short flight, Max was exhausted. He couldn't remember the last time he'd had more than three hours of sleep. The rest of his team were in the same position, way too wired, far too worried to think about sleep.

Max prepared as the plane came in for a landing, barely noticing the smooth touchdown. He was already on his feet, marching to the exit as the plane rolled to a stop, ignoring the annoyed glares of the rest of the passengers in first class.

He supposed he should be grateful that Aulus's secretary had procured him and his team flights in the more prestigious section of the plane.

As they descended the stairs and neared the tarmac, the smell of aircraft fuel mixed with hot asphalt filled his nostrils. An icy wind blew, tugging hard at Max's coat, reminding him of forest fires he'd fought as a kid back in Ralabia. The odor of dried burlap sacks, the frantic thudding of fabric against the brush as they hit out the flames.

Rows of men and women, blackened by soot, hitting at the flames, throats parched, skin drenched with perspiration, fighting nature in the hopes of saving their homes, their livelihoods.

Max blinked the memory away and focused.

Below him, Corina had reached the ground ahead of Flavius, her shoulder length white-blonde hair whipping her cheeks while she turned her face into the wind and squinted.

The Brittanic weather wasn't welcoming them, that much was clear.

As Max lifted his hand to look at his wristwatch a black Rolls-Royce drew up. A sandy-haired young man jumped out of the vehicle and trotted toward them.

He wore a pair of slim-fitting white pants and a powder-blue shirt, the high, stiff collar of which looked about to strangle him.

His pale skin was littered with freckles, which accompanied by hair a strange shade of orange, was a little bit too bright and energetic for Max.

"So glad to finally meet you, Commander Vissarion. I'm Jonathan Egent. Security attaché from the New Germanic States embassy, attached to you and your team for the duration of your stay. Anything you need, just let me know and I will make it happen." His smile was broad and white, and a little too bright given the dire circumstances.

Max supposed that it was unfair of him to take his fatigue and frustration out on the man. The attaché was clearly eager to help. But Max remained wary, and decided to keep an eye on him.

Egent drove them to the hotel, making the forty-minute drive seem endless. He peppered every island of silence with questions, and eventually Max had to pretend to have fallen asleep to avoid answering. That left Corina and Flavius to field his inquiries.

When they reached their hotel, Max and his team alighted, leaving Egent to return for them after they checked in and headed to their suite of rooms to freshen up. The embassy had booked a four-roomed suite, the likes of which Max hardly ever frequented.

He was a man of simpler tastes.

They hurried, settled themselves, and then Max headed to the dining area. Corina was already there, and she and Flavius were involved in a heated discussion as they leaned over a map of Londinium.

"What's going on?" Max asked, unbuttoning his jacket. He had no complaint about the hotel itself, but the air was flat and heavy, weighing Max down with constant pressure.

Corina looked up, frustrated. "Flavius has a bead on the seer, but is not one hundred percent sure. He thinks it's not enough."

Max met the locator's blue eyes. "What's the problem?"

Flavius shook his head. "It's just a feeling that I'm getting. I can see something, have the sense that I know where she is, but what I'm looking at feels wrong."

Max rubbed his arm absently as he reached the sash window and leaned against the casement.

"I understand, but we have to follow up on every clue that comes our way. Even if it doesn't pan out, we still have to check."

The locator nodded, although he didn't look too happy.

Max understood.

The locator bordered on the obsessive, and hated being inaccurate. He'd often go into a funk if he didn't find who or what he was looking for. It was a temperamental aspect of most locators, only on a much stronger scale with Flavius.

Max was willing to put up with his fussing simply because the man demanded so much from his own abilities.

They headed on down to the car, meeting Egent's radiance again. Max hid a grimace and climbed in beside him, telling him to start driving.

"Where we headed?" Egent asked, his eyes curious as he scanned Max's face first, then looked up at the rear-view mirror to watch the other two.

"We are not yet sure," said Max, his voice terse. "Flavius here will direct you. We don't exactly have an address, but he'll guide you there."

Max sent Flavius and Corina a warning glance. He wasn't sure how much Egent knew, and preferred to leave it at that, at least until they were more certain of the man's loyalties.

They had to take into consideration that they were in a different country, with different bureaucracies, and completely different priorities.

In addition, after the whole fiasco of losing the Pythia, and being under an umbrella of suspicion, even their own embassy's staff might look to thwart their search, or at least attempt to find Allegra before Max and his team did.

That, or they might have informants already in place, feeding information to the very people responsible for Allegra's abduction.

The attaché remained in the most agreeable mood, stopping off first at a small tavern and procuring coffee and pies for everyone, before continuing on. He followed Flavius's directions, taking every turn as requested, and without question.

When Egent finally parked the vehicle, Max was surprised at their destination. He sent Flavius a questioning glance, beginning to wonder whether the locator had been mistaken.

They alighted and headed into a large cemetery, rolling green hills dotted with black and white stone headstones, and carvings of gods, goddesses, nymphs. Here and there an owl, for wisdom, or a stylized tree of life watched over a grave, its crumbling stone or marble rendering it almost unidentifiable. The cemetery reflected some of Brittanica's past, where strange new religions and cults had prevailed for a short time before being forgotten again.

That was almost eight hundred years ago now.

Flavius hurried ahead, his bearing confident. He knew where he was going. Max let him be, walking along behind him, keeping a comfortable distance. The last thing the man needed was additional pressure, especially when he was already doubting his own ability.

Forty-five minutes later they'd searched every path and every section of the cemetery and had come up empty-handed.

"Does he not know what's he looking for?" asked Egent, not hiding the criticism in his voice.

Max refrained from telling the man to shut up.

Instead he and his team ignored the attaché, continuing their search for any sign of Allegra.

THEY LEFT the cemetery at last, having found neither Allegra's body, nor even the slightest indication of her presence.

To say that they were discouraged was an understatement, but Max was careful not to reveal too much of his mind to Flavius.

The locator was irritated, frustrated that he hadn't been able to find the Pythia. Max knew that nothing he said would make Flavius feel better so he let him be, knowing that Corina would know how to soothe him.

Egent, after asking various questions and receiving noncommittal answers, drove them back to the hotel in a more subdued mood.

As they entered the lobby, a man strode toward them, his gait confident, purposeful.

Max recognized the Londinium police insignia on the stranger's shoulder, and wasn't surprised when he introduced himself as Inspector Pienius.

Max swallowed his annoyance as he shook the policeman's hand. He'd expressly asked the States' embassy not to inform the Londinium authorities about their mission. As much as he lacked sufficient trust in the staff at their own embassy, he was even more doubtful of the Londinium authorities' loyalty.

Max forced himself to smile and greet the man, figuring that he should have it in him to deal with one polite inspector.

From the expression on Corina's face, Max could tell that Pienius had impressed her with his blond good looks, impressive physique, and old-world manners.

Max had to hide a smile because Corina was always a hard nut to crack.

"So please, how may I be of service to you?" The inspector smiled genially. "On behalf of my government, I want to assure you that we are here to help as best as we can. We believe that it's in everyone's best interest to have the Pythia returned to us all. And you can trust me when I say that should we discover that she is in the hands of a citizen of Brittania, punishment for their crimes will be just and swift."

Max nodded and smiled back. Pienius sounded sincere, yet Max wasn't entirely convinced. He knew he was being distrustful, but he would rather withhold his trust than make the mistake of handing it to the wrong person. He had already made mistakes enough in his responsibility for Allegra.

Only when Max nodded at Flavius, giving him an encouraging glance, did the locator turn to the inspector. He gave him a quick rundown of their fruitless field search and Max was glad when the inspector nodded, looking somber.

"Perhaps you should have taken advantage of my local knowledge before searching on your own. If your vision gave you a view of the cemetery, it is not necessarily one that is above ground."

Corina and Flavius both frowned at the Pienius. "What do you mean?" Corina asked.

Pienius hesitated, studying the two, checking if they really did need further information. Then he cleared his throat. "In addition to the aboveground cemeteries, the old inhabitants of Londinium, as in Rome, built elaborate underground passages and catacombs in which they stored the bodies of the dead. It's a tradition going back well over a thousand years, and there are some old families who still subscribe to the ancient ways."

Corina and Flavius glanced at Max.

Flavius looked doubtful, while the look on Corina's face said she thought the man was serious. "I had no idea," Corina said. "We don't have such tunnels in the States, though I have heard about the Roman ones."

Pienius seemed oblivious to their skepticism as he continued, "In fact, some above-ground cemeteries also have the catacombs and tunnels built beneath them. They aren't easily accessible from the surface though. For security reasons, the entrances are usually kept secret; only plot-owners have access."

That made sense to Max. "Do you know of any way we can gain access to those underground passages without upsetting too many of those plot-owners?"

Pienius smiled. "Give me an hour and I will be back. I need to find a particular map that I think will help us."

He bowed politely then disappeared from the lobby into the street, leaving Max and his team wary, yet expectant.

"You think he's legit?" asked Corina.

Flavius was quiet.

Max was still staring at the glass doors. "He damned well better be."

CHAPTER 37

While waiting for Pienius, Max led his team into the restaurant where they found a window table and ordered meals. He wasn't entirely sure what time of day it was, and Max didn't think his body cared either.

When Pienius arrived, the team headed upstairs to the suite. They preferred to refrain from publicizing their search and had already received curious glances from the other patrons in the restaurant. Possibly their accents were drawing attention as they'd taken care not to speak of anything confidential in public.

Pienius had brought an ancient-looking map with him, and spread it out on the dining table.

"This is an official council map of all the subterranean tunnels and catacombs across the city. It's rather old, so anything constructed in the last decade may not be included. Not that many people are building catacombs these days."

Max tapped a finger on the map. "It's a start at least. Let's hope it gets us somewhere."

Max watched in silence as Pienius began to mark off particular catacombs that were unlikely to be part of their search area. "These places are in a state of extreme disrepair. They are on the list, but far too dangerous for people to be walking through them all the time."

He glanced at Flavius.

"Can you give me an idea of what you saw, of your surroundings, the architecture, the types of tombstones, style of statutes?"

Flavius nodded, clearly impressed by the man's intuitive questions. The two of them continued to discuss possible locations while Max lost himself within his thoughts.

His attention was drawn back to the present with the mention of the police. Flavius was saying, "Are you sure you don't want to get additional back-up?"

Max was surprised when the inspector shook his head. "There really is no need. I am quite capable of guiding you to the most likely area. Once we are closer, I have a feeling that you will be far more successful than any local policeman in identifying the specific location."

Pienius paused and shifted his gaze to meet Max. He seemed to be asking a question that Max couldn't answer. The moment passed, and then the inspector said, "While we may not need the support of the police force, what we do require are arms. Just in case."

Max frowned. "Surely you're able to procure suitable weapons from your department. Being a police officer."

Pienius shook his head. "The situation is tenuous. I cannot trust that everyone in my department, or among my superiors, is honest about their loyalties. Trust me, now is the time to take the utmost care. And the fact that I cannot leave my trust one hundred percent at the feet of my fellow officers, should tell you something. The last thing I will be able to do is procure weapons without tipping somebody off."

Max nodded, a cool smile on his face. "People can always be bought."

The inspector smiled back. The grin told Max he was glad he didn't have to elaborate. Max figured an admission by a police officer, that he suspected someone on his own force was crooked, would be hard to come by.

"I'll make a call to the embassy. I hope it won't take too much time, because time is one thing we don't have a lot of."

Max moved toward a table beside the window for some privacy while he dialed. "Hello. This is Commander Vissarion. I'd like to speak to the Head of Security."

Colonel Braxus, a trusted confidant of General Aulus, answered a minute later, his tone stern and unforgiving. It didn't take long for Max to realize the man was extremely reluctant to help.

Max was in no mood to bargain, and soon began to lose patience. "I apologize if I seem rude, Colonel Braxus, but if you please give General Aulus in the Capital a call, I have every confidence he will set your mind at ease."

After a long pause, Braxus cleared his throat, apparently convinced of Max's authority by the mere mention of Aulus's name.

"Even if I agreed to provide you with these weapons, it's going to take a few hours to round them up."

"We can wait, sir. If that's what it takes, we will wait."

The man sighed. "I probably shouldn't even be helping you. Given the circumstances."

Max ignored him. Those circumstances were none of Max's concern at this point in time. "I understand your position, sir. I wouldn't be making such a request were it not necessary. And extremely urgent. General Aul—"

Braxus cut Max off. "I have already spoken to the general and advised him of the position that we are in."

Max stiffened, frowning. What position? Was Max expected to read between the lines? If so, Braxus was telling him that someone was currently watching his movements, someone who could influence the success of the mission.

There wasn't time to tread on eggshells, but at the same time

Max wasn't eager to throw a powerful contact to the wolves. "I'd be most grateful for any help, sir. But if you are unable to assist, I understand."

Perhaps if they ended their conversation on this note it would allow the man to claim that he'd done nothing to assist Max and his team. However, the Colonel relented and promised to do his best.

Max rang off, worried about the man's reaction, wondering what else was going on that he didn't know. This was not the first time he'd been sent on a mission with insufficient briefing.

He was getting tired of Aulus keeping things from him, information that for all he knew, might be of vital importance to recovering Allegra.

The team didn't wait long at the hotel. Despite Braxus's reluctance, he provided the weapons soon enough, sending them over with Egent.

Leaving Pienius in the room, the team met the attaché in the lobby. Gone was the bright, cheery man of their earlier encounters. Instead, they met a dour John, making Max wonder at the reason behind the sudden Jekyll and Hyde transformation.

Suddenly, after being so effusive when they first met him, the attaché appeared reluctant to have anything to do with Max and his team. He handed the keys to the vehicle to Max and disappeared with a brisk warning to take care of the van, and the 'golf bags' in the back. Then he strode off down the street, head down against the wind.

He'd said nothing more, just strode down the street, heading against the wind.

"Now wasn't that strange?" asked Corina as she watched Egent through the hotel window. "It's like we've suddenly acquired leprosy. Or perhaps he is subject to sudden mood swings."

Max, by that time, had given up wondering what was going on. He would have thought that it would have been in the best interests of the New Germanic States' embassy to help the team find the Pythia as quickly as possible. The faster they returned home with Allegra, the easier it would be for them to regain their good standing on an international scale.

Max sighed. Honestly, he'd never been a politically minded man. Not that he lacked the head for it.

He'd just never had the heart for the ruthless back-stabbing nature of that game. It had so often seemed pointless, running around in circles, constantly assuaging egos, pandering to the more powerful ones and bowing to others.

Which was why he was probably better off doing the grunt work, work that did not entail countless hours blowing smoke up someone's ass when they could see exactly what you were doing and could usually predict your next move before you even knew you were going to make it.

Pienius appeared right after Egent left, his brows bunching with curiosity as he studied their faces. Max handed the van's keys to the inspector. It stood to reason that a native would get them to their destination faster.

"Do you mind driving?" he asked.

Pienius smiled. "Not at all." He gave Max a strange look, then turned and walked off.

The team followed the inspector as they headed out in search of the van. Boxy in shape, it looked like a small delivery vehicle, two seats up front and large enough for the four of them including the weapons.

When Max flung open the back door and inspected the 'golf bags' he was surprised. Despite his reluctance, Braxus had provided them with sufficient ammunition for the mission. Guns, rifles, ammo. Even a box full of grenades. He'd gone all out and given them a broad spectrum of weapons to choose from.

Coming from a man so seemingly reluctant to help, this largesse made Max all the more certain that something was up.

He shut the rear door and headed up front, taking a seat

beside Pienius who seemed content to study his phone while the seer and the locator settled themselves beside boxes of dangerous firepower.

Pienius gunned the engine and they set off, giving Max time to think things through.

He wouldn't have been surprised if the general had gotten the president involved, overruling Braxus's hesitations. But just in case Aulus knew nothing of Braxus's reluctance, Max sent off a short message to his superior, confiding his suspicions that someone was attempting to influence the actions of the Head of Security at their Brittanic Embassy.

Then he put the issue out of his mind and settled back, eager to focus on finding Allegra.

They had the weapons they needed, now all they had needed to do was to rescue Allegra and bring her home.

CHAPTER 38

Allegra had slept fitfully over the last few hours. With her back so damaged, and still bleeding, she found it difficult to achieve a tolerable position in which to sleep. In the end, she'd finally turned over and fallen asleep on her stomach.

Her captors had left her without so much as a bandage or a bottle of disinfectant. She supposed she should be grateful they'd removed the zip ties. Not that she would have been able to treat herself, considering the wounds were so high up on her back.

Whispers, soft whispers echoed in her head, growing louder, filling her mind, then fading away to nothing. Allegra blinked as the one whispered faint voice grew louder. She concentrated, listening to verify if she knew the voice, but it wasn't familiar at all.

"My child, you must be on your guard. Do not be complacent . . . you are in danger."

Allegra frowned. That was an understatement, and entirely unnecessary advice.

Given that she'd already endured such horrible torture by child murderers, and been explicitly threatened with death, it was blindingly obvious that she too was in danger.

But was the voice warning her that something even worse was coming?

Before she could ask any questions, the voice faded away and all Allegra could hear was the clicking of the light in the ceiling, and the sound of her own ragged breathing.

She forced herself to sit up, moaning as pain shot up and down her back. A wave of shivers rippled through her body. The room had become quite cold and her back was bare where it had been torn apart.

She stiffened as she caught sight of a pair of white silk pajamas on the dresser.

Someone must've come in while she'd been asleep. Allegra was left with little option but to use the clothing, since her own things were ruined, shirt torn in half, pants soaked with blood.

Taking extra care, she got to her feet and fetched the night-clothes. She shrugged off the remnants of her bloody shirt and shifted to inspect her damaged back in the hazy reflection of the steel mirror.

Pale skin in stark contrast against torn, gaping wounds.

The twisted position sent waves of spiking pain from neck to waist. Allegra heaved a pained sighed and straightened slowly. She grabbed the pajama top and drew it on, wincing as it touched the raw and broken skin. She could feel where the silk began to soak up the blood, but there was little she could do about it.

She felt better after having herself covered. Even semi-nudity made her feel uncomfortable, considering she still wasn't sure the place didn't have cameras. Though she couldn't see any, she wasn't naive enough to think there were none.

To change the pants meant Allegra had to bend her very damaged back, forcing herself to remain silent as pain, burning pain, lanced through her bent back.

Huffing out a controlled breath, she straightened and considered her options. The voice had warned that she was in danger. What if the high priest was finally coming to get rid of her?

She scanned the room, looking for a good spot to hide. And found none. The only place she could think of, where they wouldn't see her immediately, was behind the door. Even with the door wide open, the space behind it was large enough for Allegra to hide.

Seemed as good a plan as any.

And perhaps, with some luck she'd be able to make a run for it before they realized what had happened. To gain a precious second or two, hopefully, she arranged the duvets and pillow so they could be taken for her sleeping form at first glance.

She'd just positioned herself in the corner behind the door when it opened. It let out that soft shushing sound and the intruder waited unmoving on the threshold until the door was fully opened.

Someone large and heavy rushed inside and the sound of gunfire filled the air. Bullets hit the bed, which was now a convoluted mess of blankets. A rumpled pile, the blanket thrown onto the pillow, appeared to hide a sleeping body.

Despite, or probably because of, the throbbing pain in her back, Allegra was filled with the need for revenge. She had suffered enough. She felt compelled to act, to do something to defend herself, even if her chances of survival were dire.

The weapon clicked, empty of rounds, and Allegra grabbed her chance. She shoved the door hard, enjoying the grunt of shock that her would-be assassin emitted as he was thrown off-balance. Something hard hit the wall and the gunman let out a cry.

Allegra hoped it was his head.

She rushed out from behind the door, and kicked hard at his ankle, enjoying a flush of satisfaction on seeing who he was. Her persecutor, the man who'd helped the high priest rip the skin off her back. His deep-set eyes were now scrunched in pain as Allegra's heel landed against his shin hard enough to break it.

Off balance from the blow to his head, he didn't react fast enough to defend himself.

Allegra used the opportunity to punch the man directly in his throat, a sharp jab using the narrow side of her palm. He dropped to his knees holding his throat, making a strange wheezing-gurgling sound.

But the blow hadn't been enough to knock him out, and he began to struggle back to his feet.

Memories came flooding back, of her torture, of the pain she'd endured while this man had watched with a smile on his face. And those memories filled Allegra with fury.

Stricken by the horror she recalled, Allegra reacted. She punched him again in the abdomen, then when he didn't go down she aimed a kick at his ribs. She heard the sound of cracking bone, his cries of pain too, but she didn't stop. He fell back with a moan, one hand clutching his ribs.

Allegra didn't see him.

All she saw was the cute little boy being sacrificed, and this man standing by and watching, always with that smug smile.

As he reached out toward the door, Allegra stepped forward and kicked him in the gut, glad she'd kept her shoes on. Despite the beating she was administering, he was a strong man, and began to turn onto his side.

Fear rippled through her, and in desperation, terrified that he'd get to his feet and follow her, she lashed out, desperate for him to stay down.

Her foot met his nose, and she heard the crunching of bone. Again.

Blood spurted from his nostrils and trickled down the side of his face. He fell back, and Allegra's heart stilled. Was he in shock, or pretending, or had she truly knocked him out?

Inhaling harshly, she decided she didn't particularly care. She had to move fast.

Did he have spare ammunition? Checking his pockets, she

found two fresh clips of bullets, one of which she slipped into the front pocket of her pants. Then she grabbed the empty gun and reloaded it with the second clip, her fingers shaking so hard that she had to force herself to concentrate on slipping the magazine in securely.

Adrenaline ran through her, flooding her veins, so intense that she had little idea of what she was doing. Now, confronted with the semi-conscious, moaning man she felt a little guilty.

She'd broken his ribs, and probably his nose too. Where had this violent Allegra come from?

She grimaced as her back twinged. All that violent movement to subdue her would-be killer had not done it any good. Her injuries reminded her that she still had a score to settle.

And that she didn't have time to wait until someone else came to kill her. Still trembling from shock and pain, she snuck out of her cell and inched her way down the dim stone-walled corridor.

At the end of the passage, she took a left and scurried down the empty corridor. She was surrounded by stone.

Had she been underground this whole time?

The thought of going back to her cell spurred her to move onward, to look for a way out. She was so desperate to get away that she almost walked headlong into danger.

She was about to take a left turn into the end of the corridor when she heard footsteps and voices.

Slamming back against the wall, she held her breath as a group of men walked past. Peering round the corner, careful not to expose the white fabric of her pajamas, she recognized the high priest leading the group, a semiautomatic machine gun in his hand. Thankfully she'd come up on their corridor right after they'd passed it and were moving away from her.

"He was just supposed to go and get the job done and come back. What in Hades is taking him so long?" He spat the words, so furious that even in the shadowed tunnel Allegra could make out the tense bulge of his eyes.

One of his guards mumbled something to which he replied, "How hard is it to kill one small woman?"

She remained silent, unmoving as the high priest hurried down the corridor. Backtracking quickly, Allegra turned right and ran as fast as she could. This time she didn't hear the oncoming boot-steps or the voices. She ran headlong into a firm, well-defined chest, bounced off it and fell backward to the ground, clutching her gun to her.

The man staggered, then straightened and began to walk toward her.

Controlled by her terror, and refusing to get caught by one of the Hermes brothers, Allegra convulsively squeezed the trigger. She realized too late that the sound of the gunshot would call the high priest and more of his men toward her.

Her heart pounded and her breath came in short, shocked gasps. She scrambled up, her back to the cold stone wall, aiming the gun at the face of the man approaching her. She was sure she'd shot him, having aimed at his heart.

She'd always been a very good shot. But he looked fine to her. Was she hallucinating? Even if he wore a bullet-proof vest, a bullet to the chest should have stopped him, torn his outer garments at the very least.

"Are you alright?" the stranger asked softly. "My apologies for giving you a fright."

Without moving the gun, she asked, "Who are you?" Odd that he hadn't shot her, or grabbed her to take her back to the high priest.

"My name is Inspector Pienius. We're here to save you."

Allegra gasped. She'd shot the man who'd come to save her? What a total idiot she was.

"But ... I shot you."

He shook his head and smiled. "You must've missed. I'm still intact." And his hand, stroking over the unmarred front of his jacket and shirt, confirmed his words. Allegra breathed a sigh of relief.

Before she could question him further, a familiar face popped up beside him.

Max.

CHAPTER 39

*A*llegra only had eyes for Max.

Never before had she been so happy to see someone's face. From the look in Max's eyes, he was more than just professionally glad to see her too.

Filled with joy and relief, she flung herself into his arms and looped her hands around his neck.

When Max's arms went around her in response, she lifted her head and kissed him. She hadn't expected him to respond, but he did, and for a brief moment Allegra enjoyed the feel of his firm lips against hers, the heat between them rising rapidly.

They ended the kiss when the sound of someone clearing their throat broke through. They drew apart reluctantly.

"We have to get out of here." The inspector looked on, his expression amused. His eyes twinkled, almost benevolent.

Odd.

"Let's get out of this rabbit warren," Max said with a sheepish smile.

Allegra shook her head sharply. "Before we leave, we have to find that madman."

"What madman?" asked Max, his expression now all business.

"He's some kind of high priest. He sacrificed a little boy earlier . . . in front of my eyes . . . I couldn't do anything to stop him. And he just now . . . he—" Allegra hesitated, not sure how she could put into words what the high priest had done to her.

Her back still ached abominably.

Proof enough.

"What are you talking about?" asked Max, looking at her with concern in his eyes.

"He tortured me, Max. He wanted me to tell him what I saw, but for his own personal gain. And when I refused to cooperate, he . . ."

"What did he do to you?" Max's face had paled, and the tendons in his neck stood out.

He grasped her arm, holding her gently, yet firmly. The movement sent pain stabbing into her wounds, where clotted blood tore away from her skin, releasing fresh bleeding.

She flinched and patted his hand. "I'm fine now, Max. I'm okay. The most important thing now is to find and stop him."

Footsteps echoed along the passage and Allegra gave the inspector and Max a desperate glance. "We need to find the high priest. I'm sure he has killed other people too."

They hurried after the footsteps, following as close as possible, but they were soon lost in the maze of complicated passages, their presence cloaked by encroaching darkness.

After about twenty minutes of searching, the inspector stopped, bringing them to a halt. "It makes no sense for us to keep going around and around. We aren't going to find anything. Not with this darkness, and just a few flashlights. They have the upper hand because they know where they're going. It would be best to head back. Get you to safety."

"I agree." Max's eyebrows scrunched. "Allegra does look like she's ready to fall down. She needs to rest."

Pienius led the way through the tunnels, until stone turned into narrow passages lined on either side by long depressions filled with shapes that resembled bodies. Allegra's eyes widened as she peered into one of the spaces and caught sight of a skull peeking through rotten bandages.

Catacombs.

She shuddered and stayed in the middle of the tunnel, reminding herself that the dead couldn't hurt her. Still, she walked as fast as she could and kept close to Max and the inspector.

She felt half in a daze, almost questioning her escape, almost wondering if it had all been a dream.

Almost.

Pienius led them to the surface, lifting a flat stone slab and guiding them up a set of jagged stone steps carved out of the side of the wall. It was dark outside, no moon to give them light.

Allegra was glad. No moon meant it would be hard for her captors to see them escaping.

Two figures emerged from the darkness causing Allegra to flinch. She'd opened her mouth to scream, but Max was quick, covering her lips with his hand.

"These are Flavius and Corina, my field team," Max whispered in her ear. The somber man and woman, both dressed in black, wore dark woolen hats that sat low on their brows. They carried torches that gave off a dull yellow light, which they aimed at the ground.

The light shone on the bodies of two acolytes, their weapons lying at their sides. Allegra had wondered how her rescuers had entered the tunnels without alerting the high priest.

Now she knew.

Allegra nodded at the two. No time for pleasantries.

They were hurrying away from the tunnel entrance when something hit her hard at the back of her head. All Hades broke loose as two men attacked, one landing a punch to Flavius's face, the other swiping a jagged blade at Max. The four men fought, the high priest's acolytes hampered by the long skirts of their robes, and losing the fight faster than they ought to have, considering they were meant to be keeping the tunnels safe from intruders.

Max grunted as he wrapped an arm around his attacker's neck, squeezing hard. Eventually the man passed out from lack of air, sliding to the ground in a heap of fabric and limbs.

Flavius's attacker was worse off, having received his own blade to his ribs. The man lay staring at the black sky as life drained from his body.

Allegra flinched as Max touched her back. "We need to go." Allegra said nothing. Best not to reveal the extent of her injuries to him at this point. She nodded and followed

They hurried across the grassy knoll, and headed beyond the tree line, giving them a view of the valley before them. Allegra shivered at the sight of the cemetery. To her right was a large temple, and she felt a rush of anger.

"The Temple of Hermes," she murmured. "The Order of Hermes."

"What's that?" asked Max.

Allegra looked at him, a shiver running through her. "It's the name of the order that the high priest claimed he belonged to. He performed the ceremony in the name of Hermes. And now it makes sense."

Max reached for her, hooking his arm around her shoulders. Allegra could not help the cry that escaped her throat as his arm brushed against the raw flesh of her back.

"What happened. What's wrong?" asked Max, his expression frantic.

She held a hand out, taking short sharp breaths to combat the sudden spike of agony. "It's my back. It still bleeding. And it's really sore."

"You need to go to the hospital. Now." Max barked the instruction out.

He was rather harsh with her, but she didn't mind. She understood that he was emotional about it. He was slowly grasping the extent of her injuries, but she refused to remove her shirt.

"No hospital. I'm fine. I just need a shower and a change of clothes and probably some bandages and disinfectant."

When Max hesitated, Allegra said, "Please, Max. The last thing I need now is a hospital visit. They'll ask all the wrong questions. They'd bring the cops in to question me. Too many things we can't control. And what about a press leak? I'm in no frame of mind to deal with that. I need some time."

Max nodded, his jaw tight.

THE RIDE to the hotel was bumpy and painful, and Allegra sat forward the entire time, her arms hooked around the headrest of the seat in front of her.

She spent some time giving the team a rundown of what had happened to her since she had been taken.

"I'm worried about Xales. What they would have done to him."

The inspector glanced at her from the front passenger seat. "I wouldn't spend too much time worrying about that. The method they used to capture him would not have lasted for too long."

"How do you know?" asked Allegra, suddenly suspicious of this Londinium cop who knew so much.

He smiled. "I've had previous experience with familiars. Don't worry, he'll be fine. Humans can banish them with certain rituals, but they cannot hurt them."

Somewhat relieved after the inspector's assurances, Allegra detailed the sacrifice of the little boy.

The reaction of the team was a shocked silence, then dark promises that the child would be avenged.

Allegra was relieved they were all on the same page.

CHAPTER 40

When they pulled up outside the hotel, Allegra was insanely glad, and when they entered the hotel lobby all she could think about was a hot shower and a soft bed.

Inspector Pienius cleared his throat as Allegra headed for the elevators. She stopped, chiding herself for being so rude. She'd almost forgotten to thank him. But he didn't give her a chance.

He smiled at the team. "I'd best be going, I'll send word for reinforcements to deal with the underground catacombs. Send in a team to apprehend the perpetrators."

Allegra smiled her appreciation, only now, in the light from the gigantic crystal chandelier above, fully appraising the beauty of the man's features. She'd hardly ever seen a man who was such a total pleasure to look at.

And yet, despite his spectacular looks, more appropriate for a movie star than a policeman, in her eyes the inspector was not nearly as good to look at as Max was.

As the inspector headed away, Max said, "I want someone up on rotation tonight. Best not to be too complacent in case something else happens."

"What's going to happen? They have no idea where I am?"

asked Allegra, her heart thundering painfully. She found herself scanning the room, staring at shadows behind the pot-plants, at the people checking in.

Max patted her shoulder, pulling her out of her bout of paranoia. "Just a precaution." Then he was gone to make a call, leaving the rest of them behind to watch the inspector's departure.

"That man is a wet-dream on legs," Corina whispered, pulling her knitted hat off her head to reveal platinum hair that shone in the buttery light of the chandelier.

Allegra giggled softly.

Flavius snorted. "Thought you liked girls, Corina." His blue eyes shone in amusement.

She lifted a shoulder. "When a guy looks that good, he'd do me just fine."

Allegra's shoulders shook with laughter as Max returned. She received a few curious glances, but didn't reveal the reason for her amusement.

ALLEGRA ENJOYED A HOT, though very careful and strategic shower. She'd realized soon enough that she'd be unable to enjoy the shower as much as she'd been longing to. The touch of hot water to a small area of her wounds had sent Allegra into a fit of pain and panic and she'd forgone the blissfulness she'd intended and made do with a more careful bathing process.

After she was done, Allegra asked Max to help her treat her wounds.

He was oddly silent as he tended to her, disinfecting the long bloody lacerations, and then bandaging them.

Allegra decided that it was best not to talk about it, sensing the seething anger and guilt that emanated off Max. From his expression, he was furious. Knowing Max, Allegra was certain that he blamed himself for not protecting her. He'd feel impotent now too, unable to do anything about the injuries inflicted upon her.

His passion would make him even angrier, and if she had revealed to him how upset she was, or how deeply the torture had affected her, she was sure that he'd suffer more than was necessary.

As she slipped beneath clean sheets, she thought about her prayer to Apollo. Had he been the one to help the others reach her, or was that just a coincidence?

In case it was him who had helped, Allegra sent a prayer to him, one filled with gratitude. At the end of her thanks, she tacked on a request for help to prevent the epidemic.

Perhaps she was asking too much too soon, but she had to take a chance. She needed all the help that she could get.

THE NEXT MORNING, as Allegra walked out of the bathroom brushing her hair, the team was gathered for breakfast in their suite. Max wore a confused and almost angry expression.

"What's wrong?" Allegra's stomach twinged, fear filling her. Had the high priest found them?

Max looked up at her from the couch where he'd been using the phone, his forehead scrunched in confusion. "Inspector Pienius."

"What about him?" For a moment, she wondered if he'd caught her looking at the cop as he'd left the lobby.

But Max's expression was far too serious and she watched him, worried as she drew her hair into a low bun at the back of her head.

"He doesn't exist."

"What do you mean?" Allegra asked. "We all saw him, talked to him." The words slipped out, but she'd already begun to suspect what he'd meant.

Max grunted. "I just called the Londinium police headquarters to thank them for lending us the inspector. The department head for international co-operation thought I was a madman, and just a mention of the Order of Hermes and he cut me off. Said I must have been hallucinating. Perhaps a forbidden subject?"

"But the inspector?" Corina asked, frowning. "He's not the type anyone could possibly forget or overlook."

"Once I had convinced the Superintendent that I was legitimate, he happily advised me there was no such person as Inspector Pienius on their force. And that their department had not provided us with any form of assistance. Nor will they in the future."

Allegra smiled.

Thank you, Apollo.

CHAPTER 41

*D*espite Allegra's protestations, Max had insisted on bringing in a healer from the embassy. The woman had arrived just as Allegra, who'd curled up on the comfy sofa watching old movies on the television, was nodding off.

It had been hard to fall asleep. Every sound, every voice, every creak crashed into her subconscious like a tidal wave, bringing with it memories of darkness and hoods, of kind blue eyes and red blood.

Allegra had to force herself to smile as the healer glided into the room. She reached out to shake Allegra's hand. "It's an honor to meet you, my Lady."

Allegra hesitated at the formality of the greeting. As yet, nobody had spoken to her with that much respect, the team having enveloped her with friendship and trust, and she felt a little unsure. From behind the healer, Max was frowning at Allegra.

Widening her smile, she took the woman's hand and shook it warmly. Such formality might yet become the norm, and Allegra had to learn how to take it in her stride.

"My name is Laelia Ang."

Laelia was a tiny little thing, long hair hanging down her back in a single dark braid. Her diminutive size and the hint of an almond shape to her eyes implied an Oriental ancestry, adding to the hodgepodge mix of genetics gathered in the room.

"Right, let me see what I can do for you?" she said, tacking on a question at the end of her instruction. She glanced around as if scanning the large living area of the suite for a suitable treatment space.

Allegra glanced at Max raising her eyebrows. He, in turn, tipped his head toward the double doors to the bedroom. She hid a smile at his concerned expression and said, "Come, Laelia. Privacy is definitely in order. I don't think the team is in the mood for a strip show."

She swallowed her laughter at the sound of Flavius choking on his cola.

Inside the room, Allegra seated herself on the edge of the bed, and began to unbutton her shirt. Corina had been generous enough to provide Allegra with something to wear, and not wanting to be rude, Allegra had graciously accepted.

Now, as she attempted to take it off, she knew the seer wouldn't be getting her shirt back in one piece. Allegra was going to have to replace Corina's shirt once they returned to the States.

As she lifted the fabric she winced at the pull of the fibers on coagulated blood. The shirt, soaked with blood now congealed, wouldn't budge. The wounds had stopped bleeding, but tugging at them to extract the shirt was going to rip the clots from the skin.

When the healer gasped softly, Allegra understood why.

She'd studied the lacerations herself when she'd attempted her own first aid. The result of the whipping wasn't pretty. Probably one of the reasons the Ancient Romans had loved to use the cat o'nine tails.

She supposed she should be grateful they hadn't used whips tipped with hooks. It wasn't hard to imagine a man, bones lashed bare of flesh at the mercy of those whips. It was positively barbaric.

Right now, Laelia was staring at the long strips of skin, removed with each lash, revealing red, raw flesh beneath. Allegra was sure that she would bear the scars of the torture the rest of her life.

"Hera bless my heart. They did this to you?" whispered Laelia under her breath.

A few moments later she pulled herself free from the horror of Allegra's ruined back and took a harsh breath. She straightened and said, "Hold still while I separate the fabric from the wound. It won't be painless, I'm so sorry." She paused and Allegra gave her an encouraging smile. Laelia smiled. "Then I'll clean the wound. I'd rather clean it up properly before I attempt to fix this mess."

She sounded so firm, so sure of herself that Allegra was happy to just let her take over.

She nodded, and remained as still as possible as the healer probed and cleaned. The pain existed only on the surface now, unlike the searing bone-deep intensity she'd experienced during her torture. She gritted her teeth and endured, until the healer pronounced she was done.

Allegra sighed, still a little afraid to breathe, but Laelia patted her lightly on her upper arm. "Now, this part won't be so bad at all. You should feel only a warm sensation. Unfortunately, I don't think I will be able to get rid of all the scars." She sounded more frustrated than disappointed.

Allegra wondered what Laelia had meant by 'getting rid of the scars', but she didn't ask any questions.

She'd heard of healers like Laelia, but had never met one until today. There weren't too many of them in existence. It was rumored that, depending on their skill level, they could close wounds so well that not a single scar remained.

While the healer worked, Allegra's mind wandered. Where

did they go from here? Was the high priest still on the hunt for her? He'd certainly been determined enough to abduct her and kill Ignacio and whoever else had been caught in the crossfire.

Allegra hadn't had time to think about him until now. She was the reason Ignacio was dead. And she was helpless to do anything about it.

The high priest had shown her how passionate he was about ending her life. But why? What was it that fueled his need to kill Allegra specifically? And why the sacrifice of innocent lives to achieve this end?

When Laelia tapped Allegra on her shoulder she was so deep in her thoughts that she flinched. The healer held her shoulder gently and gave it a light pat. The touch was comforting, a gentle encouragement that everything was okay.

Allegra smiled and turned around. "Thank you, Laelia."

The healer nodded and smiled. "I think I've done a pretty good job. If I do say so myself." Her grin widened.

Allegra got to her feet and walked over to the mirror, curious to see the healer's achievement. Turning around, she twisted her neck to look over her shoulder. And stared at the reflection of her back, frozen in shock.

"How in Apollo's name did you manage to do that?" she whispered, more to herself than the healer.

Allegra's mouth hung open as she stared at what was supposed to have been her ruined back. She'd expected ropy scars, twisted flesh. Or at least bright red bruised lines.

The gory, open wounds were all gone, skin smooth, knitted together neatly, leaving only a collection of fine silvery lines intertwining with each other like a white tattoo.

Allegra turned and threw her arms around Laelia's shoulders. "Thank you. Thank you so much. I'm not sure how I'm ever going to be able to repay you." She couldn't stop smiling.

Laelia shook her head and smiled kindly at Allegra. There was a certain reverence in her expression that made Allegra feel a little uncomfortable, but she stopped herself from revealing it in her expression.

The healer patted Allegra's forearm. "There is no such thing as repayment. I am merely doing my job. And for you, Allegra, I would do anything."

As cryptic as Laelia's words were, Allegra was not in any frame of mind to try and figure it out. Whatever the healer had done to Allegra's wounds, it seemed to be taking its toll on her body.

Allegra's eyelids were heavy, drooping from the inexplicable fatigue that had taken hold of her. Damned if she didn't need a nap like a little baby.

Laelia grabbed Allegra's shirt from the bed and handed it to her. "It's probably best you get some sleep. I've only healed the surface of your body. What lies beneath needs much more time. Take care that you don't bump yourself, or do anything physically violent. There is a possibility that the wounds may reopen."

She was a little human whirlwind as she returned to her bag and began to pack her things away. She wrapped all the bloodied bandages into a ball and dumped them into the trash can in the bathroom.

All done, she smiled at Allegra. "If you should happen to open them up, I don't mind coming back to fix it, but bear in mind if the wounds do reopen, the resulting scar won't be as clean as this."

Allegra nodded, and thanked the healer profusely as the two women walked out of the room. Laelia took her leave, leaving Allegra with firm instructions to rest.

As Allegra closed the door, she turned to see Max watching her closely. He was sitting beside the window at a small writing table, eyes red from lack of sleep, hair mussed, his giant phone in his palm.

She didn't say anything. But the fatigue in her face must have given her away because Max strode up to her, his expression determined.

He said, "She's right, you know. You really do need to get some sleep. Why don't you go and have a nap and we'll see about something to eat? Service here isn't all that fast so it's probably going to take another hour and a half before we see the order."

Allegra hid her smile at the surprised look he gave her when she merely nodded and headed for the bedroom.

A glance over her shoulder confirmed he was still staring at her.

Only his gaze was firmly on her ass.

CHAPTER 42

A few hours later Allegra woke to the sound of a soft knock on her bedroom door. Rubbing her eyes, she propped herself up on her elbow. She pushed her hair from her face and covered a yawn as the door opened.

Max poked his head inside. "Sleep well?"

Allegra nodded and gave him a smile as she suppressed a second yawn. "Yeah. I was out like a light."

Max's eyes traveled down Allegra's body and settled on her very bare thigh. She'd taken off her pants before jumping into bed, having never been able to sleep with too many clothes on. Now she realized a little too late that her lower extremities were on show.

Max grinned, staring unapologetically at her legs. "Laelia called and said you would need a few hours at least. Good thing too. We were planning on giving you only an hour."

As he spoke, Allegra reached for her pants and slid into them. Flashing her red silk panties - courtesy of Xenia's packing - at him had been completely unavoidable.

Not that he looked too upset about it.

Allegra began to make the bed, glad that she no longer felt the pinch of tearing skin when she bent over. "Did I miss the food?" Her stomach growled on cue as she fluffed up the pillows.

"Nope. We delayed the order."

"Oh?" Allegra straightened and stared at him. "Hope you didn't starve yourselves on my account."

Max shook his head and opened the door wider as Allegra approached. "I just need to use the bathroom. I'll be right there."

Max nodded and headed back to the team leaving Allegra to change into a blue ankle-length dress that was entirely inappropriate for such clandestine activities.

Trust Xenia to make such strange fashion choices.

She used the facilities, washed her face and dabbed on a light smattering of makeup. After brushing her hair and piling it on top of her head into something that resembled a bird's nest, Allegra left the room.

As she exited the bedroom the team began to applaud. Muted claps as they all got to their feet, a mark of respect and celebration. She blushed and smiled as she drew closer to the table, praying this wasn't going to be a commonplace thing.

She needed some normalcy, even if it meant forcing people to be casual with her against their will.

For now, she evaded their eyes and scanned the table. They'd ordered a variety of foods, and Allegra recognized their efforts with a grateful smile.

She grinned. "I hope you all don't mind, but I'm about to embarrass myself and feed my face like a Neanderthal."

Everyone laughed. "You deserve to eat however you want, Allegra. You've been through enough." Corina smiled as she reached for a helping of a meat pie.

The combination of food on the table was odd, scrambled eggs and bacon, pies, pastries, roast beef and vegetables. "Looks like you guys covered breakfast, lunch and dinner."

Max laughed. "We've been so mixed up with meals that we figured we may as well tick all the boxes."

Amidst lots of laughter and chatting, Allegra and the team served themselves and ate their fill. Despite the smiles and the banter, the room was filled with a dark tension. Allegra soon felt strained, but she maintained a calm facade.

At least, until Max took her dessert plate from her. She'd eaten the chocolate cherry trifle without even tasting it. Cream and chocolate, cherries and brandy, and yet none of the flavors had satisfied her.

Not surprising, considering what she'd been through.

Max left the plate on the table and sat beside Allegra on the loveseat near the window. "How are you feeling?" he asked softly.

She smiled and sighed. "I'm hanging on by a thread."

"I'm not surprised. This is hard on you." An observation.

Or a criticism?

"Because I'm not strong enough to handle it?" she asked. She may have sounded defensive but she really wasn't.

"Because this is all so new to you."

Allegra smiled. "You are so tactful."

"Nothing tactful about it, Allegra. I've been right here at your side since you discovered who you are. It's obvious to me, and to my team, that you are doing the best that you can. And not a single one of us think that you are weak."

"How strong was I when Ignacio was murdered inches away from me?" Allegra got to her feet and shoved the curtain aside, heading out onto the narrow balcony.

Max followed her, standing beside her in silence for a moment as she swallowed hard against the tears threatening to overcome her.

Max rubbed her back. "That was not your fault."

She glared at him. "If he hadn't been watching me, he'd be alive right now."

"That's not necessarily true. Ignacio was a Dark Ops specialist. He would have likely chosen another op that would have been just as dangerous. That was his job, Allegra. He preferred the danger. And he was especially honored to protect you."

Allegra shook her head. "What's the point of being honored when it ends with you being dead?"

Max shook his head and squeezed her shoulders. "Don't do this to yourself. A lot of people are going to die. Whether it's to protect you, or me, or themselves. The coming months are going to be unpredictable, Allegra. Yet every life we lose will count for something if we somehow make it out alive."

Allegra nodded, turning toward Max's chest without thinking. "It's just so hard," she whispered.

Max reached for her and gathered her into his arms. He stroked her hair and said softly, "I know. But you're a strong woman. And you have me. You have us."

Allegra glanced up, her face inches from his. Her lips so close to his that all it took was for Max to tip his head, just so.

Their lips met in an explosion of heat, fire racing through Allegra's veins, filling her with emotion as well as an inexplicable passion.

She'd never felt this way about a man before, this thrilling, all-consuming heat that filled her core and her heart with equal intensity.

Max kissed her hard, and Allegra kissed him back just as fiercely. Tongues dueled, hands roamed, and Allegra pressed her body against Max's length.

Allegra took a shuddering breath and backed away, her fingers touching her swollen lips. Max didn't remove his arm, and Allegra allowed it to rest around her waist. "What are we doing, Max?" she whispered as she stared out at the city skyline. "We don't have time for this."

Max smiled and gave her a squeeze. "You are right. We don't have time. But we can make time." He waited until she looked up at him. "If we wanted to, we could make the time. Our days are numbered and if we don't prevent the pandemic we are doomed."

Allegra laughed. "You sound like Xenia."

Max chuckled. "We'd better get back inside before those two come looking for us."

Allegra nodded and Max let his arm drop as they headed back inside. Flavius and Corina were lounging in front of the television both looking like they'd just eaten a Solstice Dinner.

They'd earned the respite.

The high priest, hopefully, had no idea where she was, Allegra was healing well and they'd have to wait until tomorrow to obtain a flight home.

Allegra sat with them as they watched a horror movie; something about a corpse brought back to life by a bolt of lightning.

As she watched, sitting on the sofa beside Corina and Flavius, she wondered how many days they had left to enjoy such banal things as movies and sumptuous dinners.

CHAPTER 43

The next morning the team was up early to pack, and enjoying a breakfast of scrambled eggs, smoked fish and a spiced rice dish when a knock on the door drew their attention. They watched, tense and wary as Max went to open the door.

Allegra wasn't surprised when he ushered a pair of policemen into the room. The two men stood just inside the doorway, studying them like specimens in glass jars. The taller man was portly, with a stomach worthy of the best German beer drinker. Both bore the red shoulder swag and rose badge of the Anglian Police Corps.

Both also wore the same dour, bland expressions that made Allegra want to wiggle her fingers in front of their faces to check if there were lights on inside.

"Inspector Franck," said the taller man, waving his badge at them. "This is Inspector Bainbridge." He stuck a thumb in his partner's direction.

"Franck. Bainbridge." Max acknowledged while the rest of the team watched in silence. "How can we help you?"

Franck gave Max a haughty smile, lifting his head so high that Allegra could see straight up his nose to the gray strands that populated both orifices. "We're here to collect Citizen Damascus's statement regarding her alleged kidnapping." He managed to sound accusatory and when he looked at Allegra, she got the feeling he really didn't want to be there.

Was it the interview he was averse to, or was it Allegra in particular?

Despite her misgivings, she smiled and got to her feet, responding to Corina's wary glare with a soft comforting smile. "I'm happy to give you that statement, Inspector." Allegra waved a hand at the writing desk near the balcony and Franck accompanied her, studying her from head to toe out the side of his eye. He had the dismissive look of a man filled with prejudice and Allegra wondered if it was her citizenship or her power that offended his sensibilities.

He settled his bulk in the seat while Bainbridge questioned Max and the team. Franck flipped open a small notebook and brought forth a badly bitten pencil not longer than his forefinger. "So, can you tell me in your own words what happened?"

Allegra raised her eyebrows. Whose words was he expecting her to use?

She took a breath and outlined the events of the last few days, beginning with her abduction in Barbarina Town, her incarceration in the hotel-room cell, the ritual sacrifice of the little boy and her torture.

Max had taken photos of the damage done to her back and Allegra told him they were happy to send them copies.

Franck nodded, seemingly unaffected by her dramatic story.

"Commander," Franck glanced at Max, "you saw fit to travel halfway around the world to rescue Citizen Damascus. I'm curious as to her importance to FAPA."

Max's lips thinned. "Damascus is a new recruit. A seer that has ... potential." Max glanced at Allegra but she merely watched

Franck. Max continued. "Seeing as she is a FAPA agent, we were . . . obligated to retrieve her."

Franck lifted his head and dropped it in a slow, condescending nod.

Then he shifted his gaze back to Allegra. "So how did you manage to find your way around the tunnels? You're not from around here." Franck's voice was cool, critical.

And there it was. Allegra was certain now that it was more her citizenship that was the issue. The Anglian police had a beef with the New Germanic States, or perhaps only Franck himself had issues.

Allegra pasted a smile on her face. "We had help from your department actually. For which we are most grateful." Maybe Inspector Pienius didn't exist, but she went with him anyway.

"Help?" Franck's eyebrows waggled. "Who from?" He sounded perturbed.

"Inspector Pienius. He was most helpful. Gave Commander Vissarion and the team a map of the tunnels, and he seemed to know them well, because he managed to get us out of there pretty fast."

Franck was shaking his head vigorously enough to throw his neatly combed widow's peak into disarray. "That's not possible. We don't have an Inspector Pienius anywhere on the force. I'm afraid you must be mistaken. Perhaps this man was from *your* embassy? After all you've described, it would be no wonder if you were a bit confused."

Allegra shook her head. "He introduced himself as Inspector Pienius from the Anglian police." She shrugged. "We believed him because . . . well . . . why would we not? He helped Max find me, so I don't think Max and his team would be concerned. To be honest, I'd like to find him again to thank him. I'm pretty sure I'd still be locked up by that creep of a madman if it hadn't been for Pienius."

Franck still looked confused. "Who?" He had changed his line of questioning now, but so suddenly that Allegra was a little off balance.

Now, she scrunched her forehead. "The so-called high priest. He said his organization was called the Order of Hermes. Or something weird like that."

"I see."

That was it?

Allegra glared at him. "You have to find this man. I saw his face. I can give you a full and detailed description. Look at photos of suspects if you want. He's dangerous."

Franck smiled, the curl of his lip condescending. "So, tell me what he looked like."

Allegra gritted her teeth. "He was around my height, bald, light brown eyes. Muscular arms. I didn't see the rest of him, seeing as he was covered in a cloak. But I did see his arms when he whipped me."

Allegra was sure that the inspector had begun to smile as she spoke, but it was gone in an instant, and she wondered if she was mistaken.

"And you said he sacrificed a little boy." Franck's eyes were cold as he spoke, no longer interested in Allegra's description of the high priest. She had to wonder why. Did they already know him?

Allegra nodded. "Yes. He was only three. Blue eyes, blond hair. Very intelligent. And I believe he was telepathic—"

Franck lifted one eyebrow. "We don't have any missing person's reports for that description," he said, cutting her off.

Allegra wondered how he'd know that without actually checking their database, but she'd already figured out that this man wasn't going to be of much help to her and Max.

Franck got to his feet, flipping his notebook closed. "I think we're done here."

Allegra rose and followed him as he began to walk toward the door. "Are you going to look for him? The man is dangerous and he needs to be stopped."

They'd reached the doorway where Bainbridge waited with Max, the other inspector's eyes glinted with ice. "Who is dangerous?" he asked, looking from Franck to Allegra and back again.

Allegra repeated what she'd said to Franck, explaining the high priest and the danger he posed. "The Order of Hermes. That's what he called them." Allegra stepped closer. "You have to find him and stop him. Before he kills more innocent children."

Bainbridge took a step back, his expression cold. "We will investigate, Citizen Damascus, but I can assure you that there is no such thing as the Order of Hermes."

"But that's what the priest said."

"If he did, then perhaps it was a ruse to confuse you. Seems to me that anyone who runs a secret society would be smarter than to just tell a captive the truth."

Allegra folded her arms. "Oh, really. Isn't that the whole point? These megalomaniac types are just after the attention."

The policemen moved closer to the door and Franck said again, "Thank you for your cooperation. We'll have the report filed and we'll do what we can to find out who this Pienius is."

"So you'll go looking for a man posing as a cop, but not a man who murders children?"

"Citizen, you must understand that everything you have said is a little far-fetched. And as much as the NGS police will believe such ravings, we here in Brittania do things differently. Nor do we put too much stock in a seer's powers."

Allegra snorted in disgust. "This is not a prediction, Inspector. I'm telling you what I saw with my own two conscious eyes."

Bainbridge's mouth curled in a cool smile and Allegra knew any further discussion was a waste of time. The pair took their leave and departed. When Max closed the door, Allegra let out a disgusted groan.

"Ugh. What is wrong with those two?"

Max was standing there staring at the closed door.

"It sounded to me like they don't dare go after this priest guy," suggested Corina, her brow furrowed.

"Yeah." Allegra nodded, frowning as she recalled Franck's behavior. "They seemed to back away as soon as I mentioned him."

Max walked over to the table. "I hate to break it to you guys, but in the greater scheme of things, the high priest is irrelevant."

Allegra and Corina stared at him. From Corina's expression, she was immediately convinced. But Allegra wasn't. "Easy for you to say that, but *I* was the one who saw the life being taken from an innocent little boy, not you."

I was the one whose back was ripped open by the bastard.

Allegra inhaled harshly. "That man has to pay for murdering that boy—that baby. And all the other kids he's probably already killed. I got the impression that this was routine, a habit for him and his followers."

Max sat on the seat beside Allegra. "I understand where you're coming from. I really do. But if we don't find out more about the epidemic, then what difference does it make? The high priest will be dead and so will all his acolytes and all his future victims too."

Allegra sat back, frustrated. He was right and she had no choice but to admit it. Heaving a great sigh, she said, "Fine. Yes. I understand what you are saying. Doesn't mean I've got to like it."

Then she got to her feet and stalked to the sofa. She stopped at the edge of the seat and glanced over her shoulder at Max.

"What are you waiting for?"

He frowned. "Er...?"

"I don't have all day, Agent Vissarion. Let's see if we can get a vision or two to help you out."

Allegra shook her head and settled herself on the sofa trying to hide her smile. Max's eyes had widened when he realized what she meant.

He was beside her within seconds and knelt on the carpet beside her head.

"Ready?" he asked, already down to business.

Allegra nodded.

ithin seconds Max had put Allegra into her trance and as she blinked and looked around, she suspected that soon she would no longer need his help to get her there.

This time the process had almost seemed to happen spontaneously.

His low baritone drew her attention back to his words. "You said the last time that the epidemic will not originate in the States."

Allegra nodded.

"Will it happen somewhere on the Latin Continent?"

She shook her head.

Max progressed through the different continents until Allegra nodded when he mentioned Asia.

Max leaned closer. "East Asia?"

Allegra thought about it a little harder, trying to get a better sense of the location. It was odd. Most of the time it was like a gut feeling pulling her toward a particular answer, and in this case a specific place in the world.

Now though, an image had begun to develop. Leafless trees. A network of dusty roads. Heat so thick, she could almost taste it.

And the idea of Qin or Jipangu didn't sit well in connection with the place she saw in her mind's eye.

Allegra shook her head.

She was beginning to understand the process better now. Max was guiding her with questions, but she was fully capable of finding out immediately where the disease would arise.

The only problem was she was unable to speak until after she came out of the trance. She tended to forget details once she returned to consciousness.

She made a mental note to try and find a more efficient method of imparting and recalling information while within the trance.

Just don't forget that when you wake up.

Allegra had already gotten a sense of the origin location being somewhere in the Indus kingdom when Max said, "Indus?"

Allegra nodded.

"City?"

No.

Allegra began to see the area more clearly now. A brick-and-mortar building set in a large field, surrounded by smaller white-washed though dusty, brick buildings.

Max mumbled something about rural, and perhaps farming as opposed to just lifestyle properties because of mad-cow disease and the like. She heard Corina agree.

Max said, "Livestock?"

A nod.

"Types of livestock . . . how about cattle?"

No.

The only cattle she saw was an emaciated milking-cow tied to a stake in the ground just near the entrance to the main building, which she'd already gathered was the living quarters of the farmer.

High-pitched squeals and a low purring emanated in Allegra's mind.

"Poultry?"

She gave a vigorous nod as she recognized the sound. Chickens.

"Chickens?" asked Max, the excitement rising in his voice.

Allegra nodded again. She tried hard to retain information regarding the farm and prayed to Apollo that she would remember it all when she woke.

She was beginning to tire and it seemed that Max had sensed it as he said, "Almost done, Allegra."

When she nodded, he cleared his throat. "Will it happen in three months?" She shook her head and was relieved when he asked, "Weeks?"

She nodded.

"Two weeks?" he asked and then let out a sigh as Allegra nodded in confirmation.

Allegra let out a sigh and opened her eyes. "The place is huge, at least forty acres. Brick buildings, painted white. Corrugated iron roofs. The coops are two dozen separate smaller buildings scattered around one main rectangular structure. There's a white cow tied up outside the main house. The entire place is surrounded by dilapidated wire fencing."

Allegra continued to provide more details as fast as she could, emptying her mind of everything she could recall.

"Well done, Allegra. That was excellent." Max grinned as he got to his feet and headed for his satellite phone.

Allegra talked with Corina and Flavius while Max spoke to General Aulus. But when Max returned within seconds, Allegra knew something was wrong. "What happened?"

"General Aulus was at a Senate meeting."

"So? Now what?" Allegra sat back, frustrated.

"We aren't going to waste time waiting for red tape to untangle itself. We proceed straight to Indus."

Allegra lifted a finger in question. "I was abducted from the States. They didn't give me time to gather my passport for travel."

Max grunted. "I hadn't thought of that." He got to his feet and headed for the hotel phone. "I'll get a hold of the embassy. They can issue you with an emergency passport."

He sounded confident, and even though he'd smiled as he'd spoken to the embassy, Allegra had felt her gut tighten.

Max put the phone down. "We'll have one by the end of the day. They just need time to take a photograph and then process the document."

Allegra raised her eyebrows. "That easy?"

"You need to know people."

Allegra snorted.

The team set about packing and before long, Egent arrived to take a photograph of Allegra for her passport. For once, she didn't care if the photo wasn't perfect. After the man left she realized she hadn't even bothered to brush her hair.

Xenia would have a fit if the photo didn't look flattering.

The thought of Xenia brought tears to Allegra's eyes. So much was happening and she hadn't even called her to hear her voice. Max had told her he'd rung Xenia and given her an update, but said that Allegra was resting and would call later.

Perhaps it was time to speak to her friend, especially now that they were about to head off to Indus.

After soothing Xenia's concerns and assuring her friend that she was fine and in good health, Allegra rang off. She felt guilty having not told her about the torture. But she didn't need Xenia to worry unnecessarily, especially since Allegra had gotten over the whole ordeal.

Mostly.

She was healed, yes. But that was physically. Her heart still stuttered every time she thought about the whipping, every time she was alone in a room. Even the bathroom made her tense so much that her chest hurt by the time she left the space.

She hadn't told Max either.

She didn't think that he would take it too well that she'd tossed and turned the whole night and that her sleep had been plagued by dreams of the high priest and the little blue-eyed boy, of blood and searing pain.

She'd put the room phone down just as Max walked inside.

"The embassy is sorting everything out," he announced. "They'll organize our flight and they're informing the Indus government that the Pythia and her party are *en route* to Bharat on a world-saving mission."

"Sounds more glamorous than it really is."

Max shrugged. "As long as it gets us results."

CHAPTER 45

The flight to Indus had only appeared to be glamorous. In reality, it was tedious and exhausting.

Their itinerary consisted of a flight from Londinium to Rome, then a second flight to Kemet, such short hauls being necessary due to the fuel-tank capacity of the design of the smaller aircraft.

Corina had grumbled that the airlines were taking far too long to upgrade to the recently designed planes with larger fuel capacities. But Allegra suspected she was speaking from the point of view of travelers used to access to fast military jets.

Allegra laughed. "Better than a camel?"

Corina grinned back. "*That* is such a good point I shall concede without argument."

They both laughed and settled in for the flight to Rome. Allegra slept most of the way while Max worked on reports. She felt a little guilty for her continued fatigue, but figured that after her healing, and her most recent vision, she ought to rebuild her strength.

She was also gaining confidence in her ability.

No longer did she think of it as something thrust upon her. Instead, she'd begun to feel as if the power truly did belong to her. Perhaps it was this inner acceptance that had allowed her more freedom and flexibility with her last vision.

And yet, Max's description of Aurelia and her powers didn't seem to match Allegra's own ability. She had to find some time to discuss Aurelia in detail with him. It might help her understand her own power if she got to know Aurelia a little better, though she suspected that the power did not manifest in exactly the same way in different generations.

Allegra dozed off, thinking about Kemet and its ancient pyramids, waking only when Max shook her arm. "We're landing," he said even as the pilot was announcing their descent.

Allegra followed the team as they unbuckled on landing and grabbed their luggage. They'd all traveled light, only carry-on bags and their weapons. The embassy had also thought to provide them all with international clearances for their weapons.

Even Allegra, who as yet hadn't been given a gun.

Allegra hadn't been paying much attention as she descended the stairs from the plane onto the tarmac. Only when she was mobbed by a throng of reporters, waving cameras and microphones in her face, did she realize what was happening.

Max's fingers curled around her upper arm. "Walk as fast as you can, stay with me. And don't speak to anyone." His change in demeanor startled her and Allegra had to blink away her surprise.

Max had suddenly turned hard, almost angry and it was clear in his voice.

Allegra didn't resist. She was smart enough to see for herself the danger around her. Any number of these people could be there to abduct or assassinate her. She had to wonder how the word had gotten out. Considering only their embassy in Brittania knew of their destination, she had to wonder if they were responsible for the leak.

It would seem that nobody could be trusted.

Max helped Allegra to navigate the crowd, pushing and

shoving their way until they reached the airport entrance. Thankfully, the mob was restrained by airport police, and Allegra was ushered safely inside the building where the team headed straight for customs.

They passed through quickly, grateful that their connection to Kemet was only an hour away and that they were safely behind security lines in the transit lounge.

The airport was small, though its floor-to-ceiling windows made it appear twice its size. The clear glass provided a full view of the gathered mob.

"They're not just reporters," said Allegra softly.

"Yeah. You have a fan club." Corina laughed.

"She's also got a hate club." Max's voice was low as he lifted his chin at the back of the crowd. A group of about ten people was gathered, all dressed in black, waving placards bearing varying versions of 'Death to the Pythia' and 'Prophetic Powers are an Abomination.'

Allegra found herself watching in dismay. "They aren't going to make this job easy, are they?"

Max shook his head.

Allegra glanced at him. "Was it this way for Aurelia?"

He sighed. "In some ways, yes. More so when she was young and living in various countries, traveling all over the world. Even though she downplayed her powers, and most of the public believed the line of Pythias was long extinct, among the more informed her existence was an open secret. She was not plagued with paparazzi as much, but wherever she went the zealots followed. In the end, she hid herself away in a secure remote farming compound and only gave a handful of accredited contacts access to her."

Allegra's eyes widened. Was that going to be her future? Imprisoned in her home because of her powers?

Max smiled. "We will ensure that doesn't happen to you, Allegra." He glanced over at Corina and Flavius, and Allegra smiled as both of them nodded solemnly. "See? We're in total agreement."

She nodded and turned her attention back to the crowd. The reporters were departing, leaving a small throng of people behind. A woman with a small bouquet of flowers in her hand began to harangue one of the zealots and a scuffle broke out.

Security descended upon the group and to Allegra's relief they had the sense to send them away instead of arresting them.

Zealots or not, Allegra didn't relish the idea of people ending up in jail in her name.

CHAPTER 46

Their flight to Kemet proved to be longer, probably because Allegra couldn't fall asleep no matter how hard she tried. She was wired, her thoughts returning to the zealots, and the woman with the bouquet. Love and hate standing side by side, chanting her name for very different reasons.

She thought about Xenia who'd probably see the spectacle in the news and plastered across the front pages, and hoped her friend would not get frantic with worry.

Max came to her side. "Want a drink up at the bar?"

Allegra nodded and got to her feet, smoothing the creases from her dress, and failing. She followed Max, grateful they'd secured first-class seats that provided them with an additional bar and lounge area upstairs. She wasn't sure how she'd feel crammed into economy. Just the thought made her feel claustrophobic.

Allegra ordered a brandy on the rocks, earning herself a host of strange looks from the team. "What? Never saw a girl order a brandy before?"

Max cleared his throat and was about to answer when Corina said, "Think very carefully before you speak."

Max closed his mouth but was unable to hold back the twitch of a smile as he avoided Corina's eyes. The others burst out laughing and a discussion ensued about women, bright colors and alcohol preferences. Corina and Allegra lost the argument the moment they both admitted to a liking for cocktails, colored or otherwise.

When Max left to look for food, Allegra turned to Corina. "Can I ask you a question?" When the other girl nodded, Allegra said, "Max is your superior officer, right. How come you are all so relaxed around him?"

Corina smiled and watched as Max and Flavius retreated. "It's how it's always been. Max laid down the rules on day one. We are a family. Leave no man behind. It was bullshit. The same crap you hear everywhere when they're trying to recruit you, when they are looking for your loyalty."

"But Max was different?"

"More than most." Corina sighed, then grinned. "Maximus Vissarion is capable of winning even the heart of a woman who isn't inclined to *be* with a man." Corina winked and sipped her drink.

Allegra laughed. "I see what you mean."

It didn't surprise her to hear Corina's words. Max was a good-hearted man, and his team was fortunate to have him at their helm.

Corina sighed. "So. Are you going to help us?"

Allegra dragged her gaze off Max and turned her attention to Corina. "Of course. I *am* helping you."

But Corina was shaking her head. "No. I meant, actually joining us. Being part of our team."

Allegra shook her head and smiled sadly. "I couldn't do that, Corina. Not yet. Not until I can understand who to truly trust. And it just doesn't feel right to align myself with only one group of people when the whole world deserves to benefit from this power. Isn't that what the Pythia always stood for?"

Corina smiled and shook her head.

"I'll remain as a consultant. But, that's it." Allegra leaned closer. "I'm not stupid, Corina. I can see the way the game is being played. I know I'm valuable but even though I never knew my own heritage, I've always been well aware of who the Pythia was, and what her duties were." Allegra sat back, frowning.

"What is it?" asked Corina, concern sharpening her gaze.

Allegra held out her hand before the seer decided to use her powers. "Nothing. It's just that I remembered something from my childhood. A time when my parents had educated me on the basics of Greco-Roman Mythology and the Oracles. I'd thought everyone learned similar stories at home, but now that I think about it, I always had a little more than your average knowledge on the topic."

Corina frowned. "Are you saying you think your parents knew who you were?"

Allegra nodded. "I'm beginning to think they did. And they were killed before they could tell me."

Corina leaned forward and took hold of Allegra's hand. "I'm so sorry you had to go through that. I'm not sure how I'd cope if I lost one of my family members. My parents are far too nosy, and my brother is a pain in my butt, but I'm not sure how I'd go on without them."

Allegra barely heard Corina's words as a vision of the white-blonde girl floated in front of her, blood streaming from her lips as she convulsed.

With a low moan, Allegra snatched her hand from Corina's grip staring at her in horror. Corina frowned at first then let out a soft laugh. "Don't worry. Seers can't see each other's futures. Or pasts. Only their present. It's just the way it is."

Allegra shook her head. "There must be a glitch in the system," she said softly.

Her vision of Corina's last moments was too ghastly, but not truly surprising. She too would fall victim to the plague. The worst part? The catastrophe was still coming. Despite what she had already seen. Despite what she and Max were trying to achieve.

The job was not done yet, the world still needed to be saved.

Corina's eyes went wide, her mouth opening slightly as she stared at Allegra in shock. Then she closed her mouth, schooled her features and said, "Whatever you saw, I do not want to know."

"Are you sure?"

Corina nodded. "I see far too much shit. The last thing I need is to know my own future."

Allegra looked down at her hands. Touching people was dangerous. "Perhaps I should use gloves."

But Corina shook her head. "That would only draw attention to you."

Allegra stared at her hands, and then back to Corina's face. Whatever she did, she'd be forced to conform to some arrangement with the authorities. Right now, she wasn't sure she was ready to fight against anything.

Maybe once she'd healed from the blow dealt to her confidence by the kidnappers, she'd tackle the whole problem of FAPA and their constant pressure to join with them. Working with Max and his team in itself, would not be a chore. It was something Allegra could see herself doing.

But on what terms?

And could she align herself to one country alone? That would only lead to trouble further down the road.

She sighed and looked back up at Corina. The seer was watching Allegra, a sad expression on her face.

Both girls sat back and sipped from their almost empty glasses.

Corina lifted hers.

"To the end of the world." Her voice was defiant, but not entirely steady.

Allegra shivered, hearing Xenia's words echoed in Corina's.

She hesitated for a moment, but then clinked her glass against Corina's.

To the end of the world.

It was inevitable, but if she had anything to say about it, not quite yet.

Not quite yet.

hen the team arrived in Bharat they were met with a surprisingly large contingent of military force.

Barriers had been set up on the edge of the tarmac, manned by armed guards and policemen. Beyond the metal mobile fences was a crowd of at least six hundred people, all cheering and singing Allegra's name.

The expression on the supervising officer's face wasn't comforting.

He marched forward, back straight, arms swinging stiffly, his mouth twitching as Allegra reached the bottom of the stairs. She'd just stepped off the last riser when he came to a standstill in front of her.

During the last half of the flight, Allegra had settled into a comfortable space, aware that she had a responsibility to Max and his team now. But she wasn't forgetting that she still had a larger responsibility to the rest of the world.

When she'd exited the plane and stood at the top of the stairs, at first the sight of the gathered crowd had scared her. But it was something that she was going to have to get used to, if she was going to be the Pythia that everyone needed. Aurelia had hidden herself away from society, overwhelmed by the world and its needs, but Allegra was determined not to fall into that same trap.

As the officer stared down at her, Allegra steeled herself and smiled. She offered her hand, startling the man so much that he took a full step backward.

Max touched her shoulder and whispered in her ear. "Don't be offended by General Bhana's actions," Max said, clearly familiar with the man.

General? The man definitely had a more superior air, though not in the condescending sense. Noble or regal, would be the words Allegra would use.

Max continued. "I believe some people in the kingdom are quite strict. Some traditionally believe a woman must not touch a man who is not her husband."

Allegra's spine stiffened and she struggled to keep the smile on her face as she retrieved her hand. She turned her attention back to the general and gave him a formal nod.

He offered her a low bow and waved a hand in the direction of the waiting vehicle. Much to Allegra's surprise it was not a limousine, or any type of stately vehicle.

Instead, a military armored-car waited for them, a true battle vehicle with giant wheels and bullet-proof windows, something part four-wheel-drive, part tanker.

Once Allegra and the team had settled inside the vehicle, it lurched forward, taking them rumbling past the gathered crowds. Allegra peered out of the windows—a difficult enough task considering the layer of wire mesh that covered the thick darkened glass—and studied the people. She found herself unconsciously looking for the zealots with their insulting and hateful placards.

Curiously, there were none of them.

Instead, the gathered group seemed happy and cheerful as they waved banners and threw flowers at the passing truck.

Allegra felt a little bad that they hadn't stopped to meet these people, but she knew already that finding the location of the outbreak was a matter of crucial urgency. There would be time enough for chatting and socializing after the world was safe.

The general, who'd been talking to the driver behind him, shifted in his seat to face her.

"I'm General Bhana. I apologize for my rudeness outside earlier."

It was Allegra's turn to be startled. She glanced at Max but he said nothing, the frown on his face confirming his own confusion.

"I understand that I am confusing you. Let me explain." He took a breath and pointed a finger out of the window. "See that crowd? They are peaceful, happy. Because they worship you. Here in the land of the Hind, people take those of divine power very seriously. Not those *in* power, but those who possess power. It also means that people are easily duped by charlatans. And here is the opportunity to present to them someone who is not a fake."

He sighed and smiled.

"You're almost what they consider a deity. Had I touched you, I would likely end up stoned or dismembered, my body thrown in some faraway place to be eaten by vultures and wolves."

Allegra shuddered. "Sounds a little on the gory side." She offered him a more genuine smile now.

Max grinned. "Good thing you explained. I think you may have been in for a difficult time from the Pythia, had you truly been sexist."

The general snorted. "I do believe my wife would be in total agreement."

Everyone in the vehicle burst out laughing and the rest of the ride was spent with General Bhana giving them a quick rundown on the security position and the general's opinions of the current administration.

The truth of the pandemic had been kept secret from the Indus government and administrative body.

After a forty-minute drive, they were approaching the Government House when Corina let out a low whistle. Allegra glanced at the seer who was staring wide-eyed out of the window.

"Aphrodite save me. That is one stunning architectural wonder," said Corina.

Bhana laughed softly as Allegra peered over Corina to get a view. "The palace is almost a thousand years old. It's constructed of pure white marble, quarried from the Northern Himalayan hills."

Allegra stared at the sprawling palace, its white walls shimmering in the sunlight, its curved turrets and elegant spires making the palace look like something out of a dream.

The gigantic doors, taller than a two-storied house, were wide open, guarded by two armed, elaborately dressed guards. The weapons were more likely for show than anything, considering they were bronze spears taller than each of the men holding them.

White long-sleeved shirts, red turbans decorated with glinting gold emblem of the palace. Each man wore baggy white pants, a wide red sash and bore a bronze dagger on his left hip.

General Bhana came to Allegra's side, offering her his arm. "May I have the honor of escorting the Pythia inside the palace?"

Allegra smiled and took his arm. "As long as you don't lose your head over it."

He chuckled and led them inside, down a long white-stoned pathway lined with towering palm trees which cast much-needed shade over their heads.

The sun was high in a cloudless blue sky and Allegra felt the heat of it penetrate her head. She wished she'd had the chance to at least bathe and change before meeting important people, but there'd been no such opportunity.

They walked past fountains spilling clear waters, strutting peacocks, and carvings of voluptuous dancing maidens. Despite her surroundings, which were nothing short of magical, Allegra had a hard time retaining her composure.

Being in a place this beautiful seemed to upset her more, and she faltered in her step.

General Bhana slowed and studied her face. "Are you feeling unwell?"

Allegra shook her head. "I'm just tired from the flight." Not to mention a tiny bit traumatized from the events of the last few days. She forced a smile on her face. "I'll be fine. Although, I'd rather like to get this whole thing over and done with before it's too late."

The general gave her a smile then glanced over his shoulder at Max before leading them on toward the entrance to the palace. Allegra looked over her own shoulder, meeting Max's eyes with a questioning look. But all he did was give her an encouraging smile.

He'd been quiet for the last portion of the trip, probably absorbing the news of her decision to consult, and what it would mean for future co-operation—if they managed to survive the plague. Corina had happily given him the news and he'd smiled and accepted her offer.

She'd expected him to be upset but his expression had been strained and worried. Not angry or disappointed as she'd thought he'd be.

They were guided inside the palace, but Allegra was no longer interested in the beauty of the place. All this would be for naught if the world were to end. It was like eating too much chocolate, to the point of wanting to throw up. All the deliciousness of it was too much to stomach.

Flavius and Corina were directed to a smaller waiting room before Max and Allegra were led inside a main hall, likely used by the Rajas and Ranis of the past. Now, as she headed toward a large marble boardroom table, she was surprised to see the meeting headed by a woman.

Truth be told, she knew enough of the Indus and its people, having been a voracious history fanatic growing up.

Yet she would never have expected the queen herself to head the meeting—the woman's bearing and dress leaving no doubt as to her identity.

Max headed over to her. He bowed low over the monarch's hand. Then he looked over at Allegra, beckoning her closer. Allegra obeyed and hurried to his side, her own smile fast mirroring that of the queen.

Allegra went to Max's side and smiled at the elegant dark-haired woman. Max said, "Maharani Sonali, Queen of the Hind, Ruler of all Indus, Queen of the island of Lanka and the King-doms of Ksetra and Syam."

Allegra kept her hands folded in front of her waist, hoping that her reluctance to shake hands would not be considered as rude.

"I'm so very honored to meet you, Lady Pythia," said the queen, showing no sign of wanting to shake Allegra's hand.

Perhaps she knew the danger of touching one such as the Pythia. The queen glowed, looking decidedly regal in a navy-blue sari trimmed in faded gold. The blue silk wound around the queen's body, revealing her baby bump in all its glory.

Allegra blushed. "Please call me Allegra, Your Majesty. And may I congratulate you on your impending arrival."

The queen laughed. "I will, only if you call me Sonali." She patted her belly, her eyes sparkling. "And this one is to be Maia, a nod to Rome and Indus all in one go."

She hooked an arm around Allegra's waist, the action strategic enough to avoid skin touching skin, and led her to the table where a group of aides and representatives had gathered. Among a sea of sober, respectful faces, one stood out so much that Allegra had to suppress a shiver.

Dressed in a simple white sari, the fabric draping her curvaceous form like a second skin, the woman stood near the window, the file in her hand propped against her hip. She watched Allegra closely as she was introduced to each of the Senators and Representatives and then shown to her seat at the queen's right hand. As she sat, the queen waved the woman closer.

The woman's eyes narrowed, making the thumbprint-sized dot in the middle of her forehead stand out. She glided closer and waited at the queen's side.

"This is Kantha, my advisor, and the priestess of Kali who presides over all the goddess's temples across the country."

Allegra smiled and moved to hold her hand out, temporarily forgetting her own rules. The woman—Kantha—glared at Allegra's hand as if it were a live cobra, then gave Allegra a disgusted look.

Max cleared his throat from beside Allegra. "Is there a problem?"

Kantha's gaze shifted slowly to Max, and she studied him for a few seconds. Then she seated herself on the other side of the queen without the courtesy of a response.

Sonali leaned closer. "Don't mind Kantha. She's a priestess of the mother, and too many of them are raised in seclusion."

"Seclusion?"

"Of men. And of others." Sonali met Allegra's eyes and smiled, her expression regretful.

Allegra nodded. Others as in *other races*.

Odd to find a racist in this part of the world, but if she was raised without access to other peoples, it would explain her hostility.

"She's a priestess of Kali?" Sonali nodded. "And I'm a Priestess of Apollo. By virtue of my bloodline and my power."

Sonali frowned. "It doesn't make you enemies, Allegra. It merely makes Kantha a little too rigid for her own good." She spoke in low tones, too low for Kantha to make out, for which Allegra was thankful.

The Senate was called to order and everyone paid attention as the Elder Senator opened the meeting, and formally welcomed Allegra.

Her stomach tightened and she inhaled slowly.

This is it.

CHAPTER 48

The Speaker of the Senate said, "My understanding is that the Pythia and her delegates have come with worrying information. Commander Maximus Vissarion, Guardian of the Pythia, will brief us on the situation."

Max got to his feet as a dozen heads turned to study him, expressions varying from hostility to acceptance to curiosity. "Unfortunately, what I have to tell you won't be easy to accept. There will be some who will reject my information, and I can understand that, but please bear in mind everything that is at stake. Nothing less than the survival of your entire country. And of us all."

"Commander Vissarion, you are beginning to scare me." Despite her words, Sonali's voice held not a hint of fear.

Max smiled ruefully at the queen. "My apologies, Your Majesty, but the end of the world is a terribly scary thing."

Allegra suppressed an eye roll. So much for being tactful and diplomatic.

Sonali, for all her shock, remained silent and calm. Must be the royal blood because Allegra herself was terrified.

Max looked at the worried faces around the table. "We have

known for a while that in a few weeks' time the world, or at least humanity, will come to a terrible end in the grip of a deadly pandemic."

To their credit, everyone at the table remained silent and watchful, waiting to hear more, instead of turning into a shocked mob.

"Why have we not been told?" This time the Queen's voice held an edge to it. One she was—in Allegra's opinion—well entitled to.

Max faced the queen. "Would you have mentioned this to anyone if you thought it was inevitable? That nothing you, or anyone else, could do would change it. That the information would only cause mass panic."

The queen pursed her lips as she considered Max's words. She gave him the finest of nods, conceding to his point. "And you are revealing this to us today . . . why?"

Max inhaled and glanced at Allegra. "Because the Pythia had a vision pinpointing the origin of the breakout."

"Is the disease identifiable?" Something in her voice made Allegra turn to watch her more closely.

"Not in a scientific sense. So far, all we've had to go on was the Pythia's and other seers' visions of horrible, painful deaths and a very specific timeline."

"And something has occurred to change that?" Allegra admired the queen's ability to remain so composed, when in fact she'd be the most terrified of all, especially when considering her baby.

Max nodded. "The Pythia has managed to identify the farm on which the mutation will first occur. It's not a disease that's in current existence. Not from what we've managed to identify. We narrowed it down to a possible mutation that will occur here in Indus."

This time the gathered group erupted into worried murmurs

and concerned glances. Kantha got to her feet and came to stand at the queen's side, her features twisted in anger.

Her resting expression perhaps?

Allegra thought not. Their revelation was enough to upset anyone, but it looked like the news had angered the priestess.

"This is not right," she said bending close to the queen's side. "Please don't tell me you are going to collude with them. You know what's at stake."

The queen looked at her, a little stunned, much like everyone else at the table. "What would you have me do? How can I ignore it?"

"It's wrong, is what it is. We agreed we must not interfere."

Allegra's eyes widened. "You knew about this?" she asked, meeting the priestess's gaze.

The woman gave her a look that said Allegra wasn't even worth talking to, then turned her attention back to the queen. "The people of this country need your mind and heart in the right place. The gods know what is best for us. We cannot attempt to change fate. Nor should we allow outsiders to control what we do within our own borders."

The woman's voice had lowered to almost a growl, her lips twisted. Allegra was impressed—a little afraid of her passion. She glanced at the queen who was looking at the priestess, her expression worried.

But she was still silent, as if contemplating

Allegra leaned closer. "Sonali, we need to find that farm. The sooner we get there the better the chances are for saving all humanity. It's not just your kingdom on the line." Allegra sucked in a hesitant breath. "I understand your reluctance to leave fate in the hands of the gods, but why would they give us the ability to see future catastrophes if they did not want us to attempt to avoid them? It seems to me that should any of our gods prefer us to remain entirely at their mercy, they would never bless us with the power to foresee such things."

After her speech, Allegra fell silent, feeling the weight of the room's attention on her. She exchanged a worried glance with Max then returned her attention to Sonali.

The queen took a quick breath and patted her stomach. "I have to agree with Kantha. I think it may be wrong to interfere with fate." Then she shifted her gaze to Allegra. "But I think it would be remiss for us to ignore the possibility that such god-given visions were meant to ensure we act to avoid catastrophe. Any warning of danger from such a source should be accepted, and acted upon, if possible. Then we hope and pray the threat is not real, or at least avoidable."

Allegra nodded, impressed with the queen's diplomacy and intelligence. The priestess, though, wasn't impressed. She got to her feet and began to pace, the golden skin of her face now dark with anger.

She stopped and glared at the queen. "The gods will not take this well. I've told you there is a plan for everything."

The queen shook her head. "Not for total annihilation, Kantha. We must help them. We must help everyone, including our own people."

"But you don't understand. We are not supposed to interfere. By angering the gods, we will bring more suffering upon our people." She pointed at Allegra. "People like her . . . they think they are helping . . . desperately running all over the world, trying to prevent the inevitable."

The priestess strode toward Allegra, her eyes blazing with anger. She stopped a mere foot from her. Max raised a hand in front of Allegra, but she gently pushed it away. She needed no protection from the priestess.

Kantha shook her head, a mixture of sadness and anger in her eyes. "You are like a child, racing to offer help where no help is needed. Determined to do whatever you can to save a world that doesn't need saving. That doesn't *deserve* saving."

Allegra took a step toward her and reached for her hand.

Though the priestess tried to shove her off she'd come too close to Allegra to use sufficient force. Allegra's fingers curled around the woman's slim wrists.

The vision slammed into her so hard that Allegra could barely breathe. She had to force herself to concentrate on what she saw around her.

"There is a valley, with a temple set high on the mountains whose peaks are hidden by clouds. There is a river, filled with stones." Allegra frowned. "No. Not stones. Carvings in the shape of the god of creation. There are so many they look like rapids on the water."

Allegra heard the woman gasp but she continued to study her surroundings.

"A woman is seated beneath a great banyan tree, dressed in a white sari. Her arms are bare, tattoos cover her neck . . . A flock of tiny birds is flying across her shoulder." Allegra frowned. "She will die soon. Her skin is covered in boils, and her breathing is hoarse."

Allegra let go of her hand, vaguely aware that the vision continued even after she lost contact with the priestess's hand. She felt the brush of Kantha's arm as she walked past her, almost unconscious of her surroundings. "An old woman lies beside her, a rosary of dark beads in her hand. She has already passed. Beyond the banyan is an open field. Bodies lie lined up, ready for a pyre. Someone is burning the fires."

Allegra let out a shocked gasp.

Even in her state of trance she could see the vision overlaid upon the reality and as she stared at the woman, her hair hanging over her shoulders, her white sari stained black with soot, a tattoo of the goddess Kali covering a back that was bare to the sun. A back that was free of any disease.

The shock threw Allegra out of the vision, and she found herself standing beside the window, staring at a stunned, silent room. She barely noticed them as she met the priestess's eyes.

"Who were they?" she asked, her voice soft.

"My sister. My mother." Kantha's voice was dead, her eyes flat as she stared at Allegra. "Who was burning the fires?" the priestess asked.

Allegra shook her head. "I didn't see her face." She wondered if anyone would see through that lie, but the priestess deserved the truth. However Allegra gave it to her.

She cleared her throat. "She had a tattoo on her back. From shoulder to hip. Kali in her gentle form."

"Durga," said Kantha softly.

Allegra didn't need to say anything more. Even if the priestess accused her of making it up or lying there was way too much detail in that vision even for Allegra to doubt its validity. Like all her visions there was always something within them that pointed to its accuracy and its truths.

Allegra walked over to the priestess who now stood at the queen's side, and held onto her shoulder. "I'm sorry."

She wasn't certain what she was apologizing for but it turned out her sympathy was unwanted. The priestess shrugged her off and walked to the window where she stood in the sunlight, staring out on the stunning palace gardens.

In the sunlight, she looked like something the heavens may have lost, like a goddess come to watch over them. Only she was human. A broken human staring reality in the face.

The queen watched her warily, as if wanting to comfort her but knowing the priestess would not take too kindly to revealing her weakness in front of others.

Sonali turned to Allegra. "We'll provide whatever help you need." She glanced at General Bhana. "Please see to it that the Pythia and her delegation receive every assistance? And please provide them with suitable lodgings."

But Allegra shook her head. "I'm not sure that will be necessary. I apologize if I seem rude, but our priority is to locate that farm, and then return to the States as soon as possible."

The queen got to her feet, her expression firm. "Nevertheless, we will still be providing you with a place to rest even if it's just to freshen up before you continue on your mission."

Allegra laughed softly. "Do I look that bad?" Despite the gravity of the meeting she enjoyed a moment of sisterhood.

Maharani Sonali smiled serenely. "Not *that* bad."

CHAPTER 49

Allegra and the team were shown to rooms in the palace where they were provided with hot baths along with freshly prepared meals.

Despite feeling like she was wasting time treading water, she recognized that like the priestess, she was only human and she needed to take care of herself too. It certainly wouldn't do to die on the job.

Surrounded by hand-woven, beaded silk, hand carved mahogany furniture, stunning sculptures and paintings, it was easy to forget, even if only for a short while, the stress she was under.

General Bhana arrived, having given them sufficient time to bathe and eat before he knocked. Max answered the door and ushered him in.

He gave Allegra a soft smile, a friend echoing her sadness. "So tell me where you need to go."

Allegra nodded and looked at Max who tipped a chin at the sofa.

As she walked over, Bhana whispered to Corina. "What's happening?"

The man needed to practice his whisper.

Corina had been studying a map of the Indus valley with Flavius who'd come up with a brilliant plan—to scry for Allegra using her hair, only this time attempting to combine his skills with Corina in order to scry the future.

He'd failed.

She paid Bhana no further attention as Corina ran him through the procedure.

Allegra lay down and waited for Max to put her under. She'd suspected that she really didn't need the help, but she let him do it anyway. It helped soothe and ease her mind.

They had the process down and within seconds she was swimming in bright light.

Blinking hard, she quieted as the circle of light moved left to right. Chickens squawked around her and the odor of soil and wet poultry-feathers filled her nostrils. The lights bobbed again and Allegra understood where she was.

"Are you at the chicken farm?"

She nodded.

"Can you see anything distinctive?"

Casting her gaze around she studied the brick walls and wire-mesh fencing, the heaving throng of chickens writhing within each ten-by-ten-foot pen. Unable to identify anything helpful, she moved after the men and followed them outside. The sun was still bright outside, coming in low from the west.

Afternoon.

The men headed to a truck, a large name plastered on the metal sidings. *Patel & Sons.*

"Anything yet?"

She nodded, wanting to answer, but instinctively stopping herself. Then she stiffened. Only an hour ago, she'd spoken from deep within an uninitiated trance.

She glanced at Max and saw him overlaid against the truck, merging with the vision like a strangely taken photograph.

"They're getting into a truck. Patel & Sons. That's the name of the farm."

As the truck pulled away, trundling slowly past a giant banyan in the back yard of the property, Allegra struggled to catch sight of the number plate, but only got the first letter.

Allegra sat up blinking hard. Thankfully everything was as it should be, with no overlaid visions. She glanced at Max whose face was a little pale. "I really have to get used to you talking in a trance," he said.

"Did Aurelia never speak?"

Max shook his head. "No. Her translator Mara, always transmitted her visions to us. The old bat didn't like us too much and toward the end I wondered if she'd taken the opportunity to send us on a few wild goose chases."

"And did she really?"

"One or two. Which could easily have been due to Aurelia's age." Max smiled and then got serious. "So, anything else?"

"Just the letter R on the number plate. I couldn't get anything else because of the glare of the sun."

Max and Allegra glanced up at Bhana who was staring at them as if they were welcoming him into a fortuneteller's tent at a carnival.

He cleared his throat. "R. Number plate. Right." He nodded a few times. "Rajasthan. But you said Patel and Sons?"

Allegra nodded, confident now. "That should help."

"It would. If every man and his son weren't named Patel. It's one of the most common names in the country."

Deflated, Allegra sank against the backrest of the sofa. "Can't we canvas the whole of Rajasthan? Find all the Patels who own chicken farms?"

Max shook his head. "That sounds like a witch hunt to me."

Allegra shuddered. "We don't want a repeat of the Apollo Priest Trials."

Corina stepped closer. "General. Do you have planes at your disposal?"

Bhana gave the seer an impressed glance and reached for his phone. Much like Max's, the general's phone was attached to his waist-belt and must have been a real burden to lug around. Allegra sympathized with him.

He spoke on the phone, falling into Sanskrit. The language had remained the mother tongue of the Kingdom of Indus for the last two thousand years, uniting a population of billions with a single tongue. Allegra's language was that of the New Germanic States as well as Brittania; a bastardized mashup of Latin, Italian, Greek and German. Listening to the beauty of the Eastern language made Allegra understand the ramifications of her words when spoken aloud. People around the world were depending on her and her team to save them.

Bhana rang off and gave them a lukewarm smile. "We have two planes scrambling. They'll use a grid pattern and cover the entire kingdom of Rajasthan. Can you describe to me the layout of the farm? The pilots need to know what to look for."

Allegra went with Bhana to the dining table and took the pencil and paper he offered her.

Soon, she'd sketched out the map of the farm with the main house, the chicken coops and even the cow in the yard. Just as she gave his pencil back and moved to stand, she stopped. "Wait. There was something else."

Bhana returned the pencil. "It was a giant banyan, so large that a man could stand upright within the roots. Someone had decorated the tree with red fabric and red thread. The tree was huge, I think its spread was larger than the main house on the farm."

Bhana nodded. "Now, *that* we can work with." He hurried away, leaving the room to make his calls and give his instructions.

Max walked over to her side and she glanced up at him. "What's wrong?"

"I'm worried about you?"

She frowned. "Now why in the world would you worry about me? Do I look unwell?"

"It's not that, and you know it." Max looked frustrated, "I think you're tiring yourself out. What was that stunt you pulled with the priestess?"

"What do you mean?" Allegra wasn't taking too kindly to Max's tone, and couldn't help that her voice rose in annoyance.

"Using your energy on things other than finding the origin points of this disease."

Allegra nodded. "I know. I understand your concern, but it wasn't as if I could help it. The vision came when I—"

"When you touched her."

Allegra's eyes widened.

"Fine. I get it. I'll stop touching people." Allegra's spine stiffened as she glared at Max.

Was this their first fight?

Allegra wanted to laugh. They'd have to be an actual couple first before they could have any 'firsts'.

Startled at her line of thinking Allegra looked up and met Max's eyes.

Guess he was thinking the same thing.

CHAPTER 50

The late afternoon sun was beating down on them when Bhana and his men drove the team over to the Bharat Military Airport where they would board a plane to Bhoot, a town near the Patels' chicken farm. With Allegra's exact description, the farm had been located from the air, with an estimated ninety percent chance that it was the right place. The banyan tree had been the decisive clue.

They drove through the airport complex, which buzzed with an energy Allegra couldn't define. Maybe it was the hot afternoon, heavy with petrol fumes and the odor of heated metal. Maybe it was the combined emotional quota of the platoon, eager to be part of the end of the threatening pandemic.

Whatever it was, it made Allegra more nervous.

She glanced over at Corina and Flavius who both remained unperturbed, calm and cool in the face of their mission. Experience, no doubt. Max and Bhana were discussing military politics, both knowing many of the same army people across the world.

Allegra rubbed her hands down her khaki cargo pants, wiping the moisture of her nerves away. Without question, she'd worn the dull green shirt, cargoes and boots Corina had supplied. The general had been generous and considerate, seeing to it that the team had also been provided with clothing suited to a military op. Given that they'd traveled unprepared, they were more than grateful.

Bhana's driver maneuvered the bulky vehicle along the perimeter of the complex and emerged at the back onto a tarmac filled with armored war-vehicles and planes, as well as the hustle and bustle of cargo loading and unloading.

The sight of pallets piled high with cargo, wrapped in giant green netting, soldiers with clipboards, some waving little red paddles in their hands while directing planes both large and small, diverted a little from Allegra's nerves.

The driver slowed and circled a large cargo plane, army-issue, blunt-nosed and a dull green in color. Still, the interior was large enough to haul soldiers and ammunition as well as a couple of tankers. He drove their truck onto a ramp at the back of the plane before waiting for the back door to seal.

Bhana got out of the truck and Max and the team followed. Allegra felt a little out of place as she studied her surroundings. The plane was wide and long, the sides lined with seats. Bhana waved a hand at a half dozen empty seats, giving Allegra a worried glance.

"Please strap yourselves in. Helmets *and* parachutes, please." After a second concerned glance around, he caught the eye of another soldier who was supervising the loading of dozens of narrow metal boxes marked with numbers that she assumed denoted weapons models. "If you need anything, Captain Rai here will help you."

The soldier gave Bhana a sober nod, then faced the team as they looked for seats. He was short and stocky, his skin light though marked with the signs of teenage acne, his eyes unfathomable. Allegra found herself looking away quickly, disliking the pull of nerves that twisted her gut. She was too nervous for her own good.

The rest of the seats were occupied by soldiers, safety helmets on, hiding their features. All in all they looked intense and serious.

Good.

Allegra and the team took seats while Max headed toward the front of the plane to talk with Bhana. Planning strategy, Allegra hoped.

Rai grabbed helmets and backpacks from a box up ahead and handed them one of each. "Parachutes go on the shoulders, strapped around the waist. Legs go in the bottom loops." He drilled them through the emergency procedure, indicating which cord to pull first, then second, and how to judge the distance. The entire time he kept looking at Allegra, his expression contemplative and hard.

A crash-course in parachuting was the last thing Allegra had expected but she nodded and paid close attention all the while praying she'd never need to use this newfound knowledge.

Corina and Flavius flanked her, and it felt almost as if they'd positioned themselves in order to protect her. It could well have been her imagination, but she appreciated it anyway.

Once the plane rumbled to life, talk was impossible and Allegra settled against the wall behind her. Rai sat opposite, his eyes flitting across to her every few minutes. She didn't miss the hard, almost angry looks he gave her, and again Allegra swallowed down a bubble of fear.

After a bumpy ride due to low cloud-cover, they touched down with Allegra praying to at least survive the landing.

She did, and exhaled in relief as the plane rolled to a stop. Through the bustling activity of landing and off-loading the aircraft Allegra didn't fail to notice Rai having what looked like a secretive conversation with a couple of his soldiers.

Allegra had never claimed to be good at reading body language but with these men it wasn't hard. The covert, over-the-shoulder looks, the heads bent close as if sharing a secret, all made her wonder if they were discussing her or her team.

She tried to put it out of her mind as they exited the plane at the Bhoot Airport, the sun now lower on the horizon, though still hot enough that she had to shade her eyes. The airport turned out to be merely a large clear piece of land, just long enough and wide enough to land the giant plane.

They were met by a small platoon from the Rajasthan army which served to boost their ranks.

Security was on high alert. For both Allegra and for the disease.

Bhana had said that the government had put a moratorium on information to the press. Allegra prayed to Apollo and all the gods that they'd be given the peace—and the freedom—to do their job.

The drive to the remote town was long, and offered up one long hour of bouncing around on unpaved roads through dense bush, while the sun began to sink into the horizon, turning the sky a marbled blend of soft pink and warm coral.

The scenery changed from small villages to miles of uninhabitable dry land, to farms. Nothing was expected in this terrain.

Captain Rai's leading vehicles threw up clouds of dust too, which hampered the view at times.

When the caravan slowed to a crawl, Allegra peered out the window trying to see what was going on up ahead. Bhana shoved the door open and began to speak, his voice brisk.

But something cut him off, and a hollow thud followed.

Max and Corina shared a concerned glance and both scrambled to exit the vehicle. Max was halfway out the door when he stopped so suddenly that Corina slammed right into his back.

Peering around him, Allegra's breath caught in her throat at the sight of Captain Rai, the muzzle of a rifle pointed at Max's forehead.

"Get out," he instructed, waving the rifle at them. The team complied, with Max giving them a warning glare that said, *Don't try to be a hero.*

They were instructed to stand at the side of the road, with a blood-stained Bhana and his lone military driver completing the lineup. The general was silent, only the vein throbbing at his temple betraying his fury.

The right half of his face was red from blood dripping from a gash in his scalp. Allegra felt sorry for the man who'd hit him. Should they survive this coup, his attacker was surely dead.

Captain Rai gestured to his men, yelling out instructions in Sanskrit, before walking off to the main vehicle. Allegra leaned toward Bhana. "What's going on?"

His eyes were hard as he stared at the men—his men—who were now holding him at gunpoint, having taken all the teams weapons and sat phones. "Kantha has her claws in many things and many places."

Allegra's jaw dropped. "What does she want?"

Bhana gave a tight shake of his head. A warning. Allegra straightened to see Rai stalking back toward them. He came to a stop in front of Allegra. "What you are trying to do goes against the laws of time, and of nature. One should not mess with what is pre-ordained."

Allegra shook her head. "We're trying to save the world. Do you not understand that?"

He smiled coldly. "What *you* do not understand is that in this age, mankind must pay for their fall into debasement. Humankind deserves to die, and if the gods see fit to create our destruction who are we to defy them?"

"But the whole world, all those people . . . ." Allegra trailed off, staring into the man's unforgiving eyes.

"Do not think for one moment that you are the only oracle. Mother Kantha has seen this destruction you speak off. Many of our seers have."

Contrary to what Rai thought, Allegra was under no such illusion. Her lips formed a thin, cold line. "And you chose to do nothing?"

"We chose to refrain from interfering in nature, in redirecting the hand of the gods. It is not our place."

"But we must do something," Allegra protested.

He shook his head. "What you do not understand is that there is nothing you can do. Avert this disaster, and another one will come along. Disease, disaster, death. Fate will come. Karma will be harsh. We deserve nothing less."

He was walking away stiffly before Allegra could respond. She glanced at Max. "What are we going to do?" she whispered.

"We wait for our chance, then take it."

CHAPTER 51

$\mathcal{A}$ shout went up from a vehicle along the road and one of Rai's men scrambled forward, waving at the prisoners with his rifle.

They followed his direction and turned to head into the bush single file after an armed soldier. General Bhana and his driver, then Flavius and Corina, then Allegra and Max, with a soldier slotted in after every two of them.

Their captors weren't taking any chances. The third soldier walked directly in front of Allegra and she studied him, the weapon held at shoulder height, pointed at Flavius's head, the army khakis, the knife sheathed at his waist.

Suddenly it hit Allegra as to their intention. They meant to kill them in cold blood. Line them up and shoot them in the heads, or slit their throats.

Panic rose within Allegra's gut but she pushed it down and breathed. Max was directly behind, walking with a rifle in his ribs. The ground dipped into a shallow valley, dotted with thin, emaciated trees and dry scrub. Not half a dozen steps in, Allegra heard a soft scuffling along the line behind her.

A glance over her shoulder revealed the soldier on the

ground, a short knife in his throat, the handle still sticking out of the wound.

How Max had managed to stab the man with his own knife while he held a gun on Max she had no idea.

She spun around in time to see the soldier in front of her pause, and begin to turn around. Everything moved in slow motion.

The soldier lifted his rifle at Max and began to curl his finger around the trigger. Allegra reached forward, still unsure what she was supposed to do.

Unbidden, her fingers closed over the handle of the knife at his waist and she slipped it free.

The soldier bent forward, finger beginning to pull the trigger. Allegra felt the knife slice flesh and slide deep within the man's ribs. Wet warmth coated her fingers as she watched his confused expression cloud over.

He sank slowly to the ground, his rifle falling in the dust beside him, leaving Allegra holding a blood-drenched blade.

She began to shake, her limbs flooding with adrenaline and horror.

She'd just killed a man.

Max's hands closed over her shoulder. "We don't have time for a panic attack. Hold onto the knife just in case, and let's keep moving."

Allegra nodded and put one foot in front of the other, supremely conscious of the moisture caking her fingers and growing tacky as it cooled.

She still clutched the knife in her hand, unable to uncurl her fingers and let go of the weapon.

Ahead of them, the line slowed as they entered a clearing and the leading soldier stopped and turned around. When his eyes widened, Bhana punched him in the throat, sending him down in a pile of unconsciousness.

The remaining soldier pulled the trigger.

The shot rang out, bringing everyone to a halt. A streak of fresh blood glistened along Bhana's upper arm. The soldier stared at them, frantic now as he realized he was all alone. He took a step back then scanned the line again, his face composed and determined.

When he turned his rifle on Allegra, she knew what he meant to do.

He pulled the trigger before she could do anything more than blink.

The blast was loud, louder than Allegra had expected.

Corina cried out before slamming backward into Allegra. The seer's weight threw Allegra backward and she fell to the ground, the knife flying from her grip.

Corina lay on top of her, shuddering.

Allegra's heart slammed against her ribs, threatened to burst in her chest. Her vision clouded as shock filled her, numbing her limbs.

Her ears rang harshly as tears filled her eyes, blurring her vision. Then, Corina's weight brought her slowly back to reality.

Allegra forced the panic away and slid the seer carefully off her chest before placing her on the ground to check her wound.

She knew what Corina had done and yet she was still furious. "What in Hades' name were you thinking?" she whispered harshly as she lifted the torn shirt from her stomach. Shaking her head she glared at Corina, her eyes again filling with tears.

They were out in the bush, the vehicles long gone, the sun setting, no access to immediate medical care, with Corina bleeding out from a bloody gaping hole in her abdomen.

Corina reached for Allegra's hand, fingers tightening over her forearm. "You are . . . more important. You must . . . do whatever you can to . . . to save us."

Allegra shook her head even as her tears fell. "It didn't have to be this way."

Corina shook her head slowly. "There was no time. It is what it is. Be . . . the Pythia we all need."

Blood began to spill from Corina's mouth and Allegra was hit by a wave of shock so hard that she let out a horrified moan.

Her vision had not been of Corina dying from the plague. She'd seen *this* moment in her vision and misinterpreted it.

Before Allegra could say anything else, Corina sighed and her eyes closed. She'd fallen unconscious which Allegra knew was a bad sign.

Allegra glanced around at the worried, grieving faces watching her. Max blinked hard and cleared his throat. "We have to move."

"No," Allegra shook her head, "we have to help her."

"I called for help ten minutes ago. The chopper will be here soon."

"Chopper?" Allegra frowned. "But Rai's men . . . they took your weapons and your phone."

Max's smile was cold and angry as he said, "Emergency tracking device with an SOS feature." He tapped his wristwatch.

"Oh," was all Allegra could muster in response.

"There's a NGS Army base a few miles south."

Allegra nodded and glanced at Corina. "That's good. They can take her to a hospital."

Max's hand curled around Allegra's upper arm. "Allegra . . . with a wound like that she won't survive the next ten minutes. She's bleeding internally."

Allegra shook her head. "No. The chopper can take her straight to the hospital. Then we can go to the farm."

Max's jaw tightened and he looked about to say something when Bhana touched his shoulder and pointed to the distant horizon.

A light bobbed in the sky, the chopper on its way.

They paid little attention to Allegra, and even Flavius kept his distance, his eyes shielded, his expression withdrawn.

Allegra shielded her eyes as the chopper landed in a nearby clearing, spinning a whirlwind of dust and leaves around them. She covered Corina with her jacket, trying to ensure the dust stayed out of her wounds, then stood and waited as soldiers exited the chopper with a stretcher.

Flavius drew her aside as two soldiers prepped and loaded Corina into the stretcher before strapping her in. He was a man of very few words, and even now, in the mire of grief, he remained silent, just the arm around her shoulders showing his concern.

With Corina safely inside, Max waved for them to get in. Allegra hurried to the chopper and climbed in before strapping herself into the seat beside Corina. The seer's face was pale, almost luminous in the lights of the aircraft.

Up ahead, Allegra heard Max and Bhana talking, the phrase 'directly to the farm' filtered through to her.

She sat forward. "You aren't planning on going to the farm first are you?" she yelled above the noise of the whirring blades. "Corina will die!"

Max shook his head and was about to respond when cool fingers curled around Allegra's wrist. She glanced down at Corina, whose unconscious body had been placed beside her. She'd come to, but from the look of her eyes her conscious state may only be temporary.

"You must not waste time, Allegra. Prevent the plague first." Allegra had to strain to hear her above the sound of the chopper's blades.

She shook her head, holding onto Corina's shoulder. "You'll die without medical care. I can't do that to you."

Corina smiled and coughed, and a stream of blood spilled from her already red-stained lips. "I am already dead, Allegra. Nobody can save me now. And wasting time getting medical care won't help me ... it will only jeopardize the mission."

Allegra shook her head, then glanced up at Flavius and then at

Max, hoping against hope that at least one of them would back her up and agree to take Corina to the base first.

But neither said a word, both faces remained expressionless, closed off to Allegra's emotional battle.

"What is wrong with you two?" Allegra yelled.

"They know the truth." Corina's voice was raspy, her throat coated with blood. "You are doing so well, Allegra. Your burden is heavy, but you must bear it with strength and conviction." She coughed again and blood trickled from her mouth, soaking into her hair.

"Corina, please," Allegra whispered staring at the seer's gaping wound, and then at her pale face.

Corina's fingers tightened around Allegra's wrist, but only for a moment. Then her hand went slack and she let go.

"I'm so proud to have known you, Pythia Allegra . . ."

And then, as Allegra watched, the life fled from Corina's eyes and she went still.

Allegra wiped the tears from her face with the back of her hand, swiping hard, angry with Max and Flavius, angry with Kantha, angry with the world.

Max held her gaze and spoke calmly. "It was Corina's wish that we go to the farm first. She knew she was dying."

Allegra said nothing, just turned her gaze from the men within the chopper's interior and stared out at the black night.

Corina was dead, and suddenly the future, Allegra's future, looked bleak.

How many more people would she lose in this new life of hers?

CHAPTER 52

The chopper began to descend sooner than Allegra had anticipated. She wiped her eyes and sniffed to clear her sinuses. She'd refused to cry again, determined not to show further emotion.

At last, they landed a safe distance from the coordinates that matched Allegra's vision. She jumped from the chopper, shrugged off Max's helping hand and shielded her eyes as she stared out at the inky, purple and red horizon.

The heat was tangible, like breathing a gust of dusty hot air. Her shirt was soaked with perspiration and stuck to her back, while it hung slack against her chest, the fabric stained and tacky from Corina's blood. Her throat still hurt from crying, and her eyes were gritty with tears.

Allegra stared over the rise and studied the low roofs of the farm, working up some form of eagerness or desire to confirm it matched the one in her vision.

Corina's death had dealt her a blow much worse than she'd expected. She'd grown fond of the seer, had expected they'd be friends.

And then she'd seen Corina's death but misinterpreted it. Had she been better at her job she could have saved Corina.

But she'd failed.

What good was she if she couldn't save one measly human life? How was she expected to save billions?

Movement behind her drew her attention and she glanced over her shoulder.

Bhana and Max were preparing to go in for recon with two of the NGS soldiers, leaving Bhana's driver and Flavius behind with Allegra.

She didn't protest, though she wanted to demand to go down with them, but she felt numb. Wrapping her arms around her waist, she stared at the slowly-disappearing forms of the two commanders of their team.

Flavius came to stand beside her, his elbow brushing against hers. "Corina was headstrong. She always knew her mind."

"She was dying," Allegra said coldly, keeping her eyes on the farm in the distance. "We just let her."

"We didn't let her. She wouldn't have survived those injuries. Even *if* we'd headed for the base first. She would have died before we got there." His voice was soft, yet practical and firm, and something about it broke her resistance.

Hot tears filled her eyes and dripped down her cheeks. She swiped them away with the back of her hand and inhaled harshly. He was right, but he didn't know she was dealing with her own guilt at being unable to save Corina after her vision.

Not that she'd tell him.

He had his own grief to deal with.

Allegra forced a smile onto her lips. "Well, let's hope we do save the world or she's going to be pissed."

Flavius snorted. "Damn right she will be."

Max and Bhana returned, dark shadows emerging from the bush, and headed for the soldiers to plan their attack. She watched them carry a long box from the chopper and place it carefully on the ground. When they flung the lid open, she had to stifle a gasp.

Dynamite.

Appalled she hurried over to the men who were crouched around the box, preparing the sticks of dynamite with long fuses. "You're not going the blow the place up, are you?"

Max got to his feet, dusting off his hands. "Yes, and no. We're going to blast the coops. Let's hope we don't get too much interference from the farmer and his family. Thankfully Rai and his team didn't have the exact coordinates of the farm."

Allegra had a feeling it wasn't going to be that easy. Had it been her farm, she knew she'd fight tooth-and-nail to protect it.

Max returned to help with the dynamite and Allegra paced outside the chopper, left on the sidelines to watch, despite instigating the whole debacle.

Twenty minutes later Max, Bhana and the six soldiers, including Bhana's driver, descended the hill toward the farm, leaving Allegra with the pilot to guard the chopper.

Allegra watched as the team cut through the wire fencing and entered the farm, flitting through the shadows from one coop to the next and lobbing in the dynamite.

The NGS pilot cleared his throat from behind her. "How can we be sure they've killed the origin host?"

Allegra stood straighter. "By checking, of course." She looked over at him. "What's your name?"

"Brayden Weisz, ma'am."

"Brayden, I need to touch you . . . to see if we've averted the pandemic yet."

He hesitated.

"It won't hurt," she said softly as she reached for his hand. He gave it to her in silence and waited as she slipped into the vision.

The pilot was in a living room, sitting on the sofa, a little girl on his knee. Both were covered in sores, blood dribbling from their mouths. They lay unmoving, resting back against the pillows, staring sightlessly at the ceiling.

Allegra moaned as she pulled free of the vision.

Weisz didn't say a word.

They both watched in silence as the destruction continued.

A shout went up from the farmhouse and people began to exit the low-roofed building. Shadows scattered as the farmer and his family tried to stop the intruders.

Allegra couldn't take it anymore. "I'm going down there." She headed to the chopper, grabbed a short knife and tucked it into her left boot.

"Wait. What if you get hurt?"

"Then so be it. But I'm not going to stand here and watch from afar."

She hurried away before he could stop her, knowing he wouldn't leave the chopper for which he was responsible. She ran lightly down the hillside and followed the same path into the property, over the broken fence and along the main line of coops.

She ducked as two more coops exploded. Many were still burning, the smell of flame-cooked chicken filling the air. Allegra would never eat chicken again.

Ever.

Up ahead, a shadow closed in on Max and Bhana. The two were concentrating on tossing dynamite into another set of coops when a man materialized out of the darkness and pushed the barrel of his rifle into the back of Max's neck.

Max stilled, his hands rising slowly in the air. The cotton bag of dynamite sticks remained around his neck and Allegra knew that should it explode, it would kill not only Max, but everyone within a thirty-foot radius.

The man with the gun began to speak, his words urgent, angry and unintelligible. Bhana shook his head and took a step closer. The farmer, Allegra was sure it was him proactively protecting his livelihood, pointed the gun at the general, his harsh tone filled with warning.

Allegra was a few feet to his right now, and moved away so she approached Patel from behind, bending slightly to draw the knife from her boot.

The sound of another explosion, coupled with the roar of the flames and the high-pitched squawks of terrified chickens, covered Allegra's approach and when she placed the blade of the knife against Patel's neck, he went still instantly.

A second explosion made her flinch and Patel gasped. "Sorry," said Allegra, moving aside so he could see her face. "I don't want to hurt you, but you must stop."

The farmer glared at her. "You kill chicken. Is my —" he made a feeding motion with his fingers. His livelihood.

"I understand. Believe me, we all do. But this is necessary."

Patel shook his head. "To kill my farm?"

Allegra paused, then met Bhana's gaze. He gave her a short nod and Allegra inhaled and met Patel's eyes.

"A plague is coming. One that will kill all the people in the world. You, your family, your friends, everyone that eats your chickens and everyone else they speak to, touch, sit beside. It will go on and on until the whole world dies."

Light from the flames across the yard flickered against Patel's face as Bhana translated. When the general fell silent, Patel stared at Allegra. "You crazy." He faced Max again and stiffened his grip on his rifle.

Allegra pressed her knife to his throat wondering if she had it in her to kill this innocent man. Not too long ago she'd murdered a soldier in cold blood.

But she'd had to, or he'd have killed Max. And now, once again a man was at the tip of a knife she held in her hand, all to save Max.

"Please. Let them do their jobs. You could kill one of them, but the other soldier will just kill you. And your chickens will die all the same."

The man's shoulders fell forward and the muzzle of the gun lowered to the ground as he gave up. Allegra dropped her knife hand and removed the gun from his grip.

Max and Bhana hurried to her. Allegra gave Max a defeated look, then turned her attention to the farm, still holding the knife and the gun. They watched as the next three coops went up in flames.

"You need to check again, Allegra. What if this is the wrong farm?" Max raised his voice to be heard over the roar of the additional coops going up in flames.

She nodded then looked for Bhana who was talking to one of two NGS soldiers who'd hurried over to report in. She didn't want to disturb what looked like a pretty intense conversation so she glanced over at the second soldier who waited on the sidelines.

She beckoned him closer and he stepped forward, straight-backed and serious.

"I need to take your hand. We need to check if the mission is succeeding." Allegra said loudly as she tried to sound confident and firm.

The man lifted his hand, his expression unfathomable. He waited as she closed her eyes and searched for the vision. She held her breath as she watched him lying on the ground, his helmet askew, his gun lying beside him. He too was covered in boils and leaking sores.

She withdrew and thanked him, then turned to Max, giving him a slight shake of her head.

Max's lips pursed in disappointment as they both turned to face the farm, and the ongoing destruction.

The farmer stood beside them, now flanked by a tiny old woman and taller younger one. Both wore scarves covering their heads, revealing small round, very scared faces. A little boy held onto the hand of the younger woman, big black eyes staring at the burning farm.

"Give it five minutes," Max said softly.

Allegra refocused on his face and nodded, wondering if he knew how mentally taxing the whole process was.

Seconds later, she felt his hand curl around her waist, felt him give her a comforting squeeze under cover of shadows.

Patel had begun to speak out again, his voice angry and frustrated. The two soldiers held him back, and after a few words in the man's ear, he looked over at Bhana. He shrugged the soldier off and stalked across the yard, making his way to the general who spoke softly to him

"Don't worry. The queen is compensating Patel and his family for their loss." Max spoke from beside her.

She sighed. "What if this isn't the right farm? Or I was totally wrong in the first place?" Doubt had begun to cloud her certainty.

"Check again," said Max simply.

Allegra nodded. They were down to two buildings and almost twenty fires. She shifted her gaze and searched for the NGS soldier. His lips thinned, but he stepped forward all the same, submitting in silence as Allegra called up the vision.

She saw him again, almost unrecognizable without his helmet as he pushed a shopping cart beside an old woman. She was gray-haired, tiny and extremely determined. He looked about five years older. Wagging her finger at him, she proceeded to lecture him about finding a wife.

Allegra let go of his hand and smiled at him. "Your grandmother . . . she's really determined to get you married."

The soldier did a double-take. He'd resigned himself to being her subject, but her words had startled him. He nodded vigorously and headed back to his supervising officer.

Allegra turned to Max. "It worked. The vision changed."

Another explosion went off and Allegra stared at the final two coops going up in flames.

Bhana and Patel came to stand with Allegra as she watched the fires begin to die down.

She met Patel's eyes. "I really wish there'd been another way."

He nodded and looked away, his gaze returning to the scene of mayhem and destruction below. Allegra cleared her throat. "To the rest of the world, this was just another night. They won't know we saved them from their extinction. But you will. You and your family are the only ones to bear the burden of tonight's reprieve for humanity."

Bhana translated again, and Patel's face softened as he absorbed Allegra's words. He nodded slowly, his expression now relaxing.

"It is a heavy burden." Allegra smiled sadly.

Patel bowed, then scurried away. When Allegra glanced at Bhana, wondering why he hadn't been more upset, the commander smiled. "He's just been given a plot of land not too far from here, with fully equipped barns to house new chickens, new technology to operate the farm. He's also received a bag of gold coins, courtesy of the Maharani of Indus."

Unlike Corina, Patel and his family would survive this day.

Allegra hoped it was all worth it.

CHAPTER 53

With a sigh, Allegra headed back to Max as the team prepared to return to Bharat.

Feeling a little off balance, Allegra gave the burning farm one last glance. Incredible that such a simple action should save the entire world.

But it had, and who was Allegra to question it?

THE TEAM SPENT the night at Sonali's palace, and not a single one of them rose before ten the next morning. Perhaps grief kept them abed more than exhaustion.

Allegra blinked against the sunlight streaming into the room. As she turned her head a voice whispered in her ear. "Come to Delphi, my child."

And then it was gone, just a soft voice in her mind and then nothing. Had she not experienced it before, Allegra would have dismissed it as part of her imagination.

Frustrated, she sprang out of bed and flung open the doors to the balcony. Outside the sun shone, searing and bright against the white marble.

The air was heavy, muggy and humid, but the beauty compensated for the sudden flush of perspiration on her forehead. Peacocks called and in the distance the trumpeting of elephants could be heard.

A movement at her side drew her attention to Max who'd followed her outside. "It's beautiful." His voice was soft and yet restless, as if he knew he had more to do but was reluctant to leave.

Allegra felt the same.

She met his gaze. "I'd love to stay. This place is perfect and I think it would be good for my soul."

"But?"

"But I am a woman plagued by visions."

Max's smile disappeared. "What did you see?"

Allegra faced the garden, her gaze focusing on the trickling water of a giant fountain, the droplets sparkling like diamonds as the water hit the pool and exploded into a million fragments.

"Delphi."

She didn't tell Max about the voices. Something told her that she'd be better off keeping that to herself. The only person who knew was Xenia and she'd never tell.

Max nodded. "Very well. Flavius can return to the Capital and I'll book us on the next plane to Athens."

"And Corina?" Allegra asked softly.

Max's features tightened. Then he exhaled harshly. "The army will transport her body back to the Capital. She'll be given a military funeral with full honors."

Allegra nodded, unsure if honors really mattered. "And her family?" Her vision blurred as she recalled Corina's smile when she had talked about her parents and her brother.

"They've been informed. Her brother is taking it hard but they have each other."

From the sound of Max's voice, Allegra knew that *he* had been the one to make that call.

He fell silent then, giving her a strange look before shifting his gaze to the scenery. "What's wrong?"

He didn't meet her eyes. "I just got word from Londinium." He paused and looked back at Allegra.

"What?" she asked, her stomach tightening.

"They raided the tunnels. Arrested a few acolytes." He took a breath. "They found a burial site."

"The children?"

He nodded. "A total of twelve that they have uncovered so far. Decomposition rates spread them out over the last year and a half."

Allegra shivered, remembering a pair of calm blue eyes. And the man wielding the knife that had spilled the child's blood. "The high priest?"

Max shook his head. "Not a trace of him. Not even a hint at his true identity."

Allegra's fingers curled into a fist. "You won't find him." Max sent her an enquiring glance. "He's too smart, and too powerful. Remember those cops in Londinium? I'd bet my inheritance that they are on his payroll. If I were him, I'd have my people well-positioned all over the world."

Max nodded. "Hard to find a nameless man."

Allegra smiled thinly. "He may be nameless. But he isn't faceless."

FLAVIUS DEPARTED for their home office in the States, promising to meet up with Allegra as soon as she returned to her home on the West Coast.

A day later, Allegra and Max took their leave of Maharani

Sonali amidst a farewell banquet filled with best wishes for both babies and oracles.

The priestess Kantha was present too. Sonali must be more forgiving than Allegra would ever be. She'd kept her distance from the priestess, partly because she blamed the woman for Corina's death, partly because she understood her reasoning.

Who was Allegra to judge when personal emotion, and trust in the gods came into play?

Apollo had helped, but only to a certain extent, freeing her to complete the task herself.

The ways of the gods were often unfathomable.

Allegra had been saddened to leave, the success of the mission tempered by the death of her friend. At least she'd fulfilled Corina's wishes and averted disaster. Max had tried to talk to her about Corina, but though Allegra knew he bore a grief similar to her own, she avoided the topic. His grief was uncomplicated, while hers was further intensified by guilt.

He wouldn't understand.

The flight to Athens was long and tiring, the stopover in Kemet sending Allegra into a fit of panic at the crowd that had mobbed her.

Before boarding the plane to Athens, they'd decided to pose as a couple on honeymoon, to avoid scenes like that. Max's access to fake identity documents was nothing short of amazing, and when they arrived at the hotel in Athens, they booked in as Citizens Robert and Mary Callaghan, newlyweds from the island of Eire.

Allegra sighed as she stared out of the open balcony doors of the room, absorbing the view over the city. Beautiful domed buildings inspired by the Moors and the Persians, dotted the skyline.

She made a mental note to visit the famed Michelangelo's paintings on the ceiling of the temple of Hera. Hailing from Italy, the master had spent much of his later career in Greece.

For now, Delphi called Allegra, the voices of her bloodline

summoning her. Perhaps the ancient Pythias would provide her with much-needed solace.

Who knew where she would go from there. She'd fulfilled her first mission and averted the pandemic. She'd saved the world with her visions.

She now knew her purpose.

Being the Pythia wasn't so bad after all.

THE END

Thank you for reading DARK SIGHT.
The DARK SIGHT series is ongoing, but if you dislike cliffhangers you may prefer to stop here. Thank you for reading!

Want to read more? Then continue on to the EPILOGUE.

*A*llegra and Max grabbed a taxi to the famous site of Delphi, and headed up to the temple complex. The grounds were large, dotted with a combination of temples to different gods, some in good repair, others a pile of neglected stone.

Over the centuries, many worshippers who followed the Oracle had also erected their own temples close enough to attend the Pythia as well.

Now, the temple complex provided both for pilgrimage visitors as well as for priests and priestesses who, either visit or wish to live within the grounds, not to mention tourists.

Over time, many people had chosen to dedicate their lives to the gods for numerous reasons, in modern times mostly women. The complex was never without the services of trained priestesses.

Much like the pair who closed in on Max and Allegra as they entered the Delphi temple.

They both bowed and the taller, blonde said, "Welcome to Delphi. Please let us know if you need any assistance."

Allegra smiled. "Thank you. I'd like a little privacy if that is possible?"

The women stared at Allegra as if such a request was completely unexpected.

The shorter priestess, her dark skin heralding her Nubian roots, rested her hand on the taller woman's arm, restraining her from responding further.

She gave Allegra a grave nod and a low bow. "Welcome, my Lady. We will do as you wish. May I ask if you require attendance?"

Allegra frowned. "Attendance?"

The woman bobbed a low curtsey and whispered, "All Oracles are provided with a handmaiden for assistance in transcribing the visions. Our handmaidens are experienced Readers. Though they cannot see your visions, they can read the thoughts you wish to convey."

Allegra shook her head and smiled. "I don't need a handmaiden."

The woman frowned, confused for a moment until her eyes widened. "You speak?" she asked softly, beckoning Allegra to follow her into the Oracle's temple.

Allegra didn't answer, deciding the less people knew about her abilities, the better.

The temple was small with a domed ceiling and stone columns encircling the temple floor. Half a dozen stone seats dotted the perimeter of the temple, leaving the rest of the space empty.

The priestesses took their leave in respectful silence and Allegra left Max's side to wander around the temple. After navigating the floor, and absorbing the ancient echoes of the temple, Allegra sat on a sun-drenched stone seat.

From there she watched Max, hiding a smile. He'd been quiet since they'd left Indus, and Allegra had given him space. Their attraction had been put aside, the mission to save the world given top priority.

Perhaps now, in the ancient city of Athens, they may have time to explore what they felt for each other. He'd gained her trust and respect with his passion, honesty and determination.

She took a breath and was about to fall into the depths of the vision when the sound of rapid footsteps pulled her free. She watched as Max turned to stare at the irate, dark-skinned, bald-headed man marching toward him.

They were far enough from her that she shouldn't have heard their conversation, but the acoustics within the temple were strange, tossing sounds around, allowing her to hear every word.

Max bowed quickly. "General Aulus."

So this was the famous General Aulus. Allegra had pictured someone far more discerning than the slim, taciturn man who stared infuriated at Max.

The general ignored Max's greeting. "What in Hades' name is going on here, Vissarion?"

"I'm not sure what you mean, Sir," responded Max, his spine stiffening.

His demeanor began to worry Allegra. And the unannounced presence of the general, in lieu of a phone call, meant something dire.

"You've been avoiding my calls. I'm here to ensure you both return safely to the Capital."

Allegra frowned as Max shook his head and said nothing.

Aulus let out an irritated breath and glared at Max. "What is the meaning of this trip? What are you doing *here* instead of returning her back to the States?"

"The meaning of this is that Allegra has her own opinion and if you thought to consult with her, you'd know she has no intention of being controlled by any one country or government. If you still wish to help her, then you are most welcome, but don't try to force her to do something that is both against her will, and more importantly, against international law."

Aulus glared at Max, but said nothing.

"I apologize, Sir. But I am asking for leave to remain on the Pythia's protection and advisory detail." Max glanced at Allegra and she shifted her gaze. She didn't want him to think she was eavesdropping. Max continued. "If only to retain some influence on the Pythia's activities."

Allegra stiffened. What did that mean?

She listened more intently now as Max continued, "Through me, you currently have a place at her side. Which you will lose if you attempt to control her, or her power. I'm at your service should you need me. I'll do what I can, but she is not under our control."

Aulus grunted, a thin smile slicing across his mouth. "You have failed then?"

"No, Sir."

"So you have done as I asked?"

Allegra perked up, more than curious now.

Max remained silent.

"Vissarion. Have you seduced her yet? Do you have her under your control as requested? You know how vital her compliance is."

Max said nothing but even if he had, Allegra wouldn't have heard him through the ringing in her ears.

Fury, hurt and shame filled her.

But more than that, the dizziness colored her vision with such power that she was unable to control it. She slumped down onto the stone seat staring up at the stone ceiling of the temple.

The men's voices rose and fell, the sound of chattering and footsteps echoed from the tourists within the complex. Birds on a nearby tree sang their song with exuberant joy.

And overlaid upon the peaceful scene was one of total destruction.

People screamed. A hole in the ground a hundred feet deep, lay before her. Houses, and rubble, bodies and vehicles all lay in a haphazard mess within the hole, and as Allegra blinked she got a better idea of the size of the hole.

Bigger than some towns, the hole spanned an area at least two miles wide.

Thousands of homes.

Hundreds of thousands of people.

Allegra gasped, holding a hand to her chest.

A shadow traveled along the center of the hole and the sound of a helicopter filled her ears. Scanning the sky, she identified a news chopper flying overhead, the emblem of a Quechua priest emblazoned on its side.

Peru.

Allegra blinked, inhaling sharply, her heart slamming against her ribs so hard it hurt. So many people dead.

The victims must be warned before it was too late. Evacuated, so at least the loss of their homes would not mean the loss of all those lives.

More resolved than ever, Allegra got to her feet. She pushed her pain deep inside as she turned to watch Max, now alone, staring at the retreating back of his commanding officer.

She could no longer trust him.

But, as cold as it sounded, she needed him to carry out her duty. She had a purpose now, a plan to help the world, using her ability for the betterment of mankind.

She wasn't just someone's daughter, or a mere carrier of a bloodline.

She hurried toward him. "Max?"

He turned to Allegra, his face closed off from her. "What's wrong?"

Allegra suspected all Max needed was to look at her to know she was upset. She'd have to work on that. From now on, her emotions were hers, and hers alone.

She shook her head and swallowed. They had their work cut out for them now.

"There is something that I have to say."

A frown marred his forehead. One which he quickly replaced with an inscrutable expression. It must have been the cool edge to her voice that did it.

"Go on."

Allegra stiffened her spine and her resolve. "Going forward, I will require your help. But to do so, I will need your cooperation."

"You know you have my total cooperation, Allegra." A smile teased his lips. "Our relationsh—"

She shook her head, feeling tears threaten to fall. She didn't let them.

"There is no relationship."

Max's smile disappeared and he glanced again in the direction in which the general had gone. His expression hardened again and Allegra guessed he understood now.

She cleared her throat and he looked back at her. "My visions will continue to take me to places across the world. I cannot act on those prophecies alone. If you do not wish to help me, I am sure I can petition someone else for assistance."

Max shook his head. "You don't need to worry about that. You have my full, undivided cooperation. Just say the word and I will provide whatever you require." He spoke as formally as she did, and Allegra's heart broke a little more.

She nodded, then took a deep breath.

"Then we need to leave for Peru. Immediately."

—TO BE CONTINUED—

Thank you for reading. The DARK SIGHT Series continues with CURSED SIGHT.

FREE STARTER LIBRARY - JOIN MY NEWSLETTER

Get the following titles FREE when you subscribe to my newsletter.

Tee's Newsletter

http://smarturl.it/TeesMailingList

ABOUT THE AUTHOR

I have been a writer from the time I was old enough to recognize that reading was a doorway into my imagination. Poetry was my first foray into the art of the written word. Books were my best friends, my escape, my haven. I am essentially a recluse but this part of my personality is impossible to practice given I have two teenage daughters, who are actually my friends, my tea-makers, my confidantes… I am blessed with a husband who has left me for golf. It's a fair trade as I have left him for writing. We are both passionate supporters of each other's loves – it works wonderfully…

My heart is currently broken in two. One half resides in South Africa where my old roots still remain, and my heart still longs for the endless beaches and the smell of moist soil after a summer downpour. My love for Ma Afrika will never fade. The other half of me has been transplanted to the Land of the Long White Cloud. The land of the Taniwha, beautiful Maraes, and volcanoes. The land of green, pure beauty that truly inspires. And because I am so torn between these two lands – I shall forever remain cross-eyed.

Stalk Tee here:
www.tgayer.com
tee@tgayer.com

facebook.com/TGAyerAuthor

twitter.com/TGAyerAuthor

bookbub.com/profile/t-g-ayer